17

WINTER OF DESPAIR

*A selection of recent titles by Cora Harrison
from Severn House*

The Gaslight mysteries

SEASON OF DARKNESS
WINTER OF DESPAIR

The Reverend Mother mysteries

A SHAMEFUL MURDER
A SHOCKING ASSASSINATION
BEYOND ABSOLUTION
A GRUESOME DISCOVERY
DEATH OF A NOVICE
MURDER AT THE QUEEN'S OLD CASTLE

The Burren mysteries

WRIT IN STONE
EYE OF THE LAW
SCALES OF RETRIBUTION
DEED OF MURDER
LAWS IN CONFLICT
CHAIN OF EVIDENCE
CROSS OF VENGEANCE
VERDICT OF THE COURT
CONDEMNED TO DEATH
A FATAL INHERITANCE
AN UNJUST JUDGE

WINTER OF DESPAIR

Cora Harrison

This first world edition published 2019
in Great Britain and 2020 in the USA by
SEVERN HOUSE PUBLISHERS LTD of
Eardley House, 4 Uxbridge Street, London W8 7SY.
Trade paperback edition first published
in Great Britain and the USA 2020 by
SEVERN HOUSE PUBLISHERS LTD.

British Library Cataloguing in Publication Data
A CIP catalogue record for this title is available from the British Library.

ISBN-13: 978-0-7278-8912-6 (cased)
ISBN-13: 978-1-78029-647-0 (trade paper)
ISBN-13: 978-1-4483-0346-5 (e-book)

All Severn House titles are printed on acid-free paper.

Severn House Publishers support the Forest Stewardship Council™ [FSC™],
the leading international forest certification organisation.
All our titles that are printed on FSC certified paper carry the FSC logo.

Typeset by I
Falkirk, Stir
Printed and
TJ Internatic

ONE

Wilkie Collins, *Hide and Seek*, 1854:
'The morning had been fine for November; but before midday the clouds had gathered, the rain had begun, and the fogs of the season had closed dingily over the wet streets, far and near. The garden in the middle of the Square – with its close-cut turf, its vacant beds, its rustic seats, its withered young trees, seemed to be absolutely rotting away in yellow mist and softly-steady rain, and was deserted even by the cats. The grim brown hue of the brick houses looked more dirtily desolate than ever; the smoke from the chimney-pots was lost mysteriously in deepening fog; the muddy gutters gurgled; the heavy rain-drops dripped into empty areas audibly.'

A miserable winter! It had started badly. Nothing going right for me. Hated London and longed to be back in Italy. Not to be a painter; I didn't want to paint. I just wanted to be out of the fogs of London and in the sun. My father had made a good living as an artist, but I knew that I was never going to be a painter, never anything but barely competent. My young brother Charley and his artist friends, Millais, Holman Hunt and Gabriel Rossetti were all so much better than I. No, I longed to be a famous writer like my new friend, Charles Dickens. I envied him. To have the world waiting with bated breath for my next novel; not to have to tout it from publisher to publisher, just like a jobbing salesman. And so I spent as much time as I could with him, tried to learn his secrets, to listen to his advice and even, though I was not an active man, to be his companion on those long walks of his. But I had this uneasy feeling, deep down, that the book I was writing now, *Hide and Seek*, was never going to be as good as my first book, *Basil*. Somehow, somewhere, I had lost that drive, lost that sense of urgency.

And so on that miserable day in November Dickens and I trudged along: hat brims pulled well over eyes; heads lowered; mouths and noses swathed in protective scarves; blind and deaf to the world about us; I, thinking of the book that I was writing about a painter; he, probably, thinking of his new book, *Hard Times*, both thinking so hard, wrapped up so well that it was a few seconds before I realized that someone, somewhere high above us, was calling my name.

'Mr Collins!' The fog muffled the sound; it took me moments to locate the window on the top storey where a man's head protruded below the dripping roof. The next sentences were muffled in the fog; 'painting, portrait, painters' were the only words to float down to my ears. The head disappeared; re-appeared minutes later on the doorstep. It was Inspector Field of the Detective Force.

'You're just the man that I need, Mr Collins. Come and look at this. You, too, Mr Dickens.'

A shiny round rosewood table in the hall, thick, heavy carpet of red and green on the stairs, walls patterned with birds, trelliswork and flowers – a typical rented house in this part of London, but not so typical, as the top room in the house had been turned into a studio. We followed the inspector into the large room. A painting-stand with quantities of shallow little drawers, some too full to shut; a small square table of new deal, and a large round table of dilapidated rosewood, both laden with sketchbooks, portfolios, dog-eared sheets of drawing paper. And, at the back of the room, a movable platform to put sitters on, a platform covered with red cloth. Our eyes went to it immediately. Went to it with a gasp of horror! Slumped across that platform, like a sack of clothing, the body of a man lay.

A dead man; a horribly-reddened shirt-front, throat lacerated, face hidden, head twisted as though he had sought to avoid that last deadly stroke, two livid and bloody hands and on the floor beside him an ornate, gilded frame, the picture within it slashed and scarred as though it, too, had been whipped by a knife, pieces of canvas strewn on the platform and around the floor.

There was something so artificial, so like the setting of a

scene to be painted that neither Dickens nor I said anything. Just stood. Stood and stared.

'Who found him?' asked Dickens.

'The housemaid. She works here from ten o'clock in the morning until one o'clock midday. She came in and saw that there was no milk. Went out, purchased the milk and then came back about fifteen minutes later,' explained Inspector Field. 'When she came back the door was ajar, though she is sure that she had closed it behind her. She heard something. From the studio up here. She must have disturbed the intruder. Says that she thought she heard a door closing as she pushed the door open. No sooner was she inside the hall when she heard footsteps running down the stairs from the top of the house. Says that he must have slipped into a bedroom on the second floor and waited while she went up to the top floor to see if her master wanted her.' Inspector Field rapped out his comments in a staccato fashion while looking hopefully from one of us to the other. Impatiently he kicked at a fragment on the floor.

'Don't!' I said mechanically. I had grown up in a household where the smell of oil paint was a feature of my whole childhood, where my father's work and the pictures that he painted were sacred to my infant consciousness. Not a mote of dust, not a ray of sunshine was allowed to fall upon his works of art and they were draped and sheltered like holy icons until the day came for them to be varnished and then taken carefully to the salesrooms or the art galleries. Now I knelt down on the ground and peered at the fragment. It was a title, engraved upon one of those stylized scrolls which some artists used when the title was of significance to the work of art. I picked it up and rubbed the blood from it with my pocket handkerchief.

Winter of Despair, it read and I placed it upon the table. Belonged to the mutilated picture, no doubt.

'See what you can make of the rest of it, Mr Collins,' said the inspector encouragingly and so I cleared a space on the table and began to pick up the lacerated fragments of canvas, laying them out on the deal surface and trying to match colours. The paint had flaked under the violence of the knife strokes and I despaired of making sense out of the ruined picture. My eyes kept going back to the body slumped on the platform. I tried to avert my eyes from it and I looked around the floor for more fragments of the picture, but could see nothing that would make the words appropriate. And I listened in a daze to Dickens who was asking the name of the man and what had happened.

'I'm hoping that you can help me with this, Mr Collins.' For once Inspector Field's attention was not focussed on my famous friend. I was the man that he wanted. 'You know all about artists, don't you, Mr Collins?' His voice was firm and his eyes alert. 'Recognize this man?' He beckoned us to come around to the side of the platform and then crouched down, peering at the twisted head. We knelt beside him.

'Surely that is Mr Milton-Hayes, your principal guest for tonight's dinner.' It was Dickens who spoke. He had gone a little nearer and was leaning over the body, focussing on the face. I could say nothing. My throat had swelled and my eyes ached with the horror. I took off my glasses, wiped them and put them back on again.

'Yes, that's the man,' I said and heard the unsteadiness of my voice as though it were the voice of a stranger. 'He was due to dine with us tonight, at my mother's house, inspector. He was going to bring along a few of his latest paintings. My brother Charles, who is an artist, does this from time to time, invites one of his colleagues or friends to give a showing of paintings. Just an informal gathering of people who are interested in Pre-Raphaelite art. The main guest gives names of people that he wants invited. It's always rather jolly, people go on arguing and talking about the picture or the pictures right through dinner.' I was conscious that I was babbling and was angry with myself for introducing Charley's name. The memory of that fight, years ago, between my brother and the man now lying dead at our feet, intruded itself and I pushed it away rapidly. I was conscious, though, that Inspector Field seemed to be looking at me from under his bushy eyebrows with one of his shrewd penetrating glances.

'What do you reckon that picture is about, Wilkie?' asked Dickens. He, too, I guessed, had noticed my discomposure.

'I couldn't tell,' I said shortly.

'I was wondering why it was destroyed,' put in Inspector Field. He looked from one to the other of us.

'Anger, hatred of the dead man. Could be an annoying fellow, Milton-Hayes,' said Dickens briefly. 'Or perhaps a fury of jealousy. Anyway, these Pre-Raphaelite painters are always arguing with each other, always having fights about various matters. Who knows what drives a man a step further, drives a man to murder.'

'And this portrait?' The inspector was not interested in the Pre-Raphaelites, but in the mutilated picture lying on the floor beside the dead man. He leaned a little forward, as though to penetrate the meaning from those slashed and crushed fragments on the floor. 'What do you think it's about, Mr Collins? Strange name, isn't it? *Winter of Despair*. Who do you think that this is meant to be?'

'It's a picture, not a portrait. It *was* a picture, I mean.' I corrected my first words. 'Milton-Hayes used models, of course, but his pictures were not meant to be portraits. They represented a situation. The pictures often ended up looking quite different from the model that he used. He might alter an expression, alter a feature.'

The inspector contemplated the picture for the moment while he thought about this. 'But he would use a real person as a model,' he said eventually.

'Yes,' I said impatiently. 'He would use a model. But the face, if there was a face, has been ruined. Impossible to see what . . . who . . . see who it was meant to be.' I was stumbling over my words like a man who had been drinking heavily.

'Perhaps this figure at the edge *is* a portrait, though, is a real woman. A society woman. Here's a bit of a dress, painted with great care. Look at it, Wilkie.'

It was Dickens who spoke. He was leaning over the dead man, and had gently pulled a fragment from under him. 'Look, inspector, look this was a person. But the face is destroyed. Look how the mouth is slashed and the eyes, too. And the hair. No, it's too damaged. No one could tell who it was meant to be. Only one shoulder. A shoulder from a dress. It must be a woman's dress. It may not even be a real dress. What do you think, Wilkie? Just one that the painter imagined. These tiny rosebuds look too real to be just embroidery.'

'You're an expert, Mr Dickens.' There was a note of admiration in the police officer's voice as he studied the fragment from the violated picture and I began to pull myself together. 'Milton-Hayes was like that. They all are. My brother, Charles, could spend an hour painting one lily head. He's a genius with flowers.' I stumbled over my words. What possessed me to bring Charley's name once again into the business?

'And Milton-Hayes with women's faces.' Dickens looked grimly at the ruined painting with the heavily scored lines obliterating the features, but leaving some of the delicate skin tones. 'It had been finished, don't you think, Wilkie?'

'It was finished. And framed. Look how he has even put the title.' I contemplated the title *Winter of Despair*. It sent a cold shiver down my back and I tried to distract myself, picking up pieces of broken frame from the ground. Milton-Hayes always had very elaborate frames for his pictures, carved wood, painted in pale gold and with a curled scroll at the bottom where he hand-painted the title. I picked up another fragment of frame and frowned at it. 'I think that it might have been a triptych,' I said thoughtfully. 'See there are two little hinges here. Or more likely a diptych,' I added, picking up another few broken pieces of frame. I looked at the inspector's puzzled face and launched into a slightly confused explanation of how a pictorial story, a diptych, could be painted in two halves, hinged together so that the second picture finishes the story begun in the first picture, or else in three parts for a triptych. 'There should have been two titles, I would say,' I said as I found yet another piece of frame that finished off one of the lower corners of the picture. 'No sign of the second one,' I said after a minute and I went back to matching up colours and shapes. I was beginning to make sense of the picture.

'Looks like a bridge,' I said. 'And that bit here looks like faces on the bridge. The woman with the rosebud dress would be at the end of the bridge.' Now the picture was beginning to grow under my fingers and my hand was automatically picking out the correct pieces in order to complete the shapes. 'Looks as though there is a crowd on the bridge, looking down on a body floating in the river,' I said eventually. 'I can't seem to find a face for the body, though. It's just a blur in the water and the face has been cut away – perhaps cut into tiny pieces.'

'Hmm,' said Inspector Field. 'Doesn't help us much, does it? Of course if we had a face that one of you gentlemen could recognize, well then . . .' He sighed heavily several times, watching me sort the pieces, matching the colours and shapes. 'It could be anybody, any man, couldn't it? Just as it could be any man who murdered this artist, any man who knew him, who had featured in this painting of his. There are no clues, so far, are they? Not even much of a clue about why the picture was destroyed.'

'Or any woman.' I spoke half to myself and half to them. 'It might have been a woman who killed him. It's impossible to say whether it's a man or a woman floating in the river, or whether it is supposed to be a murder or a suicide. He's painted the Thames as murky and judging by the bits that I've put together it's supposed to be foggy, murky weather.' I peered a little closer. 'Yes, I think that the body floating could be that of a woman. It may have been a suicide. The title *Winter of Despair* sounds like a suicide more than it sounds like a murder. It may be a woman with a terrible secret. And she may be the one who murdered Milton-Hayes.'

'What! A woman! A woman wouldn't have the strength for something like that, Mr Collins. Not a society lady. Nor the nerve. This Mr Milton-Hayes is a strong-looking man, young, too.' The inspector dismissed my suggestion with a short bark of laughter.

'It depends on the weapon, inspector; it could have been a canvas knife.' He laughed again and that laugh annoyed me. I knew more about artists and their equipment than either he or Dickens. After all I was the son of an artist and the brother of an artist. 'Every artist has several good sharp knives,' I told him. 'These canvases are very tough. I've done a bit of painting, and I've helped my father to prepare a canvas so I know how difficult they are to cut, but once you have the right tool, you have no problem. You need a very sharp knife and a steady hand, and then you can slice through them. And a sharp knife will cut through human flesh as easily as through canvas, inspector.'

I didn't really think that it was a woman who had killed Milton-Hayes in that brutal manner, but I resented the way Inspector Field always dismissed my suggestions as ridiculous while bowing down in admiration over anything said by my friend, the famous Mr Charles Dickens.

'Yes,' he said now, 'we've found a couple of knives, Mr Collins. Not a trace of blood on any one of them. All of them as clean as a whistle, put away in a drawer.'

'Could have been cleaned,' I said, but hopelessly, as I guessed that he might have means of examining the knives, with a very powerful magnifying glass or something like that.

He ignored me, though, going over to the window, opening it and thrusting his head out over the sill in just the same way as he had been doing when he called down to us.

'Here's the van at last,' he said after a minute. 'Now we can get rid of the body. The surgeon might have a look at him. Any notion of where his family live?' He looked at me hopefully but didn't wait for an answer before looking once more around the room. And then he cast a glance at the cluttered desk in the corner of the room. 'I've been through his papers, but nothing about a family. He didn't half make a good living, though. I've seen his bank statements from Coutts.' He left the room and then thrust his head back in again, twisting it around the door frame to make a last observation. 'Would make an honest policeman think about taking up painting. Wouldn't take long to do one of those things, I suppose, if you put your mind to it, would it?' he enquired hopefully.

'I'll ask my brother, Charles, about Milton-Hayes,' I said, ignoring the last remark. 'He's a painter, also. And he knows Milton-Hayes well.' I doubt he knew all that much, though. Charley was not a gossip. He was singularly uninterested in his fellow human beings, unlike me. I racked my brains. I had a vague feeling that someone had told me that Milton-Hayes was an assumed name. I wouldn't be surprised if that were true, I thought. The name 'Milton-Hayes' seemed to indicate a member of the aristocracy, but the artist didn't speak or behave in any way like a lord or even a squire. He had a sharpness about him that one would associate with a barrow boy who had made good and who was endeavouring to assume the manners of the gentry. I had never taken much interest in him, had not found him in any way congenial, but now I pondered over the man.

I was surprised to hear that Milton-Hayes made so much money. Millais did, but Millais was far, far more gifted. Milton-Hayes was no Millais. He wasn't considered to be one of the top artists. He had a certain facile ability as a draughtsman, but, in general, little sensitivity. His forte was in painting skin colours. He seldom showed pictures at the academy. So where had all of his money come from? Certainly my brother, Charley, made very little money and lived mostly on that £11,000 that our hard-working father had bequeathed to my mother.

'Now then, Wilkie, let's have a quick look around,' said Dickens as soon as the inspector had gone from the room. 'There's something very odd about this business. Why should anyone slash that picture unless it could harm them, unless they could be recognized? And then there is a matter of finding the partner for this picture, *Winter of Despair*.' He touched the hinge on the piece of frame and then, neatly and quickly, he began lifting the cotton sheets from the various easels around the room.

'All the usual sort of Milton-Hayes stuff,' I said as he sent back hopeful looks towards me. 'He went in for these biblical scenes. And I recognize most of the models. That's the Welsh girl. I've met her at my brother's scenes. He's used her in three or four of these paintings. And if she is in the one in that painting that has been slashed, and also the person who is floating in the river, well, I'd have no idea why she would have minded. She's a professional model. You can find her in many, many paintings by the Pre-Raphaelites.'

'Let's have a look in here, Wilkie.' Dickens, as usual, was hardly listening to me, but had picked up the dead man's keys from his table and coolly unlocked a door that led into a small cloakroom, a place where models could dress and undress. The dead man's distinctive pale-grey caped cloak hung there, also, but what Dickens was looking at was a canvas carrying bag.

'My brother has one of these and so have his friends. Will fit about . . .'

My voice tailed off as Dickens opened the bag and quite coolly took from it some pictures. He carried them into the studio, made a quick neat pile of the stuff on the large rosewood table, transferring it to the deal table and then ranged the five paintings in a semi-circular shape. We both bent over them. Each had the second side of the hinge attached to the left-hand side of the picture and each had a title on the scroll at the bottom of the frame. Dickens read them aloud: '*The Night Prowler*; *Forbidden Fruit*; *Taken in Adultery*; *Den of Iniquity*; *Root of All Evil*,' he said and his voice had a note of astonishment.

I gazed at them and it took me almost a minute to see what had puzzled Dickens, to see what was wrong. The paintings were exquisite, every brushstroke flawless, every flower almost living, every piece of fabric almost tangible; he had spent a lot of time and effort on these works, I thought. I focused on the third picture: *Taken in Adultery*. The young man, the beautiful woman and the half-open door with an elderly, grey-haired figure. The woman's dress, richly glowing, purple velvet, the young man's hand, his hair, all were glowing with colour. And furniture, carpets and lamps were as perfect as though one were in the room and experiencing their beauty.

But the faces were blank. Just ovals of white paint where a living face should have given life to the picture.

And then *The Night Prowler*. Every detail, even the line of spilt wax on the side of the candle, all painted with such care. And the perfection of the jewels on the table, shining with beauty beneath the greedy hand of the thief. The emerald brooch, glowing green as the depth of the ocean, the pearls shimmering, the sharp white light of the diamonds. But the man with the candle in his hand was also faceless.

I turned to the next picture that Dickens was holding up, his mouth a tight hard line of disapproval. It had its name: *Forbidden Fruit*. Incongruous, strange, the smooth legs of a girl-child beneath the knee-length skirt, the long hair – no face, of course, neither of the young girl nor of the man who was urging her towards the church where a robed and cloaked priest awaited them.

And *Den of Iniquity*, most ominous and most strange of all of the pictures. At first glance, every face appeared to be painted here: anonymous, blurred faces, faces of the drugged, eyes blank, and then, slightly more distinct, the seamed face of the proprietor who was blowing at a kind of pipe, to kindle it and shading it with a lean hand, concentrating its red spark of light. But the face of the central figure, the face of a man lying on a broken bed, arms and legs splayed out, helpless under the power of the drug, this face was covered with that same blank oval of white paint.

I stood and stared at the five faceless pictures, each ready to be hinged to *Winter of Despair*.

'Would that be usual?' Dickens was impatient with my silence. 'Would artists do that? Leave the face to the last? Surely not. I remember when Daniel Maclise painted me. He did the face quite early on, put in all the small details later.' Dickens went back to scrutinizing each picture, one by one.

'I suppose that every artist is different.' I couldn't think of anything else to say. The pictures were so carefully painted, strange to have the figures with no faces. We both continued to stare at them until we heard the heavy footsteps of the inspector coming back up the stairs. The thud of his feet echoed the beat of my heart.

I made up my mind quickly before the inspector reached the door. Rapidly I stacked the paintings and slid them back into the bag. And then went to the door. Dickens followed me, without a word. I could feel the guilt written all over me. I glanced sidelong at Dickens, but his face was impassable, unreadable even by me who knew him so well. The silence had to be broken and I knew that I had to take the initiative.

'Would you like me to get my brother, Mr Charles Collins, to look at that mutilated painting, inspector?' I tried to keep my voice casual. 'We could come around here tomorrow morning, if that would suit you. As an artist himself he might be able to give you some indication of what the picture was about. Strange title, wasn't it? *Winter of Despair*! And, of course, he knew Mr Milton-Hayes very well, possibly they may have . . .' I left the end of the sentence dangling. No point in going into too much detail, but I desperately needed to get Charley into this room and show him the veiled faces on the portraits, to find out from him what had happened. 'We don't need you to be here, inspector,' I continued. 'You're a busy man. If you could just give orders to the police officer at the door that I can bring my brother. He will help in reconstructing the slashed painting and may have some idea of who it is supposed to portray.'

To my relief, he gave a nod. 'You do that, Mr Collins, and I'll be very beholden to you.' There was not a trace of suspicion in his voice.

'I'd be interested in coming, too,' said Dickens and I wondered whether he had guessed, had seen what I had seen.

'I have often heard my father speak of cleaning a canvas when a picture did not please him,' I explained, talking rapidly. Dickens' eyes were on the bag that contained the *Taken in Adultery* picture and I hoped he would say nothing. I hastened to keep the inspector's attention on me. 'There must be some way of removing that top layer of paint and uncovering the features that lie beneath,' I said with conviction, adding, 'and my brother, Mr Charles Collins, will be sure to know of it.'

It was true, I thought. Yes, Charley might be able to remove the oval blob of paint that covered the faces in the pictures. But it was not something that I wanted him to do in the presence of Inspector Field.

There had been something about that young man in the picture *Taken in Adultery* that had instantly struck me and Dickens had looked closely at it, too.

However Dickens did not speak until we were out in the street and striding towards my mother's house. And then he remarked quietly, 'I suppose that Charley gets that red hair from your Irish grandfather.'

He had never called him Charley before, never other than 'your brother', or, ironically, 'Young Mr Charles Collins'. Nor had he ever spoken of him in that tone of sympathy.

'Yes,' I said in answer to his query. 'Yes, I suppose that was where the red hair came from.' And in silence we progressed to Dickens' office in the Strand where we planned to lunch and to spend the afternoon in work on his magazine.

TWO

Sesina took the silver forks to the table beneath the window and began to polish them in the last rays of daylight that came through from the area in front of the basement. Not much light was needed for the job of polishing forks, but she wanted to think and she couldn't while Dolly and Mrs Barnett kept chattering, sitting beside the warm stove. In any case, she had another and far more important job to do, but she wouldn't start that until her hands stopped shaking.

This was her second November as housemaid in this house. Never would she have imagined that she would have stayed so long. She had told Mr Wilkie that she would give it six months, but somehow she had stayed on and here she was, eighteen months after she had left Adelphi Terrace. Not a bad place, Hanover Terrace, she supposed. She liked Mr Wilkie, liked his mother, Mrs Collins, a decent sort of a mistress, she conceded, but the reason that she had stayed was not because of either of them, but because of the third person in the house, Mr Wilkie's young brother, Mr Charles.

Sesina had never met anyone like him: tall, pale skin with red-gold hair and a lovely sweetness about him. Very handsome. A sad look always in his beautiful blue eyes, poor fellow. So polite. Just like she was a lady, she sometimes thought. She liked to do things for him, save little treats for his supper, give his clothes an extra brush. Make sure that the fire in his painting room burned well while he was working. Keep an eye on him.

She had known that something was wrong last evening when he came home. Came home very late. Poor Mr Charles never looked strong, never looked happy, but last evening he looked sick to his heart, his face bleached white. She had been shocked by his appearance when she opened the door to him, had told him that a cold supper was waiting for him in the dining room, but he had brushed past her. Not even looked

towards the dining room. His eyes blind. Had gone straight
upstairs, straight to his mother, dashed into his mother's sitting
room and slammed the door behind him. She had followed
him. Had stood outside the door and she had heard him. He
had sobbed. Brought a lump to her throat. Like a little boy,
he was. Wanted money. Sounded desperate, she thought, as
she knelt down and pressed her ear to the keyhole. Lots of
money, he was asking for – too much money. Mrs Collins was
telling him that she hadn't got it. Not a sum of money like
that. Not even in the bank. Something about a 'trusty' or was
it a 'trustee', someone looking after her money – she seemed
very upset that she could not get him the money. Sesina heard
a sob in her mistress's voice. Something badly wrong. Saying
something through the sobs. Both of them crying.

'Don't tell Wilkie, Mamma, will you?' That was Mr Charles.
Like a cry of despair.

And then a crash. Knocked over a chair. Coming to the
door. Sesina sprang to her feet, moved to the other side of the
landing and began frantically rubbing at a banister bar. Needn't
have bothered. He went past without even seeing her. Up to
his own room. Sesina heard the door slam and then crept
downstairs to her own place in the basement.

She lay awake for a long time, listening to Dolly snoring
in the room next door. Five hundred pounds! What did he
want with money like that? Still, if he wanted it, he must have
it. Needed to rob a bank to get money like that. She might
have a word with him in the morning. Might be able to get
himself in with someone in the business. There was that fellow
in Seven Dials. Always talking about robbing a bank in
Lombard Street. Trying to work out ways of getting in, getting
past the snooty guard at the door. Good-looking fellow. Give
him a suit of Mr Charles's clothes and tell him to leave the
talking to Mr Charles. Two respectable young men strolling
into the bank. Surely the pair of them could rob a bank. Sesina
resolved to talk to Mr Charles in the morning. Find some way
of seeing him before he had his breakfast, find him on his own
and then tell him her plan. He'd be ever so grateful to her.
She smiled to herself, turned on her side and fell asleep.

But the plan went wrong. He was up and dressed in the

morning, coming down the stairs to the hallway, just as she was coming up from the basement. Looked terrible. Face as chalk white as a bowlful of lye, hands shaking, could hardly turn the lock of the door. And then left it open. Tripped on the steps going down. Just saved himself with a frantic grab at the railing. Staggered down the remaining steps. Off down the road like a drunk. Looked back, once. Didn't look at her. Didn't see her. Just looked up towards his mother's room. Tears running down his face.

And she had followed him. Didn't hesitate. Tore off her apron, screwed it into a tight bundle and went after him. No shawl, nothing. But she wasn't cold because he was running and she kept up with him. Running like a lunatic down Park Road. Frightened a young fellow wearing a school cap who dodged into a back alley. Pretty empty, Park Road. More people around here. Give him time. He was slowing up. Noticed that people were looking at him. She'd catch up with him then and say something, casual-like, keep with him, anyway.

That look on his face. She had seen that before. He was going to throw himself in the river or something.

Slowing down, now. That was good. Calming down. But no, turning into a small street. Walking fast. Then into a square. Not running but going very fast with his long legs. Sesina had to run to keep up with him. Knew where he was going. Crossed the square. Not looking to right or to left. Almost bumped into an old gent with a scarf over mouth and hat pulled over eyes. Kept going. Up the steps.

Sesina waited. A bit relieved. She knew that place. Mr Charles had sent her on messages there. Another artist. A Mr Milton-Hayes. He had been working with that man during the last few weeks; she knew that. Had gone there with his painting coat and his palette and paints. A bit early to work today, but perhaps he had another reason.

He'd go in, she told herself reassuringly. See his friend. Perhaps try to borrow money. Could anyone borrow a huge sum of money like that? She didn't know. Anyways, he'd be safe in with a friend. Up the steps he went. Hand lifted to knock, but the door was open. Just a little open. Went straight in. Didn't close it. By now she had reached the end of the steps and she waited. Sooner or later he would be out and then she would walk home with him. He wouldn't mind that. They were easy-going, like their mother, both Mr Wilkie and Mr Charles. Not a bit of a snob in any of the family.

But it didn't take him long. Came pounding down the stairs. She could hear him, running like a lunatic. Out through the door, leaving it wide open. Down the steps. Turned back, down the road. At least, she thought, after minutes of hard running, he looks like he's going home. Changed his mind about going to work. Or had something happened? She kept near to him though, and somehow, as he calmed down, he must have noticed her because he slowed right down and waited for her to catch up with him. He didn't ask her any questions, just walked slowly with his head bowed.

They had entered Hanover Terrace before he spoke. And then his words were addressed more to himself than to her. 'I should have taken my painting coat, my father's painting coat, I should have taken it away from that place; I'll never go there again.' He said the words in a dazed sort of fashion.

'Don't worry,' she had said and she had done her best to make her voice sound comforting and reassuring. 'Don't worry. I'll run back and fetch it. You go inside, Mr Charles. Go back to bed. It's still early. Have a little sleep.'

THREE

Wilkie Collins, *Hide and Seek* 1854:
The police, on their side, lost no time; but they had to get out of the crowd in the passage and go round the front of the house, before they could arrive at the turning which led into the court from the street. This gave the fugitives a start; and the neighbourhood of alleys, lanes, and by-streets in which their flight immediately involved them, was the neighbourhood of all others to favour their escape. While the springing of rattles and the cries of "Stop thief!" were rending the frosty night air in one direction, Zack and the stranger were walking away quietly, arm in arm, in the other.

'What's troubling you, Wilkie?' Dickens had said nothing for a good fifteen minutes, but from time to time I saw him look across at me. He, himself, wore a puzzled look. Now, quite abruptly, he stopped walking and turned to face me.

'It's no good, Wilkie. I'm not happy about this. And you're not happy about it. We must be on the side of the law, no matter what our private feelings are. I think we must go back. And we must tell Inspector Field about those pictures and, what's more, we must give him all the help that we can about identifying the people in them. You know and I know that, even if there were no faces, even then we began to think of names.'

My heart sank. When Dickens spoke like that, not even the Queen of England could move him. In fact, when Queen Victoria wanted to congratulate him on a part that he played, he wouldn't walk the few steps from the dressing room to her box in the audience. He just refused, just said that he wasn't going to meet the Queen of England still wearing a clown's make-up and that was it. And Queen Victoria was not only a million times more important than I was, she was also a very

forcible lady and not even my best friends had ever compli-
mented me on strong-mindedness. In the end, I nodded, but I
felt like a traitor. A strong picture of my brother, pursued by
the police, and running frantically through the streets of
London, had taken possession of my mind and do what I might
to banish it, the horrible image just would not be erased.

'I suppose that you are right, Dick,' I said as we walked on,
but I couldn't keep a note of misery from my voice.

'I know that I am right,' he returned with his usual air of
quiet confidence. 'Don't worry,' he said kindly. 'I know what
you're thinking, but I tell you that you are wrong. Lots of men
in London have red hair.'

Red hair, tall, slim, conducting an illicit affair with a young
married woman, an acquaintance of Edwin Milton-Hayes, in
possession of a good income, thanks to the generosity of my
mother and the money-making ability of my father. That was
Charley and no, there were not others in the circle of
Pre-Raphaelite painters who would fit that description. Those
thoughts were in my mind as we went back. Still, I tried to
tell myself, perhaps Dickens was right. There were other paintings there, other names had sprung to my mind. I had guessed
who the person in *The Night Prowler* might be, the name of
the young man in *Forbidden Fruit* sprang to my mind as soon
as I had seen the picture. The world of the Pre-Raphaelite
artists was a very small one; was a world full of gossip and
innuendo. Sooner or later, someone would start mentioning
names and then Inspector Field would be more suspicious.
In the meantime, as the friend of Dickens, a man whom the
inspector admired so immensely, I might have enough influence to shield Charley from his own stupidity.

'We don't need to say anything, Wilkie, you know.' Dickens
had been looking across at me from time to time and now the
essential kindness of the man came to the surface. 'It's not
up to us to make surmises. We'll just show him the pictures,
lay them out, have another look at them ourselves and then,
if you think that we should go no further, why then we'll be
off before your mother's dinner will have got cold and we
both get beaten around the head with that enormous handbag
of hers.'

He laughed, but with such an anxious and concerned expression in his eyes as he scanned my face that I, too, laughed and tried to tell myself that I was making a mountain out of a mole heap. Charley was such a gentle fellow, so religious, so in earnest about everything. That fight with Milton-Hayes was completely out of character for him. But, of course, he had felt that Milton-Hayes was mocking his intense love for the girl whom he had painted in his beautiful portrait. It surprised everyone who knew him. When we were boys, in Italy, I was the one who always had to stand up for my young brother and to fight his battles for him. I remembered how, when my mother went away on a visit when Charley was twelve years old, he was so 'mother-sick' as my father put it, that she had to be summoned home to comfort him, poor little fellow. I saw my companion cast several glances at me as we progressed down the street and I knew that he was reading my face as though it were in one of his own manuscripts, or slips, as he always called those sheets of paper which he filled up so conscientiously every day.

After a time he began to speak. Did not stop this time, but continued his rapid walk, not looking at me, but speaking fast and persuasively.

'Come on, Wilkie,' he said. 'Why should you fear the truth? You, of all people, know that young brother of yours. Your father, God rest his gentle soul, worried about both of you, just as most fathers worry about their sons. He used to say to me, and this was long before you and I met, he used to say, "I worry about Wilkie getting into scrapes, he's that kind of boy, but I worry even more about Charley because he's too fearful to get into scrapes".' Dickens laughed gently to himself as I stared ahead and thought hard.

'It was his own fault, of course,' resumed Dickens. 'He was a religious man, your father. Religion played a big part in his life and he was approaching, bit by bit, to the Church of Rome. But, you know, Wilkie, he made a terrible mistake when he sent that nervous, sensitive boy of his to that Jesuit school, Stonyhurst College, wasn't it?'

'That's right,' I said and I thought about Charley waking up with nightmares, worrying about whether he had confessed all of his sins. 'You're right,' I added. 'He was – is – too religious, too worried about doing wrong.' I hesitated for a minute. 'You know when we were boys in Italy, I broke a window, playing ball. I didn't want to own up to it, because it was my third piece of mischief in the day and my father had threatened that I would miss my daily ride to the outskirts of Rome and so when the window was found, I utterly denied everything, blamed the street boys. My father was suspicious, though, and kept on questioning us and then Charley – and I was furious with him – suddenly said that he was the one who had broken the window. I think that he couldn't bear the tension, whereas I was quite enjoying myself, cheerfully lying with an innocent face. I can tell you I was pretty annoyed with him as I then had to own up myself,' I added and suppressed the words 'and I'm afraid that he might do the same thing again now'.

Dickens smiled a little at my story. 'How old was Charley, then?' he asked and when I answered that my brother had been about ten years old, Dickens broke into a laugh.

'Well, he's a man grown now,' he said. 'I can't see what you are worried about.'

'I suppose that you are right,' I said, though there was still an uneasiness within me. People didn't always change in their essential character as they grew from childhood to adulthood.

'Of course, I'm right,' he said impatiently and left barely a second before he rushed on. 'So what I am saying, Wilkie, is that this gentle, nervous, scrupulous boy would not have committed murder, but there is no doubt that he has got himself into a mess, got himself entangled by that little flirt, Molly French, and sooner or later that is going to come out. So what can we do?' Dickens turned to face me, eyes brightly glowing, thin lips firmly compressed.

I did not hesitate. 'Shield him for as long as possible,' I said decisively.

'Wrong,' he said. 'No, we bring it all out into the open, draw the poison. Bring everything out into the open. Between us, with a bit of effort, I think that the two of us could put a name to every one of the figures in those damnable pictures. Broaden the horizon, my dear friend, heap the information on the lap of the inspector, be on the side of law, Wilkie, old man, flood the man with names. After all,' he said earnestly, 'who in this world of ours cares too much if a handsome young man plays about with a silly young woman? Of course, no one. The world would laugh. But who would be condemned by the world as we know it? Why, Molly, of course. All the good ladies would hold up their hands in horror if that picture was shown with the face of Molly sketched onto that blank oval of white paint, and rightly so, Wilkie, rightly so. A woman has to be without stain. Now let me put another question to you, Wilkie, who would be laughed at, sneered at, would feel that he could not hold up his head in society ever again? Why, the husband, of course. John French may feel that he has to go away and shoot himself, or at the very least, retire from London society, bury himself in the country. And you know what the world would say? Why the words: "No fool like an old fool" would be on everyone's lips.'

'What are you saying, Dickens?' I asked the question, but there was a feeling of despair lodged like a leaden weight in my stomach. He was going to talk me into something; I knew that. And it was going to be something that I didn't really want to do.

'I'm saying that we go back to the Milton-Hayes house. We make some excuse about Charley. Let's keep him out of it, Wilkie. He's not up to this sort of calm, blank-faced, poker game stuff. We, you and I, reveal those pictures to the inspector, that's if he hasn't found them already. But, in any case, like good, law-abiding citizens, we open our minds to him, we give him the benefit of our knowledge.' And then when I said nothing, a note of impatience came into his voice.

'Come on, Wilkie, be sensible. Don't you see we broaden the canvas, open up the field, flood the man with names,' he repeated, 'let him race around London investigating. Inspector Field is enamoured with the thought that he is one of the first detectives in the whole of the country. He'll love to dig into all the backgrounds. You know and I know that it wasn't young Charley who took a knife to that man. He's incapable of it, Wilkie. So if he didn't do it, what we must do is give every assistance to Inspector Field to find that man or the woman who did do it. Come along now, Wilkie, let's step it out.'

And he set off walking at a tremendous speed, powered by his belief in himself and in the wisdom of his decisions. I followed, trying not to allow the heavy feelings of trepidation and anxiety to slow my footsteps. Perhaps, I thought hopefully, the inspector would not be there. Perhaps another crime in another part of London was now taking his attention and the matter of the death of the artist would have been put to simmer on the back burner in his mind and I could go straight to my mother's house and talk with Charley before he could be questioned by the inspector. Wild thoughts of ferrying my brother to Norfolk and getting him on board my friend Pigott's yacht were flashing through my mind as we turned into the square and approached the Milton-Hayes house. It looked the same as all of the other houses beside and across from it. No sign of any police activity as we approached the door and rang the bell. Only the white and scared face of the silent housemaid showed that anything unusual was taking place inside.

And, to my disappointment, Inspector Field was still there, barking out orders to a subordinate policeman who was staggering under the weight of an enormous picture of Covent Garden. The door to the cloakroom was now standing open and the bunch of keys was in the lock. I did not hesitate, but went straight in, walking past Dickens.

'Look at that, inspector,' I said, taking the initiative for once and pointing to the canvas carrying bag. 'Exactly what I expected to find. I came back to see if there was a bag like that somewhere in the house. My brother, the artist, has one of these. I wondered whether Milton-Hayes did.' I didn't move to touch it, wouldn't have had the time, anyway, because the inspector had seized its handles, almost before I had finished speaking.

The police had a trestle table, brought from somewhere and now erected on the platform, across the place where the body of Milton-Hayes had been lying, slightly shielding the ugly, darkening stains of blood. Inspector Field picked out the pictures, one by one, and laid them out on the table and then stood back, giving a long, low whistle to denote intense excitement and interest.

'Look at that,' he said enthusiastically. 'Look at that, Mr

Collins. Do you see, Mr Dickens! Look at these screw marks in the frame, in each one of the frames. All ready for the finishing touches, ready to attach the second half of the picture. Get me that piece of frame.' He snapped his fingers at an underling who was back in a second. Inspector Field ignored him, though. His eyes had widened as they took in the details of the pictures.

'No faces,' he said after a minute.

'Strange,' I said in a neutral fashion. Dickens said nothing. The inspector looked from one to the other of us.

'Would that be the way they would do things, normally?' Inspector Field spoke as though artists were some strange tribe from some remote part of the world.

I tried to look knowledgeable. 'Everyone has a different way of working,' I said wisely.

'Could be blackmail.' Dickens spoke quickly and decisively, just as if suddenly he had made up his mind as to the correct mode of action. 'This might be your clue, inspector. You were saying that it looked as though the man made plenty of money. Perhaps he found out secrets and threatened to display the picture to the world. This one, for instance.' And Dickens leant over and picked out the picture named *The Night Prowler*.

The inspector gazed at it, knitting his brows. 'A housebreaker,' he said. 'Like Bill Sykes in your *Oliver Twist*, Mr Dickens.'

Dickens shook his head. 'But not like Bill Sykes, though. Not a common or garden thief, inspector. Look at those clothes. Latest London fashion. Look at that hat! Beautifully painted, isn't it? You can see the quality of the silk with the fine brushstrokes.'

'Milton-Hayes specialized in the painting of the effect of light on silks and velvets,' I said. I felt happier discussing *The Night Prowler* and hoped that the inspector would keep focused upon that picture. I had a feeling that, if I had the skill, I might be able to get him to put a face to that faceless figure. While Dickens and the inspector were exchanging meaningful glances over the *Forbidden Fruit* picture with the young-looking man urging the girlish figure towards the church, I pondered over the idea. And just before they moved on to *Taken in Adultery* I spoke out.

'You may be interested in this, inspector,' I said. 'As I mentioned to you earlier, my brother had persuaded my mother to throw a party for Mr Milton-Hayes. On this very night, in fact. She often did this, enjoys the company, but this time it was a little different. Mr Milton-Hayes asked my brother to invite a canon who was a possible purchaser of a set of pictures and instead of inviting other artists to discuss the works, he presented a list of other people, possible purchasers, perhaps. One was the owner of an art gallery – and his wife. That, I suppose, was understandable. Another was a most talented young artist, Walter Hamilton, but the others, for instance Lord Douglas, the son and heir of the Earl of Ennis. He's certainly not an artist nor were any of the other guests, which is strange . . .' I pretended to hesitate and then said, as one who is struck by a good idea, 'Why don't you pop in tonight, inspector. Number 17, Hanover Terrace, Regent's Park. You would be very welcome. My mother is the most hospitable of women and . . .' Again I hesitated and then I said, 'And you could come to announce the death of Mr Milton-Hayes. Who knows but you might see some signs of guilt, might guess who came here this afternoon and used that knife with such deadly effect.'

The inspector nodded vigorously. 'That's very kind of you, Mr Collins. I'll do that if I may. About ten, do you think? Give everyone a chance to eat their dinner. Don't you worry, sir! I'll have my eyes open and will be watching all of the faces.'

And with a feeling of triumph, I saw his eyes go back to *The Night Prowler* picture. I looked at Dickens. His face was grave and it was impossible to read his expression. Nevertheless, I was pleased with myself. The inspector was now carefully studying the last picture, *Den of Iniquity*, and as far as I could tell, his eyes had moved quite quickly past the third picture, *Taken in Adultery*.

But then, just as we were about to leave, I was arrested by the inspector's voice as I made my way towards the door.

'Do you know anyone in the artistic world with red hair, Mr Collins?'

I turned back, swivelled on my heel, shocked and surprised. The inspector was pointing to the *Taken in Adultery* picture.

I pretended to look at the red-headed young man with his arms around the woman, but then to my horror, my eye was drawn to a table in the corner of the room. Milton-Hayes had drawn and painted it in a most realistic fashion.

And on that table, placed neatly in the middle of the shining surface, painted with meticulous care, was an artist's palette. I knew it well. It had belonged to my father and it was now Charley's favourite possession. For a moment, I was savagely glad that Edwin Milton-Hayes had met his death at the hands of an assassin.

'Could be your young brother, Wilkie, couldn't it?' said Dickens in a casual fashion. 'Or, wait a minute, wasn't that Irish friend of Daniel Maclise a red-head? Do you remember the fellow, Wilkie, came from Maclise's native city of Cork? You must remember him. Played the fiddle, didn't he?' said Dickens giving vent to his artistic imagination. 'Or am I thinking of someone else,' he concluded blandly.

The inspector had lost interest. He had gone back to the *The Night Prowler* picture and was inspecting it carefully, nodding his head from time to time. 'Interesting, that,' he said after a minute. 'I must check a few records in Scotland Yard.' And then he roused himself from his thoughts. 'Well, I'm most obliged to you, Mr Collins.'

'Of course,' said Dickens walking from painting to painting and then stopping opposite one of them. 'Of course, inspector,' he went on, 'the idea of burglary, adultery, smoking opium and mixing with criminals in one of those low dens in Limehouse and such places, are all something that no respectable citizen could approve. But speaking as the father of two young girls, I am sick to my heart to think of any man taking advantage of youth and innocence.' And he pointed with his stick to the second painting on the table, *Forbidden Fruit*.

The inspector studied it. 'Quite a young man,' he said after a moment.

'Old enough to know better,' flashed Dickens and thumped his stick on the floor to lend emphasis to his words.

The inspector looked from one to the other of us. 'You wouldn't happen to know the name of the man?' he asked, impartially addressing the space between the two of us.

I hesitated, but Dickens spoke before I could frame an answer.

'Come to Hanover Terrace this evening, inspector. I can guarantee you a hospitable reception from the charming Mrs Collins and, so long as they allow me to carve the beef, why then you will be very well fed, indeed.'

'It's very kind of you, Mr Dickens,' said the inspector, for all the world as though he had been invited to the Dickens household, 'but I think that I will turn up after dinner and if you will be good enough to arrange for me to have a room where I may lay out these pictures, perhaps as Mr Milton-Hayes was going to do. I'll arrive at ten in the evening, if that is all right. Oh, and I'd be obliged if you could keep my visit a secret until I arrive.' He looked enquiringly at Dickens, but his eyes strayed back to the pictures.

'I think that can be arranged, can't it, Wilkie. The drawing room, don't you think?' Dickens gave a perfunctory look in my direction, but did not wait for any comment from me before going on. 'Yes, we'll arrange all that for you, inspector. I think that Mrs Collins will have to know about this death and the change in arrangements, but otherwise we'll say nothing to any of the guests.'

The inspector nodded at that and I presumed that he agreed that my mother should be informed. A relief to me as I could imagine her fury if she were kept in the dark – could almost hear her declaiming about arrangements made to invite police officers into her own house and allow them to occupy her cherished drawing room and no one having the manners or consideration to inform her about the matter beforehand. I resolved to leave my mother to Dickens and to immediately disappear into my own bedroom as soon as we arrived at Hanover Terrace. I wondered whether to warn the inspector that my mother, though very good hearted and a wonderful mother to her two sons, could be a bit hot-tempered. But the inspector's eyes left me and my friend quickly and when I looked back before going through the door I saw that he was bending over *The Night Prowler*, seemingly absorbed in memorizing all details about that fashionably clad figure with his silk top hat and his sleek fitting trousers.

FOUR

'For the love of mercy, Sesina, look at the time. Near on five o'clock. Will you leave off scrubbing Mr Charles's painting coat and go and chop the apples for me. I swear you've been at that stain for the last twenty minutes.'

Mrs Barnett was in a bad mood. It was the fault of the missus, of course; Sesina knew that. Mrs Barnett was a good cook and she could turn out good meals whenever she was left to herself, but Mrs Collins would keep fussing her, would keep coming in and out of the kitchen and tasting things and changing her mind. Although Mrs Collins had stayed in her room all day, looking pale, and not feeling well, apparently, already there had been a stream of messages, relayed by Dolly, the each one contradicting the last. The fact that the cook had discovered that Sesina had not cleaned the front step nor polished the knocker on the front door as she had been sent out on an early-morning errand by Mr Charles added to the cook's fury.

Sesina shot a look at Mrs Barnett's face. Like a fire, she was. The hotter the temper, the redder the face. Sesina shrugged her shoulders. *Got worries of my own.* She silently addressed the words to the cook's back and began to hum loudly and then to sing 'Angelina Baker', trying to remember the words that she had heard in Covent Garden. Dolly, the parlour maid, averted her gaze and went on chopping onions and little Becky gave Sesina a scared look.

Don't care, thought Sesina. Her nerves were on edge, stretched out like guts hung up to dry for sausage casings. She began to sing a little louder. Another song, one that she remembered better.

> Now this young lady cried,
> I can't be satisfied,
> I wish I was his bride.

'Be quiet, Sesina,' snapped Mrs Barnett. 'And I'll thank you, young lady, another time, to come and ask my permission before you go off on some errand for Mr Charles without permission,' she repeated angrily, 'or without even having the manners to tell me that you were going off.' Mrs Barnett sounded at the end of her patience, so Sesina gave a shrug and stopped singing. She'd go on with the song in her mind. It blotted out the memory of that house and those dead eyes staring up at her . . . Sesina shuddered and scrubbed a little harder, until the ache in her arm made her stop for a moment.

Mrs Barnett had gone towards the pantry so Sesina relieved her feelings by sticking out her tongue at the fat, waddling figure. She took care not to let Dolly see her, though. Thick as thieves, those two. And Mrs B. was in a very bad mood. She was back in a moment with a face like thunder. She had taken a lump of steak from the meat safe and was chopping it like she was killing something. The blood flowed over the board and Sesina found herself feeling slightly sick. Strange how animal blood and human blood look just the same.

She gave one last rub at the painting coat, sprinkling some more salt, but the stain was still there. She could even feel it with her fingers. Sticky when she had first picked it up and taken it away, but now it was beginning to harden. Something coating the threads of the old black coat, sticking tenaciously to them and no amount of salt or water seemed able to shift it. She tried to avert her mind from what had occurred this morning. No good thinking about things after the deed is done. Her friend, Isabella, used to say that and she was right. *Only get yourself into a state of nerves.* Sesina hummed the tune under her breath. No need for anyone to know.

'What is it, anyway, that stain?' Dolly had to put her oar in.

'Paint,' said Sesina shortly. 'Red paint.' Not red, of course. Almost black now, she thought. And she knew very well that it wasn't paint. Had known the minute she had seen it. She had known that she could not leave it there. Not beside that body on the floor.

'You'll never get that out with salt,' stated Mrs Barnett. 'A drop of turps might do it, but it looks set to me. Anyways, leave it now. It's only the old coat he uses for painting. He won't care, bless him. Not fussy. Now get chopping them apples or you'll feel the weight of my hand.'

Just you try, thought Sesina, but she thought that enough had been said about the stained painting coat. She took it out and left it in the scullery and then came back into the kitchen just as the sound of footsteps on the stairs made the cook rap out a swear word. Should have been expecting it, though. Not like the mistress to leave it so late. In the usual way she'd have been fussing in and out of the kitchen from an early moment. Dolly had said that the missus wasn't well, ever so pale, according to Dolly.

'Oh, Mrs Bennett, how are you getting on?' Mrs Collins came in with a waft of perfume. Not dressed yet, but all ready for it. Not pale now, neither. Hair done, face heavily powdered and painted. Bright pink cheeks. Stuff around her eyes, too. Still wearing her dressing gown although it was five o'clock in the evening. Would just pop on her new crinoline as soon as the clock struck six. Loved a party, thought Sesina. Got her sons to organize one as often as she could. Sixty years old if she was a day! A fine sight she made herself, dressing up like a twenty-year-old, drinking wine, flirting with all the young men, acting like she was the same age as all of her two sons' friends. Sesina often had a good laugh about that. Even managed to get Dolly to laugh a bit too. Good as a play, she said to Dolly. A play with the title *The Missus and her Men* said Sesina. Dolly thought that the missus might be on the lookout for a new husband, but Sesina knew better. The woman was just having fun. Much more sensible to keep your own hand on the money strings and not let any man boss you around. And Mrs Collins was a woman who liked to have her own way though she pretended to be so sweet and went around praising everything. For all the world like a big fat purring cat, thought Sesina. She was at it now.

'Oh, Mrs Bennett, aren't you wonderful! What gorgeous smells! Oh, I just must taste this gravy. Just get me a spoon, will you, Dolly, like a good girl? Marvellous! Quite, quite perfect. I do want this party to be a success. It's not often that Mr Charles asks for one. Not like Mr Wilkie, is he, Mrs Bennett? I vow that Mr Wilkie would have a party every day of the week if he could. Now, I must do something to help. Shall I do the table? And I'll just borrow Sesina to fetch and carry for me. That will be one thing off your mind, won't it, Mrs Bennett? Come along, Sesina, let's get started.'

All worked up. Must be the excitement. Quite the actress. Had always wanted to be an actress. She had told Sesina that, time and time again. Kept her figure well; nice and slim, too, thought Sesina as she followed Mrs Collins up the stairs. Was having such fun, too. Pretending she was one of the young lads. Easy to see how she got away with it. Didn't look like a lad, of course, with her crinoline on. But she was free and easy with them as if she was one of the crowd, even though she was wearing a crinoline. Didn't care if they smoked at the table or told off-colour stories. And afterwards in the drawing room, sat there like a queen bee with her crinoline spread out and the lads sprawled on the rug in front of the fire. Sesina wondered what it would be like to wear a crinoline. Must make your waist ever so small.

She tried to think of what Mr Charles – Charley, she liked to call him when she had dreams about him – what would Charley say if he saw her wearing a crinoline and an orange velvet dress over it? It was a nice daydream. There was some-thing about him; something that gave her a slight ache at the back of her throat. Something about the extreme pallor of his skin, the pale, red-gold of his hair, the paint stains on the fingers of his hands and the wounded look in his dark-brown eyes. He had cut himself shaving that morning and she longed to put some Brookes ointment on it. He needed someone to look after him. Made a mess of things when he was left to himself. *Kill the rat and let him lie; he'll do no harm to you and I.* Good job that she had got that painting coat. And a good job Sesina had eyes in her head. He'd have never noticed the stain. Like his mother. Short-sighted the pair of them! Not as bad as Mr Wilkie, of course, but then he had the sense to wear spectacles. Mr Charles was afraid the girls wouldn't like him if he wore spectacles.

'Too soft for his good,' she muttered to herself, feeling a slight smile curve her lips and then cleared her throat when she saw her mistress look back down at her.

'How many guests, ma'am?' she asked, as soon as they got into the dining room. A bit of a gossiper, Mrs Collins. Loved to talk. Would drag out this business and then Sesina would be in trouble when she got back to the kitchen. Let her talk, though, she thought. Nice to be out of the kitchen for a while and I can just get on with setting the table while the woman chattered.

'Let me see.' Now Mrs Collins was fishing around in a drawer. 'Here we are. Here's the list.' Blind as a bat, she was, peering at the piece of paper, nearly holding it touching her nose. 'Now, Sesina, just let me copy out the names onto these little cards and then you can put them in the right place.' She had seated herself at the sideboard, had the pen and ink out in a moment and had piled up the gilt-edged cards in front of her. 'Well, here's one for Mr Wilkie. He goes at the bottom of the table, Sesina, and this one for me. I go at the top of the table. Now, who is the most important female guest? She has to go on Mr Wilkie's right-hand side and the second most important on his left-hand side.' She consulted her list, biting her bottom lip.

Sesina ignored her. This could take for ever. She took out the cutlery drawer and began to lay the places. Twelve seats around the polished mahogany. She'd lay twelve places for a start and then either take some away or add some more if needed. Her hands had been trembling but the mindless, mechanical work steadied her and she found that the images and the strong smell of blood were beginning to fade. She had gone halfway around the table by the time that Mrs Collins had made up her mind.

'Fourteen,' she said. 'That's what I make it. Fourteen altogether.'

'Fourteen,' repeated Sesina. 'Well, three at each end of the table and four on either of the long sides. Will that suit you, missus?'

She didn't wait for an answer, but went on laying the cutlery. 'Every second one, man, woman, man, that's the way, isn't it, missus?'

'That's the way it should be, Sesina, but those sons of mine never think about that when they are asking me to stage a dinner party and, of course, when it's a dinner given by two young men, well, the wives don't want to go. There's Mr Dickens, now. How many times has he been to this house, Sesina? He even took over the carving the last time he came, said Wilkie was making a mess of it. Quite at home, here, isn't he? And never once have I seen his wife! And the canon – well he's not bringing his wife, just coming to look at Mr Milton-Hayes' pictures, thinking of buying them for a church hall, so I hear. Well, of course, he's not bringing his wife. And Mr Milton-Hayes hasn't a wife. None of them have a wife, not my two boys, not Walter Hamilton, or Lord Douglas. Still Mr John French has a wife – Molly's a jolly girl. Even my Charley, shy as a wild bird, poor fellow, well even he likes her a lot.'

'Who are you going to have sitting next to you, missus?' Sesina laid down the last dinner spoon and took up the bundle of cards. She'd see if she could put Charley next to Mrs Molly French. Give him a bit of fun. Cheer him up. Make him forget his worries for a night, at least. She'd make sure that she kept his glass filled.

'I'd better have the canon on my right-hand side,' said Mrs Collins with a resigned sigh. 'Rough sort of man. New to the parish. From Essex, you know, Sesina. And then after that he came to London, but he was just a vicar down by the docks, then. Don't know why he was chosen for a nice place like Regent's Park. Not like the canon we had before – such a gentleman. This fellow drinks like a fish. Went to sleep with his head on the table last time I saw him. Still, that saves talking to him once the meal is half over. He'll be insensible by then. And I suppose that I'll have to have Mr Milton-Hayes on my other side since the dinner is for him to talk about his paintings and we'll put Lord Douglas on the other side of the canon. The clergy like people with titles and then let's have Mrs Gummidge, Mrs Hermione Gummidge on Mr Milton Hayes' other side and her daughter Florence down next to Lord Douglas. Or should I put the mother somewhere else? A terrible woman, would talk the hind leg off a donkey. What about next to Mr Dickens? He'll manage her. Still, he's capable of changing his place and disturbing everything if his dinner partner doesn't suit him. Capable of anything, that man! No, we can't have that. Now, who are you putting there, beside Mr Dickens, Sesina? Oh, little Molly French. Well, that should work out. He's a married man, Mr Dickens, but you mark my words, she'll flirt with him and he'll flirt back with her. She's a terrible flirt, so they say. Of course, you can hardly blame her, married to a man so much older than herself! Oh well . . .'

'Mr Charles likes her,' put in Sesina. 'Mr Wilkie's been teasing him about her.'

'Hm,' said Mrs Collins. 'That mightn't please her husband, Mr John French. Very jealous, he is, but thank goodness, he won't dare say anything to Mr Dickens. Though Molly might hear about it when they get home. That's the trouble with rich husbands, Sesina. They feel that they can do what they like. And he's so rich! You wouldn't believe it. A great catch for Molly. Mind you, he's nearly thirty years older than she is if he's a day. But never mind. You should see their house! And the carriage that she has for her own use. Now where on earth shall I put that wretched Mrs Gummidge?'

Sesina left her to it. She remembered this Molly, Mrs John French. She and her rich husband had been at a dinner a couple of months ago. Charley had a nice time then, sitting beside Mrs Molly and telling her about his painting of a convent garden, stuttering a bit and his pale face flushing up and his green eyes all excited. Lovely fellow he was, ever so handsome, thought Sesina, tall and good-looking with that lovely red-gold hair. Funny, when you think what a plain and odd-looking little man his brother was. Still, Mr Wilkie had the gift of the gab; he was the one who got all of the ladies and poor Charley was ever so shy. Needed a bit of encouragement, poor lad. She was glad that she had done what she did. Never know! Might have been terrible trouble. Without waiting for an answer she neatly extracted the card with Mr Charles Collins written on it and slipped it down on the right-hand side of Mrs John French. Let him have a nice time with flirty Molly. Been looking so peaky and worried, more sort of frightened, during the last few days. She hoped she hadn't been seen rearranging the cards and was pleased when she heard Dolly clumping along the passageway. Make a bit of a distraction. Though Mrs Collins was in a giddy mood. All excited about her dinner party.

'Mrs Gummidge, madam.' Little Becky, who helped in the house a couple of days in the week, gave the door a perfunctory knock and then pushed it open. She was almost swept to the ground as a very large woman in an immensely wide crinoline pushed past her and through the doorway.

'Oh, Mrs Collins, I've just come to beg a favour of you, I do apologize. But I just know that as a mother yourself . . . well, I'm sure that you will understand my feelings. All London talks about what a good mother you are to your two sons. Dear Mrs Collins, how are you? Oh, how well you look and I do love your hairstyle.'

Nothing like laying on the compliments with a trowel, thought Sesina.

'And you, like me, have lost a dearest husband, so I know you'll understand . . .'

That hadn't gone down quite so well. Sesina could see her mistress stiffen. But that Mrs Gummidge had brass nerve enough for anything, pushing past Sesina as though she was a stray cat. Looking up and down the table now and then snatching up the card marked Miss Florence Gummidge.

'Oh, Mrs Collins, I really can't have her sitting next to Lord Douglas. Lots of strange things said about him, you know. I suppose you mightn't have heard, dear Mrs Collins. You are here in your delightful house, devoting your life to your dear sons . . . Oh, dear, dear Mrs Collins, it must be such a relief to you just to have sons, but you see with a daughter, I have to be so careful. And of course, Florence, she can't help it, poor pet, but she is so devastatingly attractive that I have to keep a weather eye out all of the time.'

'How very tiresome that does sound, for both of you!'

Sesina swallowed a giggle. Good old Mrs C. She certainly could give a smart answer. Mrs Gummidge looked undecided for a moment, but then chose to ignore the words. She waved the card marked Miss Florence Gummidge in the air and looked up and down at the fourteen places arranged on the table and examined the cards already laid out on the table.

'Perhaps my little pet could go up somewhere near to the top of the table, somewhere where you could keep an eye on her, dear Mrs Collins, perhaps here, just beside Mr Milton-Hayes. I've heard such very nice things about him. A friend of mine was saying that he was doing very well from his paintings. Has taken a new house in Dorset Square, so I've heard. A most worthy young man, so they say.'

'And Florence? Will she like sitting next to him? He's not that young, you know. I'd put him as nearer forty than thirty. I was going to put Mr Dickens next to him. Or the canon. They are about the same age. But please do feel free to choose a suitable dinner partner for her. I was just hoping to give the poor girl a bit of fun.'

Not half irritated, thought Sesina. Easy-going in the normal way of things, but a bit ruffled up like now. She didn't blame her. Who owned the house, anyway? Didn't stop Mrs Gummidge, though.

'Oh, dear Mrs Collins. You quite mistake my Florence. Just because she is so pretty! But she's a very earnest girl and interested in sensible conversation. And so I think, yes, we'll leave that card there, just around the corner from Mr Milton-Hayes. I do want her to make a good match; I'm sure, as a mother, you'll understand.'

'Yes, of course, my dear, do put your daughter's card over there next to Mr Milton-Hayes.' There was a mischievous gleam in the mistress's eyes. Surprising that Mrs Collins had given in so easily to have her arrangements overturned like that, but Sesina understood all, when, after a dramatic pause, Mrs Collins, behind her hand, whispered to the woman, 'Of course, I can understand how worried you are. Don't worry; no explanations needed. I did hear . . .' And then she bustled over to the condiments cupboard and started giving loud-voiced commands to Sesina, just interrupting them to call across to the purple-faced woman. 'Goodbye, Mrs Gummidge. So lovely of you to pop in. And, of course, you understand how busy I am. See you this evening, then. And I'm so looking forward to meeting dear Florence. And you can trust me to say nothing. Now, Sesina, count those salt cellars, one between two. Oh, on second thoughts, take ten sets of them.

I hate conversations being interrupted with people looking for salt or pepper.'

'Yes, ma'am,' said Sesina demurely, watching Mrs Gummidge flush a dark red and then walk from the room. She was wishing that she could ask for details of what Florence Gummidge had been up to. Some sort of scandal, she thought, judging by the missus's voice, and by the fashion in which she had managed to get rid of the woman so quickly once she had dropped that heavy hint. 'Do I leave that card where Mrs Gummidge placed it, ma'am?' she enquired. 'Is that all right, ma'am? We'll leave the card there where she put it, is that right?'

'Oh, who cares,' snapped Mrs Collins. 'Let her try to get a rich husband for the plain-faced girl of hers. Not that there's anything wrong with being plain. I was never a beauty myself, but this girl, Florence Gummidge, well, I wouldn't like to tell you the things I've heard about her. If I were her mother, I'd take her back to Essex.'

Well, thought Sesina, as she arranged three glasses beside each place, this should be fun tonight. Funny stories about Lord Douglas – and he a lord! Funny stories about Florence Gummidge and her mother keen to get her married. And Molly French was a flirt. And the canon a drunk. Sesina had hoped for a little more gossip, but Mrs Collins had turned sour and snapped out orders impatiently, glancing at the watch in her waistband from time to time.

'So it's all right to leave Miss Florence Gummidge beside Mr Edwin Milton-Hayes, then is it?' she repeated, hoping to hear some more gossip.

'Oh, you might as well. That frightful woman is capable of making another fuss when she arrives. And Wilkie will give into her immediately. Who cares anyway if she nabs Edwin Milton-Hayes?' Mrs Collins swallowed down a slug of wine from one carafe and then tried out another. Drank it straight down, too. 'Unpleasant man,' she said indistinctly. 'Serve her mother right if he mistreats her precious lamb. Wouldn't trust him with a dog, not to mind a child of mine.' Then Mrs Collins had another swig from a third decanter and then washed down the wine with a glass of water, swilling it around in her mouth before she swallowed it. 'Now let's do a quick check and then I must go and get dressed. Read out the names to me, Sesina.'

'Top of the table there's you in between the canon and Mr Edwin Milton-Hayes. And then down one side, there's that Lord Douglas, Mr Dickens, and Mrs Molly –' (the flirty one, Sesina said to herself) – 'and Mr Charles. And across the bottom, there's Mr Wilkie in between Mrs Helen Jordan, the wife of the art gallery man and that woman that's just been here, that Mrs Gummidge.'

'And her dear little Florence on the other long side,' said Mrs Collins crossing over to read the labels, 'and that young painter, Walter Hamilton beside her. Well, that should keep the dear girl busy if Mr Milton-Hayes takes no notice of her. Wally Hamilton has the name of being a ladies' man. And then we have the art gallery man, Mr William Jordan, I hope poor Wally takes care to butter him up and to impress him. Let me see, yes, and just next to him, in between William Jordan and his wife, Helen, we have Mr John French. He's the husband of Molly, you know, Sesina, but you would never know it to look at him. He must be a good forty years older than she.'

No wonder that this Molly flirts with Mr Charles, thought Sesina, but she kept her mouth shut. It was very hard to know with Mrs Collins. One minute she was as familiar and chatty as if you were a member of the family and then, the next moment, she would slap you down for taking liberties.

FIVE

Wilkie Collins, *Hide and Seek*:
But whatever department of painting Valentine tried to excel in, the same unhappy destiny seemed always in reserve for each completed effort. For years and years his pictures pleaded hard for admission at the Academy doors, and were invariably (and not unfairly, it must be confessed) refused even the worst places on the walls of the Exhibition rooms.

'This is Jordan's place. He has his art gallery here in the bottom rooms of his house.' I looked up at the tall, three-storey-high terraced house as I was speaking and then turned towards Dickens. 'Let's stop here and go in and see him,' I proposed. 'We don't need to say anything about Milton-Hayes; the inspector will want to be the first to break that news when he comes around, but it would be interesting for us to pop in and judge whether he's heard the news and to see how they both are.' Dickens and I had been walking fast and I had begun to worry that we would arrive far too early back at home for the party. My mother was, on the whole, very easy-going, but she did like to be dressed and her hair arranged before the first guest lifted the knocker at number 17 Hanover Terrace and I didn't want to annoy her. I stopped, therefore, at a gate marked with a tasteful sign, featuring some of the plants in the garden and bearing the words, *Art Gallery*, lettered with imaginative flair. I saw him look puzzled; obviously he didn't know the name and so I explained in a low voice that I thought the art gallery owner's wife was the card player in the gambling picture entitled *Root of All Evil*.

'Out-of-the-way sort of place for an art gallery,' said Dickens, looking with disfavour at the rather overgrown rustic garden which contrasted very much with the neatly planted patches in front of the neighbouring houses. Nevertheless he nodded at my explanation. He was always a man who liked to get to the bottom of any mystery.

'Plenty of very wealthy people around Regent's Park,' I explained. 'William Jordan does a good business, sold a lot of my father's paintings, for very good prices, also. Milton-Hayes was lucky to get in with him. To be honest, he isn't, wasn't, a particularly outstanding painter.' I was anxious to go in, anxious to see if Helen was all right. She and I were friends and I hoped that no harm would come to her and that she and her husband would make up their differences. 'His wife, Helen, painted the board,' I said, seeing that my companion's eyes were fixed on it.

'Hmm,' said Dickens, giving it a cursory look. 'She'd be better off doing her garden. Pulling up weeds, rather than painting them.' He looked severely at a clump of delicate herb Robert, whose elusive pale pink flowers contrasted with the clusters of dark green ivy, grown like a hedge against the garden wall.

'They're wild flowers,' I said mildly. I found Helen's garden and her paintings rather charming. As she was herself. 'Let's ring the bell,' I proposed hastily. Helen might be on her knees behind some bush. She spent a lot of time in her rustic garden and she would be upset at his remarks if she overheard them.

However, when she opened the door to us, I could see that he was mollified. The sight of Helen Jordan was enough to enchant any man, no matter how critical.

One of the most beautiful women in the art world of London, I had always thought her. Auburn hair, very dark, long-lashed eyes – that wonderful combination that I had always admired. Dressed beautifully and expensively as always. Her corn-coloured hair braided into innumerable soft braids and piled onto the crown of her head. Her eyes glowed at the sight of me. Helen was always a charmer.

'Wilkie!' she exclaimed. 'What a wonderful surprise. You brighten up a dull afternoon. Come in out of the fog. And this must be Mr Dickens. What a privilege to meet you, Mr Dickens. I cannot tell you how much I loved *Bleak House*! I have read it again and again. Come in. Come and see William.'

Her voice was low and melodious and again I could see

how impressed Dickens was, despite his hatred of gambling. He had no time to reply though because the inner door opened and William came through, burst through, in fact. Very hastily, indeed, rather as though he were expecting some bad news and the sound of the doorbell had alarmed him. He stopped short when he saw me, almost seemed startled, and yet he knew me very well indeed. I was the one who, over the years, had taken many of my father's pictures to him to be sold to the owners of houses in the terraces and streets within the Regent's Park district. And I was the one delegated to come and collect the money due to my father once William had subtracted his own substantial commission. The art gallery owner had done very well from the dozens and dozens of small, medium and large paintings which my father, a hard-working man, had turned out. William and I had always been on excellent terms, but now he looked at me with an apprehensive expression on his face.

'Anything wrong?' he asked and, yes, there was certainly a note of tension in his voice. His eyes slanted rapidly towards his wife and then returned to scrutinize my face.

'What should be wrong?' I said and then lightened the atmosphere with a jolly laugh. 'Don't worry, my friend,' I said. 'I haven't taken to painting, again. Haven't come to ask a favour. Don't want you to sell any painting of mine.'

He laughed, also, but it was a forced and artificial laugh and I saw him look once more at his wife. And that lovely face had grown very white under his scrutiny.

'Don't see why I shouldn't be a painter,' I grumbled while keeping a sharp eye on Helen. 'After all the Academy did exhibit my *Smuggler's Retreat*. And if only it had been put in a more favourable position then I would have made a fortune.'

William Jordan laughed once again and this time it sounded a little more natural. 'Stick to the literature, Wilkie,' he advised. 'What do you think, Mr Dickens?' He definitely sounded more relaxed now, but I wondered whether the sound of the doorbell had made both husband and wife expect bad news. Odd that Helen had opened the door to us herself and had not left the task to a servant. They would not, could not, be short of servants, I thought. Well, I hoped not, anyway. But as I looked

around I, the most unobservant of men, could see signs of
household neglect. There was dust on the mantelpiece and on
the window sills. The vases had flowers in them, but not
hothouse flowers, just a few wild flowers from her garden.
The window, like all untended London windows, was streaked
with sooty fog and did not appear to have been cleaned for
days. The rug looked unshaken and the fireplace was filled
with ash and dead pieces of coal. The room, I thought, was
decidedly cold. Could Helen's gambling have reduced their
income to the extent that a servant had to be dismissed? Or
had money been demanded of Helen by someone who knew
that she had continued to gamble despite promises to her
husband. Perhaps the housekeeping money had gone to swell
the coffers of Edwin Milton-Hayes.

'What a surprise to see you, Wilkie. We're looking forward
to your mother's dinner party. Can't wait for our company,
eh?' The art gallery owner had a stilted note to his voice and
I saw him glance again at his wife. And then when I made no
reply, he asked suddenly and slightly maliciously, 'What's
young Charley doing these days? Haven't seen sight nor sound
of him for some time. Has he finished the Regent's Park
painting?'

'I think he has been working for Millais,' I said and then
added, with my eyes on his face, 'and I think he has been
painting in the clothes on some figures that Edwin Milton-Hayes
has sketched. Charley is very good at material, at textures.'

His face had paled at the mention of Milton-Hayes. I was
sure of that. He did his best to rally, though, observing curtly
that my brother would be better off concentrating on his own
paintings rather than bringing praise to other artists because
of his expertise and meticulous care in painting the details of
a scene. His heart wasn't in the lecture, though and he soon
ran out of words. No offer of refreshments had been made
and both husband and wife seemed uneasy in our company,
uneasy and apprehensive, rather as though they were expecting
us to make some sort of an announcement.

'I suppose that you have seen Milton-Hayes' latest master-
pieces, have you?' I said carelessly. 'What did you think of
them? Allegorical, aren't they?'

I saw Helen pale, pale so noticeably that Dickens turned to look at her with concern. He even took a step nearer to her and put his hand on the back of a chair as though about to offer her a seat. She stiffened, though, and stood very upright, very still, her eyes on her husband. He also stiffened.

'I have no idea,' he said abruptly. 'Haven't seen anything by Milton-Hayes for some time. Not sure who he deals with, but not me.'

'You surprise me,' I said. I took off my spectacles to give them a polish and peered at him. 'I would have thought that you would have been his first port of call. You live so near, don't you? You could even have popped in this morning before your breakfast, couldn't you?'

'I'm not in the habit of "popping in" on artists, as you put it,' he said coldly. He had an angry flush on his face.

'You live so near,' I repeated innocently. Did he know that the man was dead? It was possible that he had heard. After all the police had been there for hours. But if he had heard, he was not going to betray any knowledge. He eyed me with a strong air of dislike and then turned to Dickens.

'Could we offer you anything before you go? A cup of coffee? Tea? A glass of wine?'

The emphasis on *'before you go'* made the offer barely polite and Dickens didn't bother to reply. His eyes were fixed upon Helen and I saw a measure of concern in them.

I decided to put an end to the tension.

'We must go, now. We won't keep you. I know that you are busy. Just passing the gate and couldn't resist introducing my friend here. I knew that Helen is a great lover of his books.' I said the words blandly and with conviction, though, before this evening I had never heard Helen say anything of the sort. It was a stupid thing to say, in any case, since Helen was due to meet him within a couple of hours, but it got us out through the door and then when we were safely past the gate I looked back at him standing there in the doorway. He was frowning heavily and I wondered what he was thinking of. I raised an umbrella in a gesture of farewell and endeavoured to keep up with Dickens' rapid walk.

The more that my friend was pondering over a puzzle, the

faster he always walked. I had learned that during the past
few years. Eventually, though, he stopped and waited for my
short legs to catch up with him and then slowed his pace.

'Blackmail,' he said after a minute. 'I said it before and
now I'd lay a bet on it that there is blackmail involved. This
man, Milton-Hayes, devised a very clever method of blackmailing. A most effective method. He paints someone in a
compromising position and then shows them the picture and
tells them that if they don't pay up, why then he will show
the picture all over London, beginning with a small select
party in number 17 Hanover Terrace where the face will not
be revealed, but then moving on to other and more public
occasions where, undoubtedly, that oval of white paint would
have been removed and the victim would have been ruined for
ever in polite society.'

Dickens stopped for a moment, carefully removed a clod of
earth that disfigured a newly painted gate and then walked on
again, thinking hard. After a few minutes he spoke again and
his voice was very thoughtful.

'I hope to goodness,' he said, 'that I would never have
been inveigled into committing one of those sins, that I would
not steal, or gamble, or covet my neighbour's wife, or frequent
low dens of iniquity or seduce a very young girl . . . but if I
did and was faced with dishonour and disgrace, well what
alternatives would be open to me?'

I did not answer. I didn't suppose that I was expected to. I
could see that he was trying to put himself into the shoes of
one of the subjects of these pictures.

'I suppose,' he continued, 'Milton-Hayes' victims were
faced with two alternatives. One, pay the sum of money that
he demanded, and so swell the man's coffers. Or secondly,
get rid of the man; kill him.'

'The second would be the surer method,' I said, trying to
sound sagacious. I began to be more cheerful when I thought
of the number of people that could have been involved in
this blackmail plot. When it came to police suspicions, well,
Charley was only one of at least eight people featured in those
paintings that we had discovered. 'There would be no guarantee
that he would destroy the picture even if he promised to do

so, would there be? Another demand might come a month later,' I finished.

'Indeed!' Dickens nodded his head emphatically. 'And so, my friend, we have a dead body and a slashed painting, though fortunately others were left untouched and despite the blank faces, they may help in the tracing of the person that did this deed. And now let's make haste out of this fog and into your mother's hospitable premises. I have a feeling that this is going to prove to be a most interesting evening.'

I said nothing in reply. Interesting for him, I thought, but for me, with every detail from the painting *Taken in Adultery* fresh in my mind and above all the picture in my mind of that young man, his arms around the young woman, and him with the very distinctive red-gold hair, so carefully painted that it was the first thing that I noticed.

And what had struck me would, doubtless, strike the inspector as soon as he met Charley. I didn't care too much about the death of Milton-Hayes, but I cared intensely for the life of my younger brother.

SIX

Sesina was the one that opened the front door to the peremptory double knock. She had been on edge all of the afternoon. All was ready for the party. Mrs Barnett and Dolly were busy in the kitchen, Mrs Collins had retired to her bedroom to get dressed, Mr Wilkie was out and Mr Charles had refused lunch, just had immured himself in his painting room. Sesina had gone in once or twice under the pretext of seeing to the fire, but each time he was just stretched on the sofa, gazing at the ceiling and he would not address a word to her.

So when the knocker sounded she had the door open in under a minute. A cabbie with a sealed note.

'Mr Charles Collins,' he said, handing it to her. 'I'm to wait for an answer.'

'Come in,' she said. Nice looking young fellow. Might get something out of him.

'Dreadful fog out there,' he said, removing his hat and shaking the wet from his coat.

'What about your passenger? Is he all right? Doesn't want to come in, too, does he?'

'It's a woman,' he said. 'She's all right. Got a roof over her head.' Hoarse voice. These cabbies were out in all weathers, standing perched up behind their passengers, reins over the roof, all the rain and fog dripping down over them and wet slobber from the streets sloshing up against their legs. She'd never known one that didn't have a permanent cold in his head. She was tempted to take him downstairs to the kitchen for a warm drink, but she'd better deliver the note first.

The door to the painting room was locked. It took two knocks before Mr Charles came to the door. She had been on the point of knocking again, but then heard a sound, not words, just a groan which went through her heart. Then he was at the door, paler than ever.

'I've a note for you, Mr Charles. A cabbie brought it. There's a lady waiting in the cab outside.'

He tore it open, really tore the envelope. Hands shaking, eyes staring. Hair needed brushing. She'd love to have done it for him.

But then he was running down the stairs. No hat, no coat, not a minute to think. Didn't even close his door behind him. Running down the stairs as fast as he could go. She followed as quickly as possible, but heard the front door slam as she crossed the drawing-room landing.

The cabbie was still in the hall when she came down the stairs. Comfortable as you please. Sitting on one of the best chairs with a cushion at his back.

'Your horse will run away if you're not careful,' she said. She was dying to open the front door and see who was in the cab, but she didn't want to seem to be spying.

'Not him,' said the cabbie. 'Quietest horse in London. Too old for any capers. Glad of the rest.'

'Better make sure,' she said and went to the door and opened it a slit, just enough for her to be able to peer out. The horse was still there, his reins tied to the gas pole.

'Looks like your fare is gone, though,' she said over her shoulder and had the satisfaction of seeing him jump to his feet and join her.

'Nah, not her.' He was peering over her shoulder. 'Having a walk, the pair of them, ain't they?'

Sesina narrowed her eyes. Hard to tell much from the back view. Had an umbrella too. He had taken it from her – always the gentleman, Mr Charles. Holding it over her, head turned looking down at her. And now they were stopped, standing face to face.

'What's she like, your fare. Don't tell me that you didn't get a good look at her?' she said to the cabbie.

'Young. Not much more than a girl. Good figure, a bit thin for my taste, but the gentry like them thin,' he said. 'Now I'm different. I like 'em small and plump.' He slipped an arm around her waist and she ignored that for the moment. The two figures had turned and were coming back. Sesina elbowed the cabbie back into the hallway and just allowed a chink between the hall door and its frame. They were definitely returning and she wondered whether Mr Charles had persuaded the girl to come into the house. But no, they stopped just by the back of the cab. He opened the door for her and she handed him something. Sesina strained her eyes, could see nothing for a moment, but then they moved underneath the gas light overhead. A small box, she thought, like a pill box, studded with jewels. She could see them flash as the box was passed from hand to hand. And then the girl got into the cab.

'Better get back. Your fare might make off with your horse.' Sesina threw open the hall door. She wanted to get Mr Charles back indoors, didn't want him going off in the fog. Might forget all about the party. She wondered if the lady visitor could be that Mrs Molly French. Ever so romantic, if it was. And she had given him a little present. Sesina was glad that she had put the pair of them sitting side by side for the party tonight. Didn't want to give him his present then. Her husband would be keeping an eye on her. She'd have a good look at this Mrs Molly when she was serving tonight. In the meantime, she'd get Mr Charles indoors and make sure that he had his hot water in plenty of time to wash and shave and his nice new suit laid out ready to wear.

'Go on, get down there,' she hissed to the cabbie and hoped he'd have the sense to get off the steps before Mr Charles came up them. She watched anxiously, but it was all right. The cabbie had gone to the back of the cab, untied the reins, and then walked round to the horse's head and waited there until the young man mounted the steps.

'Nasty fog, Mr Charles,' she said cheerfully as he came through the door.

He did not reply, but clenched into his hand was the small, jewel-studded box. Perhaps a present. A ring? Or perhaps some of them new shirt studs. Mr Wilkie had a present of a couple of pairs of them. He had shown them to her, one day.

Whatever it was, he would probably wear it tonight, as a secret signal between them both.

For a moment Sesina felt a pang of jealousy. Nice to be

rich, to be a lady, to have beautiful clothes. But when it came down to it, Sesina was the one that would save him. This Molly might be having a bit of fun, but she would stick to her rich husband. Ladies were like that.

SEVEN

Wilkie Collins, *Hide and Seek*, 1854:
If the rich proprietors of the "mansions" in the "park"
could give their grand dinners, and be as prodigal as they
pleased with their first-rate champagne, and their rare
gastronomic delicacies; the poor tenants of the brick
boxes could just as easily enjoy their tea-garden conver-
sazione, and be just as happily and hospitably prodigal,
in turn, with their porter-pot, their teapot, their plate of
bread-and-butter, and their dish of shrimps. Not so with
the moderate incomes: they, in their social moments,
shrank absurdly far from the poor people's porter and
shrimps; crawled contemptibly near to the rich people's
rare wines and luxurious dishes; exposed their poverty
in imitation by chemical champagne from second-rate
wine merchants, by flabby salads and fetid oyster-patties
from second-rate pastry-cooks; were, in no one of their
festive arrangements, true to their incomes, to their order,
or to themselves; and, in very truth, for all these reasons
and many more, got no real enjoyment out of their lives,
from one year's end to another.

M y mother was in a bad mood when Dickens and I
arrived at home. She greeted Dickens, never a great
favourite of hers, in a fairly cursory manner and then
launched into a stream of complaints. How she slaved and
slaved to please her sons and how neither of them ever lifted
a finger to help. One of them went walking around the town
and the other shut himself up in his bedroom. Not an offer of
help from either of them and then there was all that she had
to do and the care that she had taken and how one of the
guests, not a woman that she liked or would ever have invited
if the guest list had been left to her, that Hermione Gummidge,
had the unbelievable nerve to interrupt her preparations and

to demand, 'Yes! Demand!' said my mother with huge emphasis, that she rearrange the table, undo all of her hard work, just solely in order that the woman's plain and tongue-tied daughter, Florence, could be moved to sit beside the man of the moment, the man, who unlike her idle sons, made a fortune from his work.

'No, Florence is not tongue-tied; she just never has a chance to get a word in as her mother keeps talking all of the time; just like Charley and myself. We can never get a word in edgewise,' I said. I had learned by experience that the way to handle my mother, when she's in one of those moods, is always not to answer any of her real complaints but to seize on some small detail and to set up an argument about it. Dickens had taken himself off and was busy wandering around the table in the dining room, re-adjusting a glass here or there, and coolly picking up the name cards and inspecting them. I took out an imaginary sword, waved it in the air and I prepared to defend my analysis of Florence Gummidge to the bitter death, hoping to trick my mother into laughing, but then something she said earlier suddenly penetrated and I dropped my hands to my sides.

'What's wrong with Charley, Mamma?'

My mother might have a hot temper, but she was the soul of loving kindness to her two sons. Now her annoyance had vanished and she stood very still. For a moment she appeared as though she were holding her breath and her fingers opened and closed a couple of times as though she sought for words or for an explanation, or perhaps to capture a feeling or an apprehension.

'I don't know, Wilkie,' she said after a minute. 'Perhaps he'll tell you.'

I doubted it. Charley was always very close to his mother, close to both parents, very influenced by them in every respect, but in awe of his father and the baby of his mother. I was the rebel, the one who insisted on going his own way. Nevertheless, I knew that I would try.

'Don't worry,' I said. 'I'll run upstairs in a minute.' I hesitated for a moment. I had to tell her about Edwin Milton-Hayes and I had to tell her about Inspector Field's visit, bearing these last works from a dead man. Now I wished that I had come out with it instantly, the minute I had come into the room, instead of having silly conversations about Florence Gummidge and her bumptious mother. This news about Charley shutting himself into his bedroom was bound to connect in her mind with the visit from the police.

There was a look of apprehension in her eyes. She had picked up something from my expression and her mouth tightened. She had never been easy to deceive. Dickens, who had finished his examination of the table and of the fourteen places named in my mother's fine Italian hand, turned back to look at us and then strolled across to the window, twitching the Pompeian red curtains into a mathematically exact similitude. My mother did not even look at him and that was most unusual for her. He always annoyed her when he fiddled with mirrors and rearranged furniture.

'What is it?' she said quietly to me.

There was nothing I could do, no way of glossing over the facts, no point in trying to break it gently now, no course open to me except to tell the truth.

'Milton-Hayes is dead,' I said. 'He has been murdered. Someone murdered him probably with a canvas-cutting knife.'

'Murdered,' she said. There was an odd note, almost of hysteria in her voice. The sound attracted Dickens' attention. He turned again and this time he stood very still and kept his eyes on us, but he did not approach, didn't come to add his words to mine. I looked across at him, looked an appeal, but he did not move and I suppose that he was right. This was a time for family and family only. I turned back to my mother, taking her cold hand in mine. And then, almost as though she had been stunned by the blow of my words, she looked, wide-eyed across at the table and said in a stupefied tone, 'But I've just written a card for him, put him beside me on purpose, well away from Charley . . .'

My mother had always wanted to be an actress and at times like these her full histrionic powers came into force. I had to go on, though I hated to do it, hated to spoil her little drama. But she needed to know the full seriousness of the news.

'An inspector of the police, Inspector Field, is coming here

tonight, Mamma. Milton-Hayes painted some pictures, very
strange pictures, they may depict people we know, show them
to their disadvantage; perhaps be food for blackmail. I think
he was going to cause trouble when he . . . if he . . .'

'Trouble,' she repeated. 'Trouble for Charley . . .' And then
she stopped and when she spoke again, her voice was brisk
and assured. 'Go and change, Wilkie. Mr Dickens and I will
go up to the drawing room and prepare to receive the guests.
You and Charley come and join us there as soon as you are
ready. Make sure that you bring him down with you.'

And then she swept out of the room, her head held high.

'A tigress in defence of her young,' murmured Dickens. I
went towards the door, but he stopped me with a hand on my
arm. 'What was that fight about, Wilkie?'

I didn't pretend to misunderstand him. Everyone in our set
had heard about the fight. 'Charley painted a picture, some
years ago, must be in 1850 or 1851,' I explained. 'It's called
Thoughts in a Convent Garden. Milton-Hayes made a mockery
of it. And, of course, Charley was still sore about the Rossetti
girl, Maria Rossetti, going off to be a nun and rejecting him
and when . . .' I could not go on. Charley with his hands
around the man's throat. I had found it difficult to believe
that my gentle, sweet-natured little brother had turned into a
savage wolf.

And now. And now the memory of the terrible slashing
wounds across the dead man's face and neck came to me and
the bile rose to my mouth, but I did my best to speak, to try
to banish the picture at the back of my mind.

'Charley is incapable of murder. He is a very gentle fellow,'
I said hoarsely, but I did remember how it had taken two of
Charley's friends, Millais and Holman Hunt, to drag him off
Milton-Hayes and to unfasten his hands from the man's neck.
I still seemed to see those red marks on that thick neck.
Although it had happened so many years ago, I had still been
amazed when Charley had not only consented to work for
Milton-Hayes, but had even requested my mother to hold a
dinner party where the man could show off his latest paintings.
Now I began to understand.

Dickens patted me on the arm. 'Go to him, Wilkie, get

him downstairs; get him to take his place at the table as though nothing had happened. Tell him to pull himself together. Don't underestimate Inspector Field. He has a dogged persistence and he will question all who are present here tonight and he will question and re-question until he feels that he has established the truth. Charley needs to have his wits about him.'

He left me then, springing up the stairs in his sprightly fashion. I heard him open the drawing-room door with some quip to my mother. And then the door closed and the two were in there together.

And so I went slowly up the stairs after him, not pausing by the drawing room, but continuing on upstairs. I could hear Dickens cheerily teasing my mother about her dinner-table arrangements, reminding her how, when he and Millais had quarrelled over the Millais picture of the Christ Child in his father's workshop, that she had deliberately put them side by side during a long and merry dinner and they had ended up as good friends. My mother had been very triumphant about that and told half of London about her success and how she had made a menu of twice the usual length, where dish after dish had been served, and how she had chosen food that needed lots of chewing, all so that the two enemies, seated side by side, had eventually ended the long drawn-out dinner as the best of friends.

I couldn't raise a smile at the memory, though. Dickens' last words rang in my ear. Good advice, but my brother Charley never did have his wits about him, never was able to stand up for himself. When we were children he was a gentle, scrupulous, worried boy, four years younger than myself and he had grown into a gentle, scrupulous man who went through torments of self-doubt and agonies of fear for his immortal soul, the sort of person who feared that he might be damned if he stayed out to the small hours of the morning. I had to save him from himself, I decided as I went to find him.

I knew where he would be.

My mother, when she had leased this house in Hanover Terrace, had made generous provision for both of her adult sons. I had my study and Charley had his painting room with its north light. And that is where I went.

A half-finished picture stood on an easel. It was a landscape painting of Regent's Park as seen from the veranda outside the drawing-room window of my mother's house. The bushes, with their clusters of meticulously painted flowers, had been finished months ago, but the central figures had been barely sketched in with the faintest of pencil strokes and had not been touched since I had seen it last. I suppressed a sigh. My brother, as I had come to expect whenever I entered the room, was stretched on the sofa, gazing drearily at the ceiling above.

I decided on shock tactics. 'Charley, Edwin Milton-Hayes is dead,' I said, purposely brutal, hoping that he would leap from the sofa and bombard me with questions.

But he didn't. He stayed as he was, stretched out, and his eyes did not move from the ceiling.

'May gentle Jesus have mercy on his soul,' he said eventually.

'Never mind *gentle Jesus*, never mind his soul. It's his body that we need to think about and that body is at Scotland Yard with some policemen looking at it.' Again, I made my tone as brutal as I could. I had to shake him out from this daze.

That shocked him, but in the wrong way. 'We all need to think of our souls, Wilkie. They matter. The body is corrupt and will decay, but the soul will live forever,' he said and then he placed his hands over his stomach and grimaced.

'I have such a pain, Wilkie,' he said and he whimpered like a small child.

I looked at him with despair. If ever a man looked suspicious, well that man lay on the sofa in front of me. The story of the fight had gone around our little world. It had been so unlike Charley that a blow-by-blow account had been narrated in all the haunts of the Pre-Raphaelite brotherhood and by their fellow artists. I had even heard a discussion of it within the precincts of the Inns of the Temple.

So pain, or no pain, Charley had to be on his feet and joining the guests in the dining room within fifteen minutes. He had to eat some dinner, address a few words to his neighbours on either side of him and then he had to be in good shape and good form to endure the questioning of Inspector Field. There was only one thing for him. I left him abruptly and without a word went straight to my room, mixed a dose of magnesia and then laced it heavily with laudanum. I had a moment's doubt as I carried the glass back to the painting room. Charley, I knew, did not like to take laudanum. He took it, of course. But then he suffered agonies of self-hate. It was all part of his fanatical religion. I had given him what I gave myself and, perhaps, that would be too much. Still, I dismissed that particular worry from my mind. He would be excited and stimulated by the company and I would make sure that he had plenty of brandy, would leave a bottle beside his place. Charley was fond of brandy and relied upon it.

'Drink this, Charley,' I said as I entered the room. 'Down the hatch, old fellow.'

He took it obediently. Charley was always an obedient boy. I waited beside him anxiously, waited as the minutes ticked by. Getting too late to change for dinner. Luckily everyone was used to my eccentricities and my oft-repeated desire that everyone should dine wearing a comfortable and colourful dressing gown. Charley, despite his agonies of depression, looked his usual neat and clean person. Some of the guests would, like Dickens, be wearing a dinner jacket and a black tie, but others, like young Walter Hamilton, would not bother,

'Come on, old fellow,' I said, as I heard the first gong sound, 'come on then, Charley. You'll be fine.'

He was a little unsteady on his feet as I ushered him out of the room, but the haunted expression had gone from his eyes and his pale cheeks had a slight flush upon them. There was a buzz of conversation from the drawing room but I steered Charley past it and guided him down the next flight of stairs towards the ground-floor dining room. Only Sesina was in the room and she was putting finishing touches to the table. I cast a quick glance down the table. There he was, quite near to me, and with delightful little Molly French on the other side. I pushed him into a chair and then suddenly remembered that picture, *Taken in Adultery*. The red-headed young man and the slim young figure of a dark-haired girl. Still, it couldn't be helped. My mother had arranged the cards and was liable to make a fuss if any of her arrangements were upset. And, after all, the inspector was not going to be present at the dinner. The important thing was to free Charley from that pall of depression, to make him relaxed and carefree.

'Where's the brandy?' I asked Sesina.

'Next to the canon, Mr Wilkie,' she said. But without an additional word, she went to the top of the table, fetched the decanter and placed it beside Charley's place name. 'There's another one in front of Mr Milton-Hayes,' she said casually and with a wink in my direction. 'They can pass it between them.'

Milton-Hayes, I thought, was far beyond needing any brandy, so as soon as I had Charley settled in a chair and sipping his favourite drink, I went up to the top of the table and moved the brandy decanter from the dead man's place and positioned it neatly between the canon and Lord Douglas. I had my own reasons to hope that his lordship would be a little drunk, a little incautious by the time that he met Inspector Field. Let him blurt out something, let him blurt it out before his noble father, the Earl of Ennis, could get hold of a team of lawyers who would prevent his son and heir from incriminating himself. That's if the earl could still afford lawyers. I had heard that he was on the verge of bankruptcy.

The first dinner guests, my mother on the arm of the canon, were at the door by the time Charley had finished his first drink. Dickens had managed to secure Molly for himself and was flirting loudly with her, probably much to the annoyance of her grey-bearded old husband who was saddled with the loquacious Mrs Hermione Gummidge. I went to meet them, smiling to myself at John French's expression. He was a coward, though. Dickens was such a famous man that all a husband could do was to smile feebly and then look away as he watched his wife Molly giggle and pretend to hide her blushes. He glanced across the table, picked out his own name card and made his way towards his seat, deliberately averting his gaze and pretending to study a small oil painting of some fisher boys that hung on the wall behind him.

'Wilkie, you haven't changed your clothes!' exclaimed my mother with mock fury.

'Dear, oh dear,' I said with a quick glance downwards. 'Never

mind, Mamma, I'll just fly upstairs and slip on my best silk
dressing gown – my new purple one.'

Dickens, good fellow that he was, immediately backed me,
wanting to go home for his own favourite dressing gown,
or at least to send a cab to Tavistock House, and there was a
chorus of voices, each trying to cap each other's choice of
dinner attire. My mother laughed, the canon smiled benignly,
everyone took their places, nobody casting a second glance at
the silent, taciturn figure of my young brother.

But it only took a few moments for William Jordan to notice
that the star painter of his art gallery was missing. While
everyone speculated on possible reasons for that absence – my
courageous mother, after joining in with a long and, I'm sure,
fictitious account of an accident in Albany Street, called upon
Sesina who enthusiastically corroborated her mistress's account
and added, I was sure, several fancy additions of her own –
while all of this was going on, no one noticed my brother
quietly sipping brandy and saying nothing at all.

From time to time, during the spirited discussion, I peered
around Mrs Hermione Gummidge's bulk. Nothing unusual
about Charley's silence, but Molly, now that Dickens had
deserted her in order to insert his novelist's creativity into
fabricating more and more reasons for the non-arrival of our
dinner guest, was slipping several conspiratorial glances at
Charley's white face. I tried to send a warning glance at her
while keeping up an animated conversation with my mother
on the other side of the table. All against the rules of etiquette,
of course, to talk across a table like that, but we are always
informal in my mother's house.

And, puzzlingly enough, I could not get a word out of my
right-hand neighbour. Very unlike Helen Jordan who was
normally full of jokes and witticisms. She did not look well
at all, I thought. Her cheeks had been embellished with a
touch of rouge, I felt sure; and it was not a success as the
skin beneath the rouge was unusually white and her large
dark eyes, fringed with those immensely long eyelashes,
were filled with misery. There was something wrong, I thought,
as the oysters were removed and replaced by the clear Mock
Turtle soup . . . yes, there was an unusual air of constraint.

Had there been some sort of a row between herself and her husband after we had left? Perhaps the news of the death of Milton-Hayes had come to the house after we left and then there had been accusations between them.

My mother was an excellent hostess, knowing well how to blend an informal atmosphere with top class food, top class wine and she knew how to keep a free flow of conversation going as her guests savoured the meats and the fish and allowed the intoxicating fumes of the wine to mount to their brain and stimulate their wits. But tonight, this was not happening, not even when the turbot and the smelts were served accompanied by an excellent Chablis. Neighbour eyed neighbour with suspicion. That empty chair, at the top of the table, beside my mother, seemed to mesmerize the guests. No one spoke of it. Most tried to avert their gaze from it, but it stood there, like Shakespeare's Banquo; a ghost at the feast, stood dumbly there, its silent presence a mute accusation. It was quite strange, I thought, that after that first burst of almost hysterical foolery that no one mentioned the missing guest again, or even expressed any curiosity about the pictures that he had promised to display for their opinion. Not even the canon, the purchaser of the works, said a word or asked a question about the pictures.

I watched the clock, heard it tick loudly in a sudden silence as the croquette of chicken was removed by a saddle of mutton. The conversation was beginning to die out. Even Dickens now had his eye upon the clock and Molly, turning in despair from Charley who was still drinking steadily, cast a defiant glance across the table at her husband and then fixed her eyes upon her plate. William Hamilton tried to make conversation with Florence Gummidge while her mother, Hermione, at my side, gave an impatient sigh at seeing her darling daughter, whom she had hoped might make a splendid marriage, marooned, with an empty place on her right-hand side and an impecunious young man on her left.

As the saddle of mutton was removed by a dish of pheasants, I looked from face to face, and eventually at the canon. There had been no sign of a canon's robes in any one of the pictures that we had seen, so perhaps he was here purely in order to see whether this set of pictures would be appropriate for a church hall. Nevertheless, despite his stolid demeanour, his fingers were nervously shredding a bread roll.

I cast a few uneasy glances over at Charley. He had refused the wine and continued to sip brandy. Nevertheless, it was a controlled process. He did not, as others might do, toss glass after glass into his mouth, just took the liquid, sip by sip. Nor did he become loud, or noisy, or give vent to uncontrolled fits of laughter. No, he sat quietly in his chair, ate a little, exchanged a few polite sentences with Mrs Hermione Gummidge, his neighbour on his right-hand side, but he seemed to be avoiding the glances of little Mrs Molly French, and that, I thought, showed a certain presence of mind. Perhaps, I thought, Charley would be all right when the inspector arrived. Brandy never seemed to make him noisy or incoherent. My brother, I told myself, was a gentle soul. Not someone who would ever slash a man's throat in that brutal fashion.

And then my eyes went from guest to guest, studying each face in turn. Not all, but most showed signs of tension. It could have been a scene from one of those crowded pictures painted by my godfather, David Wilkie. *The Empty Chair*, it might have been entitled and that chair, up at the top of the table, beside my dauntless mother, could almost be seen to cast a shadow over the invited guests; his invited guests. I had read the list that Charley had presented to my mother. Mrs and Mrs William Jordan, Mr and Mrs John French, Mrs Hermione Gummidge and her daughter Florence, Lord Douglas, Walter Hamilton and the canon, the proposed purchaser of the set. Not a person had declined the invitation. I wondered about them. I had little difficulty in matching most of them to the figures in the pictures that Dickens and I had uncovered in Milton-Hayes' cloakroom, but there were a few puzzles.

The doorbell rang just at the moment when Sesina and Dolly were arranging clean plates for the Curaçao soufflé and the marbled jelly and apricot cream. I saw how Dolly widened her eyes at Sesina with dismay. The soufflé would collapse if not served quickly. The guests glanced at each other uneasily, wondering, doubtless, whether the missing guest was arriving after all. My mother's fingers tightened so much on the spoon

that the candelabra in front of her illuminated the dead white
of her knuckles.

I got to my feet. 'I'll open the door, Sesina. You carry on.'
My late father would have died of shock to even hear of the
man of the house opening a door, but my mother, brother and
I led a bohemian existence and no one would be surprised.
Eyes followed me, nevertheless, as I left the room. They had
been expecting Edwin Milton-Hayes throughout the evening
and now they were bracing themselves for his arrival.

But, of course, it was not the artist; it was the police.

Inspector Field had a minion with him, a young policeman
carrying a bulging bag – more bulging than it had looked in
the morning, I thought.

'Come in, inspector,' I said affably. 'Everything is ready
for you.' It had been all arranged for Milton-Hayes, of course,
but that didn't matter now. I closed the door behind them and
then led the way up the stairs and through into the drawing
room.

My mother was nothing but innovative. Her drawing room
was magnificently unusual. The walls were painted black, but
there was nothing gloomy about the room. These walls were
just a background for my father's magnificent landscape paintings which were framed in gold. There was gold everywhere.
The ceiling was gold. The carpet was gold. The numerous
sconces on the walls had the sheen of gold and the heavy
black velvet curtains that framed the view of Regent's Park
were sewn with swirling garlands of golden leaves and stems.
By day, the view of Regents' Park was beautiful with graceful
weeping trees and ponds and dominated the room, but, by
night, the room was romantic and beautiful and the paintings
were the focus of all eyes.

Inspector Field gave a glance around, took out one of the
pictures from his bag and held it awkwardly in his hands. It
was one that I had seen this morning but had not looked
closely at it. Now I examined it with interest. It had its name
engraved on the same carved scroll as the others and obviously was part of the Milton-Hayes collection of paintings
commissioned by the canon.

'*Root of All Evil*,' I read the title aloud. A gambling den, I guessed. Cards on the table. A woman with one long white hand to her heart and the other pushing a pile of gold coins across the table. The face, as with the other pictures, had been erased, covered with that familiar oval of white paint, but the hair was distinctive.

The inspector was busy looking around him. 'I thought you would have stands, or something,' he complained. 'Where am I to put these pictures? What had your brother arranged for Mr Milton-Hayes?'

'Well, usually at these affairs, the artist takes his picture out and holds it in his arms, or props it up against the back of the chair.' I wasn't too sure, really. I took scant interest in these affairs and normally retired to the balcony to smoke a cigar, sip some brandy and contemplate the stars over Regent's Park. Suit yourself, inspector, I thought. I have other things on my mind.

'Brandy? Cigar? A piece of larks' pie?' I enquired airily.

'No, no.' He fumbled with his picture, walking around with it in his arms as though it were a baby.

'There won't be much room once everyone is in here,' he grumbled.

'We had a dance for over seventy people one night recently,' I said coldly. The face of poor Charley, waltzing dreamily with Molly French in his arms, came before me and I wished even more fervently than before that I could have got him on to my friend Pigott's yacht and transported him out of danger before he came under the inspector's eye. Too late for that, now, but at least I could do my best to shelter him tonight from Inspector Field's suspicions and then remove him tomorrow. He was looking at me keenly, looking at me as though he were not sure that I was on the right side, after all. I remembered Dickens' words and cursed myself. I needed to flatter this man, to appear to be lending him all possible help. I should be carefree, but at the same time keen, just like a fox hound on the trail of the enemy.

And then the door opened and Dickens, himself, came in.

'Let me help you, inspector.' The words were quietly spoken, but in a moment he had sized up the situation and had taken all of the small chairs from around the room

and lined them up against that splendid backdrop, the black
curtain with its gold silk embroidery. One by one he carried
over the pictures, placed each carefully in the centre of the
chair, leaning its frame back against the back rungs of
the chair. And then Dickens left the room and returned with
the patched-up *Winter of Despair*, and set it upon another
chair that had been placed well in front of the others in a
place where one of the lamps threw a direct light upon it.

'This, I think,' he said in his most authoritative manner,
'will be the key to the mystery.'

Neither the inspector nor I, neither of us, asked him to
support that piece of reasoning. Both of us were overwhelmed
by his air of firm self-belief, by his air of authority. We felt,
well I did, anyway, that this was a man who always knew the
right thing to do, just as he always knew the correct note to
strike when he turned out yet another new book or made a
speech to a roomful of people.

I watched my friend as he walked up and down, appraising
the pictures, just as though he were a shopkeeper setting out
his goods. He gave a grunt, took out the *Forbidden Fruit*, the
picture of the very young girl being urged towards the church,
and he placed it upon a chair just beneath one of my mother's
elaborate oil lamps, the flame burning brightly within the
gold-engraved glass bowl. Now it was strikingly illuminated.
And then, almost casually, he moved the picture *Taken in
Adultery* towards a more obscure corner.

'I'll tell you what you could do, inspector,' he said in a low
and confidential voice, 'you could just watch faces for a
couple of minutes when they come in first, give them a few
moments to absorb the strangeness of the pictures, those faceless pictures, and then you could make the announcement
about the death of Edwin Milton-Hayes. Don't hesitate to pile
on the details. Mr Collins and I will watch faces, though you,
yourself, an experienced man like you, will have your eye on
all of them.'

'I'll see to the coffee,' I said hurriedly. It was the only
excuse that I could think of to get out of that room. I needed
to see Charley, to see how he was. If necessary, I thought, I
would get him out of the house, find a friend who would put

him up for a few days if I found that he was in no condition just now to stand up to Inspector Field.

I was too late, though. Sesina and Dolly were on their way up the stairs carrying trays. And all of the guests were following my mother up from the dining room. I stood helplessly on the landing and awaited their arrival.

My mother was making a huge fuss in her theatrical way about the coffee cups and calling upon me to corroborate her grandiose claims. 'Ming,' she was saying to the canon. 'Just so valuable. Now stand back everyone. Make room for Dolly! Be careful, Sesina! Watch your step. Stand back, Wilkie. Stand back and wait. Don't get in the way.'

'Ming; nonsense, Five Towns Potteries,' I said loudly and scornfully, while my eyes scanned through the crowded figures on the stairs. Sesina's right eyelid twitched as she passed me bearing her tray carefully aloft. She was no respecter of the household gods of my mother's dubious antiques and this amused me so much that my eyes followed her as she made her way with careful footsteps up towards the drawing room. By the time that I looked back, Charley had slipped past me and I saw his head of richly red hair, bending down to speak to Walter Hamilton.

Well, at least he is in control of himself, I thought. It was surprising that he could even walk, considering all the brandy that he had consumed, and that on top of the strong dose of laudanum which I had given to him. There was nothing that I could do, now, as my brother had already gone into the drawing room. I followed with a heavy heart.

There was a strange atmosphere in the room. My mother, waving aside the two housemaids, was pouring the coffee herself, holding up the precious pot and engaging Lord Douglas in a stream of banter as he endeavoured to look for a mark on the bottom of one of the coffee cups.

'*Yongzching*,' he said with an authority that surprised me. He was reputed to be quite badly off. Still, perhaps there was an ancestral home, well furnished with antiques, in some part of Ireland, called Ennis. His father, after all, bore the title of Earl of Ennis.

'Nonsense,' said my mother. I could have taken an oath that

she had not the slightest idea of what he was talking about and that she had never heard the word before, but that was my mother. A woman who was never at loss for a good lie. I joined in the debate enthusiastically and placed a bet on the authenticity of her Ming china. My mother enjoyed this sort of thing and it created a diversion. People had turned back from contemplating the pictures to join in the argument, all of the ladies, except Molly French, joining in the defence of my mother. Charley, I noticed, had moved towards Molly, but she had instantly turned her back on him. I saw her give one horrified glance at the picture, *Taken in Adultery,* and then walk resolutely down to the other end of the drawing room and tuck her hand inside the elbow of her elderly husband. He, I noted thankfully, was very short-sighted. He had taken out an eye glass and was peering myopically at one of my father's paintings on the wall. I joined them instantly.

'I remember very well the day when that picture was painted, Mr French,' I said cheerily, trying not to look across to see where my brother stood, helpless and devastated. 'It was a terribly wet day on the island of Skye in the Highlands of Scotland. My father knelt on the ground, braced against the wind, sketching this picture and the rain was so heavy that I had to hold an umbrella over him so that his work would not be destroyed. I still remember how the rain dripped down the back of my neck. I always feel that I should have got half of the sum that the picture was sold for,' I ended and hoped that my voice betrayed none of my desperation.

Mr John French waved my heroic part in the production of the masterpiece away. He stared at me coldly. 'Your father, young man, was a most talented artist and a very good man. I'm sure that it was a pleasure and a privilege to be allowed to assist him.'

I bowed my head meekly and cast a respectful look up at the picture that he was admiring. He looked a little mollified by my submissive attitude and unbent a little.

'Such lovely pictures, weren't they; those pictures that he painted. Nature in all its glory.' And then he turned back and pointed contemptuously at the five pictures lined up against the dramatic black and gold curtain.

'Look at these pictures by that man Milton-Hayes that everyone is gawping at. Mere daubs, mere daubs, wouldn't you agree, my dear?' Mr French turned to his wife, Molly, and white to the lips she murmured something that could pass as an agreement.

Mr French, I hoped, was far too short-sighted to see what everyone else was seeing as they examined the paintings lined up for their perusal. With any luck he could not see the resemblance to the shape of the head and the white line of parting through her unusually dark hair, Spanish dark hair. Something about the neck and the slightly drooping shoulders now struck me also since I had the woman before my eyes. Just as Charley was immediately recognisable by the red hair, so Molly, the very young woman with a husband three times her own age, would be recognized by everyone here. All conversation had stopped and coffee remained untouched as one by one, with suspended breath, the guests invited by Mr Milton-Hayes widened their eyes at those faceless pictures. No one spoke. Suddenly there was silence in the room as, man and woman, glances were exchanged. And then sounds, but very hushed. A slight sucking of breath by one person goes unnoticed, but the sound is unmistakable when ten or more people inhale. There was a movement, a decided stepping back as person after person sought to detach themselves from a painting that featured their likeness or a resemblance to a spouse or a friend.

And then Inspector Field came to the front of the room.

EIGHT

M rs Collins fussing as usual. Wish that she'd hold her trap, thought Sesina. Stupid woman. Trying to pretend that the coffee cups and the jug were something special. Serve her right if me and Dolly dropped the lot of them. She gave Dolly a wink but Dolly just looked stiffly into space, holding her chin up like she were posing for a statue. Just the way to trip. Still, no business of mine, she thought. Why did I let Mr Wilkie talk me into coming to this place? Should have stuck to my plan of having a coffee stall. Would like to be down in Covent Garden now, having a bit of back-chat with the drovers, patting their horses, taking their money. I'd be off tomorrow, but for Mr Charles. Have to look after him, poor lad. Got himself into a trap, didn't he? Everyone looking at that picture. Pity he didn't have a hat on or something. No mistaking that hair. Still she'd done her best. That nosey . . .

Sesina took out another cup, placed it carefully onto its saucer and then held it out to the missus. Nice steady hand Mrs Collins had for a woman of that age, had to give it to her. Face as white as the lace fichu around her neck, but a smile pinned on her lips and a nice line of chat with everyone who came for their coffee. Just as though everyone wasn't whispering about her son; and him in that picture with a label under it saying: *Taken in Adultery*. Really spelled it out, didn't it? Be funny if it was about anyone else, except that poor lad.

Have to do something about it, though. Sesina bit her lip as she moved the cream jug a bit nearer to the missus. That poor Mr Charles, my Charley, she said to herself, well, he looked like death warmed up. Have to stop everyone looking at him. Sesina searched across the room and found a victim.

'Let me take a cup over to Miss Gummidge, mistress; she looks ever so ill. Looks like sommat has upset her,' she said in a confidential whisper to Mrs Collins. Sesina was proud of her whisper. *Sesina, the girl with the loudest whisper in London*, her friend Isabella used to say. She and Isabella used to have fun with it when they wandered around Covent Garden, or made their way through Smithfield. It always turned heads.

Even people on the other side of the room stopped talking and turned around to look at her.

Mrs Collins cast a perfunctory look across the room, but now all were looking between Mrs Gummidge and her daughter Florence, who was examining the pattern on the curtains, tracing the gold swirls on the silken black velvet. The picture of *The Night Prowler* was quite near to her, but she averted her head from it. The colour, Sesina noticed, had ebbed from the girl's cheeks.

'Oh, go on,' hissed Mrs Collins as the small cup was filled to overflowing.

Sesina took her time. Found a small tray, daintily arranged upon it a bowl of sugar lumps, a pair of tongs, a teaspoon and a small jug of cream. By the time that she was finished, almost everyone in the room had stopped talking and was looking across at Florence, peering from her to *The Night Prowler* picture and then back to her again. Sesina went slowly across the room, timing her moment beautifully, waiting until all eyes were upon her.

And then she gave a sudden startled gasp. 'Oh, my word, miss, is that going to be you in that picture? Looks ever so like you, doesn't it? I'd know it anywhere. It's the way you do your hair.' She pointed at the picture and spoke loudly enough to be heard by those nearby, but not loudly enough to force the mistress of the house to take notice of her. Carefully she placed the tray on a nearby Pembroke table, had another and closer look at *The Night Prowler* picture and then smiled sweetly at the white-faced Florence.

'It is you, isn't it, miss?'

There was a buzz of whispers as she made her way back across the room. What was it that Mrs Collins had said to Miss Florence's mother when she agreed not to put the girl sitting beside Lord Douglas? '*Of course, I can understand how worried you are. Don't worry; no explanations needed. I did hear . . .*'

And it looked as though Mrs Collins were not the only one to hear of a connection between Lord Douglas and Mrs Gummidge's pet daughter. Sesina looked back again at that picture. It did look as if it might be a picture of him, title and all. She had served a coffee to Lord Douglas only a few minutes earlier. She had very good eyesight and could even see the pale patch on his finger as he drank his coffee. Wore a ring normally, then.

Left-handed, she said to herself, looking at how he held his cup; wonder if that's important. She felt very satisfied with herself. She cast a quick glance over at the picture. Yes, the 'prowler' in the picture was holding the candle in his left hand. And yes, he had a ring on that finger. She wondered if she was the first person to notice that and glanced around. Not too many people looking now. All chattering in twos and threes. Nobody much looking at the pictures except that policeman. And he was dividing his attention between the picture named *Taken in Adultery* and Mr Charles.

I'll kill him if he does anything to that boy. The words in her head must have shown in her face as she stopped beside Mr Charles and the poor fellow looked quite startled.

'Would you like me to bring you a cup of coffee, Mr Charles?' she asked.

He made an effort. Blinked a couple of times and then shook his head. 'No, I'm alright, Sesina. Coffee makes me sick.'

And brandy, was her secret thought. *Not to mention a bit of the laudanum, either.* Probably had that before he came down. Both of them, Mr Wilkie and Mr Charles drank pints of the stuff, but it didn't seem to do Mr Wilkie much harm. But then he wasn't sensitive, like his brother. She made her way back to the rosewood table where Dolly was carefully piling the used coffee cups onto one of the trays. Sesina joined her instantly. Lots of people had not finished their coffee, she noticed as she tipped the remains into the slop bowl. Nothing wrong with the coffee. There wouldn't be. Mrs Barnett was ever so careful about coffee. Trained by the mistress herself, she always said. Always tested it with a few sips, too. No, the chances were much stronger that people had been too busy whispering and looking at the pictures and from one to another that they had allowed the coffee to get cold.

The inspector came up now. An empty coffee cup. Well, he drank it, unless he had poured it into one of the potted palms.

'Many thanks, Mrs Collins, excellent coffee.' And then he raised his voice. 'Well, if everyone is finished, perhaps I could have a word.'

There was an instant dead silence. Every eye turned to him. Had been wondering about him, thought Sesina. Every one of them there had been puzzling over the absence of Mr Milton-Hayes. And they'd want to be very dumb if they hadn't connected up the presence of the police with the absence of that man.

'Take the trays back down to the kitchen.' Mrs Collins' voice was low and Sesina could swear that it shook. The mistress had looked over towards Mr Charles, just one quick look, but it was easy to read her face. The woman was terri-fied and Sesina felt for her. He would have been a lovely little boy, she thought sentimentally. And he did look such an innocent still, poor lad, standing there, like an idiot, gaping at the inspector. While Dolly's back was turned and Mrs Collins was busy with the inspector, she quickly removed one of the china cups and put it onto the mantelpiece. And then she took up her tray and walked out with a virtuous air, making sure that she was ahead of Dolly.

She would need an audience.

She waited until Dolly had closed the door and then gave a gasp. And then another as the first had not registered. She lowered herself down onto the top stair, keeping the tray carefully poised on her knees.

'What's amiss?' Even Dolly was roused by such strange behaviour.

'I've been took!' gasped Sesina.

'Took!' Dolly looked back at the closed door which hid the sight of the policeman.

'Took bad!' Sesina strove to hide the note of impatience. Thick as a feather bed, that was Dolly.

'You sick?'

Now light was beginning to dawn in that stupid head.

Sesina groaned in reply. 'Terrible pain,' she gasped.

Sickness made you pale, but a pain only showed through a pantomime and she was a good actress. She groaned and leaned over the tray.

'What am I going to do?' Dolly sounded panic-stricken. 'Don't throw up on that tray,' she said sharply as Sesina groaned again.

'Take your own tray back down and come back for mine,' gasped Sesina. She retained hold of her tray in order to imbue Dolly with a sense of urgency. Dolly never could hold two ideas in that noddle of hers, she reflected, as she groaned again.

That was enough for Dolly. Holding her own tray securely, slightly forward so that she could see her own feet, not too high, not too low, just as she had been trained nearly forty years ago, Dolly went down the stairs at a steady pace. Sesina put aside her own tray at the very instant when Dolly had left the landing below and she could hear the woman's footsteps progress down to the hall. In a second Sesina had reached the drawing-room door. She turned the doorknob noiselessly. No point in wasting time by putting her ear to the door. She had a legitimate excuse.

Noiselessly, she shut the door and crept into the room. The inspector had just begun to make his little speech.

'Very sorry to bring such bad news. Hope the ladies will excuse me . . .'

Pompous old goat. Sesina slipped silently along the side wall, making her way to where she had placed the coffee cup. Mrs Collins' eyes flickered in her direction but she said nothing.

'. . . have to tell you that Mr Edwin Milton-Hayes was brutally murdered, probably at some time this morning. His throat was slashed with a knife.'

So much for not upsetting the ladies, thought Sesina, as she squeezed her way behind the green velvet sofa, keeping as close to the wall as possible. She stopped for a second when she emerged from behind the sofa and risked a glance around the room. Well, ladies or no ladies, no one was fainting, or even looking upset. There had been an odd sound, almost like a sigh of relief, and everyone was facing the inspector, waiting

for more. And looking quite interested, thought Sesina as she
slid behind the mahogany buffet server.

And then she noticed her mistress's hands were clenched
behind her back, clenched so tightly that the nails must be
digging into the palms of her hands. So, perhaps others were
just hiding their feelings, putting a brave face on things. Mrs
Gummidge had taken a step towards her daughter, Florence,
but then stopped when the inspector looked alertly in her
direction. Molly French, the flirtatious Molly, pulled her shawl
more snugly around her shoulders and gave a sweet smile
towards where her husband stood beside Mr Wilkie. Lord
Douglas pulled out a cigar and then put it back again into his
pocket and moved a few steps closer to Florence Gummidge,
Mrs Gummidge's little pet daughter, but Florence turned
her head away and did not appear to notice the noble lord
who seemed to be coupled with her in one of the dead man's
strange, faceless pictures.

There was another glance from Mrs Collins and Sesina
knew she could not stay any longer in the room. She shot one
last look at poor Mr Charles, but she could do nothing for
him at the moment. Somehow, she told herself, I'll find a way
of getting the inspector to think about the others. I fancy Mrs
Hermione Gummidge, myself, she thought. A tough-looking
lady. Couldn't afford to have her only daughter involved in a
scandal with that Lord Douglas, especially if it was true that
he went around robbing people of their jewels by midnight.

Good idea, that, though, she thought, and wondered where
he found a fence to give him money for them. Something to
be said for being a lord. He could always pretend that he was
just selling off some family jewels. Wouldn't work with her,
of course, though, thought Sesina, I'd really enjoy it. Any
case, Mrs Collins didn't really have any rich friends. And
when she did go visiting, she didn't take a maid with her.
No, she and Dolly were left behind and made to do a lot of
extra scrubbing by Mrs Barnett.

Another look from Mrs Collins. The inspector was asking
if anyone knew why there were no faces painted onto the
figures in the pictures. Talking about *The Night Prowler*,
moving close to the picture, pretending to discover, just that

minute, a ring on the finger of the thief. Sesina closed a finger and thumb around the delicate handle of the coffee cup. She held it up, angling it towards Mrs Collins' eyes in a silent pantomime explanation of why she had returned into the drawing room and Mrs Collins gave a nod. But nobody else moved or spoke. There was a dead silence after the inspector's question. He was the only one talking in the room, going along the pictures, one by one, reading out the titles: *The Night Prowler, Forbidden Fruit, Taken in Adultery, Den of Iniquity,* and *Root of All Evil.*

Sesina moved softly and quietly along the wall, dodging behind the mahogany tallboy and then bent down to retie her shoelace. No one was looking at her, not even Mrs Collins.

The canon was explaining to the inspector about commissioning the pictures from Mr Edwin Milton-Hayes. They were to hang in the church hall and to be an example to his parishioners about the terrible end for anyone committing one of those sins. Then the inspector pointed at the picture that I had endeavoured to restore.

'*Winter of Despair.*' He read the words out very clearly. A lot of murmuring. They couldn't tell much from it. A right mess that picture, thought Sesina with satisfaction as she moved stealthily back towards the drawing-room door. Slashed with a knife. She wondered what the visitors thought about it. They'd be able to see that it was a body, a body floating in the river, down near Hungerford Stairs. Wouldn't be able to tell if it was a man or a woman, though. Not after the knife had made such a mess of it. That inspector was watching all the faces, peering from one to another. Waiting for someone to say something.

But no one obliged him. They had had enough. The canon cleared his throat. 'Well, very interesting,' he said. 'I'm sure I speak for everyone, inspector, when I say that if you need any additional help or information, we will all be delighted to be of assistance. And now, Mrs Collins, I have to thank you for a most pleasant evening, but I have a morning service and need to be in my bed before eleven o'clock.'

That did it. Everyone got their bottle up. All of them on their feet. Telling the usual lies to Mrs Collins. 'What a *lovely*

evening! Really enjoyed it! Wonderful hospitality!' As if!
Sesina had a job to keep a straight face.

'Sesina, the coats!' Mrs Collins was as glad to get rid of
them as they were to go. Sesina sped back to the kitchen to
fetch Dolly. Leave the coffee cup, she told herself. Be interesting to hear if the inspector says anything more. His eyes
were on Mr Charles and he didn't look like he were going
nowhere. Sesina decided that personally she would find the
inspector's coat and hat and then hand it to him. Hard for him
to stay then.

But he was too clever by half. He sent them out of the
room. Must have done. They were all down the stairs and
standing in the hall by the time that she came back with Dolly.
Ten visitors that night, but only eight of them wanting coats.
Not him. Not Mr Dickens. Sesina grabbed as many men's
coats as she could. Always better with the vails, men were.
Dolly hadn't worked that out yet after being in service for
twenty years or so. All the time though, as Sesina was bobbing
at them and thanking them, pocketing the vails and holding up
coats and finding scarves, her mind was on the drawing room
upstairs. What was happening? Mrs Collins, Mr Wilkie and
Mr Charles. And that inspector, probably looking at Mr
Charles, looking from him to the picture *Taken in Adultery.*
She had a look at Mr French. What did he think of that woman
in the picture, with a head of hair just like his Molly? He
wasn't all that old and doddery. Grabbed the umbrella from
her ever so quick, swung it a bit, swishing it. In a very bad
mood, she thought. Had to keep on holding his scarf until, in
the end, he reluctantly put his hand in his pocket, otherwise
she wouldn't have got a penny from the old dolt. Come to
think of it, why not suspect him? What did he think of his
wife having a bit of fun with a handsome young man? Perhaps
he was the one that cut the artist's throat.

Still, she was glad to see the back of them all. Glad to close
the door behind the canon. No vail from him, of course. Some
nonsense about giving all his goods to charity, she guessed
as she slammed the door on his heels. Spent plenty on himself,
she didn't doubt that. No walking home for him. Raising his
umbrella for a cab as soon as he got to the top step. And what

did he want them pictures for? Wasting money; that was. Not his money, of course. No, he'd take church collections for that, thought Sesina, as she closed the door behind them all and crossed the hall to the stairs.

'Where are you going, Sesina?' Always one to be minding someone else's business; that was Dolly.

'Left a cup in the drawing room, din't I?' Sesina spoke the words without even turning her head. She went speedily up the stairs until she reached the landing and then she stopped and trod as quietly as possible. When she reached the drawing-room door she turned the smooth marble doorknob as gently and smoothly as she could. There was just the sound of one voice, the inspector. The door was a heavy one, lined with green baize and no individual words could be distinguished, but the tone was rough and aggressive. Sesina turned the knob a little more. Now she could hear that aggressive voice.

'And you don't deny that this coat is yours, you use it when you're painting – that right, sir?'

'It's my father's.'

Poor fella, thought Sesina, he's all upset. Too soft to deal with that policeman. She would enjoy giving the stupid man a slap across the face. She felt bad. Her fault. Should have burned the thing as soon as she spotted the bloodstain, burned it in the kitchen stove. That's what she should have done. Burned it and then denied ever seeing it. Easy enough to do.

'I must tell you, sir, that you were seen visiting Mr Milton-Hayes this morning.' Now she was inside the door, standing just behind the velvet curtain that kept out the draughts. Couldn't see, but could hear everything. Nothing to hear at the moment. None of them said anything. There might have been a gasp. Not the poor fella. The missus, she thought. Felt a bit sorry for her, too. Ever so fond of the two sons, she was. Laughed like anything at Mr Wilkie's jokes, put up with all his ways, allowed him to come and go as he pleased, doled out the money to him whenever he wanted it, turned a blind eye to what he got up to with that girl he had tucked away in a room down Nash Street, but her Charley was different. Loved that poor fellow, did the missus, almost like he was still her little boy.

'You were seen by the maidservant, sir. By Mr Milton-Hayes' servant. She saw someone with red hair coming through Dorset Square when she went out for milk.' Leaning forward, that inspector. A bully if ever she had seen one. Peering into Mr Charles's eyes. Leaving a bit of a pause and going on again. Good trick that. Makes everyone nervous. 'That's what she told us, sir. She said that she had been sent on an errand by her mistress in another house; she divides her services between the two houses – so she told us. And when she reached the corner, she looked back and saw a tall young man with red hair going through the square and reckoned that he was coming away from Mr Milton-Hayes' house. Of course, she would have known you as you have been helping Mr Milton-Hayes with his pictures – or so I understand.' The inspector had stopped now, but no one spoke for nearly a minute until Mr Dickens chipped in.

'Our young friend here, of course, is not the only man in London with red hair, as I am sure that you were about to remark, inspector. And that doesn't sound a very reliable witness statement. How could the maid know where this red-headed man could have come from? Or, indeed, how she could have told that the hair was red since Mr Charles Collins wears his hair extremely short and I would imagine that it would be almost completely covered by a hat. And no one, inspector, except a lunatic goes out without a hat on a November morning, is that not correct?'

Mr Dickens putting his nose in. Couldn't bear to be left out of the conversation for too long. Still, might do some good. Sesina flattened herself against the door. If only she had thought, a bit earlier, of disguising the bloodstain instead of trying to remove it and then hiding it in the scullery. Stupid place to choose!

'No, Mr Dickens, you are quite right.' The inspector had a little laugh at that. 'Of course Mr Charles Collins is not the only red-headed man in London. I remember very well that you had a red-headed man in *David Copperfield*. But I don't think that Mr Uriah Heep was knocking on Mr Milton-Hayes' door this morning. As for the hat, well, that girl struck me as a sharp piece and I don't think that she would make a mistake like that.'

There was a bit of a silence after that. Sesina bit her bottom lip. *Just deny it! Go on! Tell him it wasn't you!*

'And I must tell you, sir, that when I asked the maidservant if she recognized the young man with red hair, well, she immediately mentioned your name.' Getting on my nerves, he is, thought Sesina. That inspector's got a really boring sort of voice, all on one note, just like a foghorn on the river.

'Probably because my brother is a frequent visitor to Milton-Hayes and she assumed that it was he when she saw a man with red hair.' Mr Wilkie was keeping cool. That might shut up the inspector for the moment.

'Possibly, possibly,' said the inspector, but he didn't sound too convinced. 'But why don't we ask your brother, himself. Now, sir, could you tell me whether, or not, you called in at that house this morning?'

All holding their breath, they were, waiting for Mr Charles to speak. Sesina held her breath, too. *Just tell a good lie. Don't hang about. Out with it straight away.*

'He asked me to come. Wanted to consult me. Wanted me to help him to paint some more backgrounds. I help him quite a lot. It's easier than doing my own picture. I just follow his directions. Said he was behind with the pictures. He knows that I'm good with flowers and silks, and velvets. Wanted to have them ready by tonight for the canon.' All breathless. Hard to hear him, even. Still, it was a bit of an explanation. But would he be believed? Sesina thought again of that large bloodstain on the painting coat.

'My brother, inspector, is rightly esteemed for his wonderful portrayal of nature and of the texture in fine clothing.' Mr Wilkie doing his best. Sesina swallowed a giggle when she thought of the portrayal of nature in the picture *Taken in Adultery*. Real nature, that would be. A handsome young man and a young woman having fun behind the back of that old geezer of a husband.

'Yes, sir. You were telling me. You rang the bell. The door was opened by . . .'

'It was already open, the lock was just on the snib. I went in, took my coat off in the hall, found my painting coat, I had left it there in the hall, and went upstairs to the studio.'

Voice all dull and very low. Had to strain her ears to hear him. Wasn't going to be all stupid, now was he? Go on, tell him someone else was there, someone else came before you left. Sesina felt her throat ache with the effort of trying to send a silent message.

'And . . .'

'And I opened the door and went in . . .'

Dead silence. Sesina held her breath.

'It was horrible. He was lying there. Blood everywhere. I leaned over him. Touched him. And he was dead.'

'Was the body warm or cold?' Like a sudden bark, the question made him jump.

'I don't know. I can't remember.'

'So how did you know that he was dead?'

There was no answer to that. Sesina slid from behind the curtain, no noise, soft-soled shoes, moved towards the mahogany tallboy. The cup was still there. She had her hand upon it. Had made up her mind what to say. And then there was a crash! A table first, a card table made from walnut. Sesina had often polished it and cursed its fragile, spindly legs. And then a heavier crash. A man's body.

Everyone moved, everyone exclaimed, all except the mistress, who stood very still. After a moment she took something from her handbag.

'Give him this, Wilkie. Just let him breathe it in. He'll be well, in a moment. Sesina, you go back to the kitchen now. I'll ring when we need you.'

'I'm telling you this, Sesina, and I'm telling you for your own good.' Mrs Barnett took in a deep breath and her enormous bosom swelled to the limits of her apron.

'What?' Sesina picked though the crumbs of the soufflé and did her best to seem normal. Mrs Collins was always very generous with the leftovers, never wanted to see them again in the dining room and there were plenty of pieces of sweet and savoury goodies on the table from the night's dinner party. Change the subject, she thought. 'Lucky for some, unlucky for others,' she said.

'What are you talking about, girl?' Dolly liked to give

herself airs, from time to time. Liked to remind Sesina that she had been working here with Mrs Collins for donkey's years. Thought she knew everything.

'Thirteen,' said Sesina sweeping a handful of crumbs onto her hand and swallowing them hastily. 'Fourteen places laid and only thirteen at the table. That's bad luck, bad luck for them and good luck for us with all the leftovers.'

'I'm not talking about that.' Mrs Barnett had a nervous habit of trembling when she was angry that made her round flabby face look rather like a wine jelly. 'I'm talking about your behaviour. Mr Charles is not for the like of you and you shouldn't be talking to him the way that you do, bending over him, whispering in his ear, giving him an extra spoon of jelly. Bad enough with Mr Wilkie, then again I have to say that he does encourage it, but Mr Charles is a quiet young man. Don't you behave like that with him, or ever call him Charley again, or I'll have to have a word with the missus about you.'

You'd be better off minding your own business in the kitchen and not coming into the dining room just so that the missus could tell you what a wonderful dinner you cooked, thought Sesina, but she contented herself with cleaning out the dish of apricot cream. Mrs Barnett should have chopped the apricots a bit finer, she said to herself, but she had to admit that the cream was set well and the mixture deliciously thick. That had been Mr Charles's plate. She had noticed that he had left most of it behind. Shame after all the work of heating and sieving and mixing in the yolks of eggs. Still, he was a delicate young man. Not too strong. Things upset him, poor fellow. Look at the way he just keeled over and fainted. She felt all motherly towards him, wondered what was happening upstairs. Would the inspector leave him alone now that he had fainted? Or would he think that it proved him guilty? It wouldn't work if he was poor, she had known a girl who used to scream and faint when she was arrested, but the constable would just drag her off by one leg. Different for the gentry, though, she told herself as she shrugged her shoulders at Mrs Barnett.

'Why didn't that fellow, that Mr Milton-Hayes turn up anyway,' she demanded. 'Struck me that everyone was a bit strange, jumpy, like.' Especially my poor Charley, was her

secret thought, but she knew better than to utter it in front
of the cook. Aloud, she said, 'And that copper with him?
What did that fellow want? Disappeared, didn't he? What did
you think, Dolly?'

That was a good move. Dolly was an easy-going type and
she had been with Mrs Collins even longer than the cook.
When it came down to it, Dolly was always favoured, always
the one to be confided in. Harriet, as Sesina secretly liked
to call Mrs Collins, would have long confidential chats with
Dolly, the pair of them giggling over something. Dolly was
known to favour Mr Charles, to say that he was sensitive
and to hint that the master had made him too religious,
always worrying about his sins. She had a troubled look on
her face, now, but when she spoke it was not of Mr Charles,
but of his mother.

'The mistress was looking very worried,' she said quietly.
'Don't know what got into her tonight. Was in a bit of a
state, wasn't she, Mrs Barnett? Did you think that when you
came in?'

The two women looked across at each other. Sesina chewed
on a piece of cold pheasant. Should have had it before
the jelly and apricot cream, she told herself, but she was too
interested in the exchange of looks to concentrate too much
on her taste buds.

'All her fault.' Dolly gave a nod at Sesina. 'Leaving that
painting coat in there in the scullery.'

'Stupid place to leave it. Makes people get ideas.' Mrs
Barnett rounded upon Sesina, her face as red as a fighting cock.
'You could have guessed what would happen. That policeman
poking around the place. Of course, he took it. What was Mr
Charles's painting coat doing in the back pantry? If you had
any wit you'd know that 'ud look suspicious. And anyone
could see it was a bloodstain. And don't pretend you didn't
know that. Pretending it was paint and then soaking it in
salt. You must think that we was born yesterday. And that's the
sort of thing that makes the police suspicious. And now they're
after poor Mr Charles.'

Sesina gawped at her. Couldn't find words for a second and
then, she, too, launched into the attack.

'It's your fault, the two of you. You're always on to me, the pair of you, one after the other. Everything I do is wrong. Nothing but moan, moan, moan. Well, I'm getting out of here. Wish I'd never let Mr Wilkie talk me into coming to this place. Well, I've stuck two years of it and that's enough for anyone.' With a warm rush of triumph, she pulled at her apron, tore it off and threw it onto the floor.

And then she kicked it under the table, turned on her heel and made for the door.

But it opened before she got to it and there was Mr Wilkie, his little round glasses all fogged up as if he might have been crying.

'She's leaving, Mr Wilkie,' said Mrs Barnett. 'Going to hand in her notice.' There was a slightly gloating sound in her voice and Sesina felt like giving her a sharp slap across her big fat face.

'That's right,' chimed in Dolly.

'No, no.' Mr Wilkie was always kind. 'You mustn't do that, Sesina. What would we all do without you? The house would be lost without you.' He took her by the arm, in his friendly way, and pulled her through the door and shut out the cook and her echo. 'We need you, Sesina,' he whispered. 'There's my poor brother. Wouldn't hurt a fly. You know that, Sesina. I have to get him out of this mess. You keep your eyes peeled, won't you? We must find the truth. We must save him. My poor mother is in a state.'

She knew what he was talking about. He knew that she had brains. 'I'll stay,' she said. And then she took a chance and whispered to him, 'But if the cook is found murdered, then you'll have to keep the police away from me.'

He patted her on the arm. 'Good girl,' he said. 'Now, do you think you could bring a cup of tea up to my mother? She's in a bit of a state.'

Sesina nodded. 'What about you, Mr Wilkie, and Mr Charles?'

He patted his waistcoat pocket, bulging as usual with the little flask he kept inside it. 'No tea for me, Sesina,' he said with a grin. 'I can think of something better. Come on, let's see about that tea.' He led her back into the kitchen. 'Mrs

Collins is a bit upset and I've asked Sesina to bring her a cup of tea,' he said to the cook. He bent down and picked up Sesina's apron from the floor. 'What do you think I'd look like in this, Cookie,' he said to Mrs Barnett and she and Dolly split their sides laughing, just like he was ten years old again. Twenty years they had worked in the same house. Go mad with boredom to even think about it! Sesina thought to herself.

'Go on with you, Mr Wilkie.' The cook was in a good humour now and she didn't even look at Sesina when she took the apron and put it on again. The pair of them were holding their sides laughing at his jokes as she busied herself with a tray and a set of cups.

'Put it in her sitting room; I'll persuade her to take it in there,' he said over his shoulder as they came up the drawing-room stairs so Sesina turned and went into the small sitting room beside Mrs Collins' bedroom. She took a little time, fixing the table and closing the curtains, checking on the fire and then she thought she'd go and see what was happening in the drawing room. Very quiet it all was when she came up to the door. Couldn't hear a sound. Wondered whether to knock, but then decided not. She'd just pop in, whisper in Mrs Collins' ear and then take herself off. Best not to interrupt anything.

And so she turned the handle.

As soon as Sesina came in, she knew that there was something wrong. Mr Charles was standing there, standing facing that inspector; white as a sheet, he was, standing there, just looking, stricken-like, at the inspector. Mr Charles was a tall man, much, much bigger than his brother Wilkie, but, nonetheless, Sesina thought that when she looked at him that there was something about him that reminded her of those calves at Smithfield Market, something about his eyes, something that told you that he knew he was heading off to be slaughtered. Poor fellow. It was that sick look! Sick and frightened and hoping for nothing.

And his mother, standing there at the end of the room. She, thought Sesina, as she looked down at the woman, she knew. She'd know; know what the poor fellow was thinking. Knowed that he'd got no hope of nothing.

'Just let me go through this again,' the inspector was staying. A sneaky sort of fellow; pretending to be all nice, pretending that he wasn't gloating or nothing. Oh, no, not him, but he was of course. Could hear the sound of it in his voice. Remembered once going to a rat catching with her friends, Isabella and Rachel Meyers, and all the geezers in the audience suddenly roared with excitement and you could smell the excitement in the air. Sesina could hear that note in the inspector's voice, just like he was a ratting terrier with his teeth snapping.

'You received a summons from Mr Edwin Milton-Hayes. That was right, wasn't it? He summoned you to give him some assistance, wanted you to help with finishing off a picture before this evening's display of them.'

The inspector stopped, but Mr Charles said nothing. Just bent his head, like he was getting ready for a noose to be put over it. Mr Wilkie opened his mouth, but the inspector, not looking at him, but seeing everything out of the corner of his eye, held up one large hand.

'Just a minute, please. Yes, Mr Collins, go ahead, tell me about the argument between yourself and Mr Edwin Milton-Hayes. He invited you into the house, didn't he? Of course, he did. Invited you to come and see that picture. Were you alone, or were you with someone? Perhaps Mrs Molly French came too. Would that be how it happened?'

Charley opened his mouth, closed it again, looking a bit like a stranded fish on the edge of the river. Looked sick and bewildered. Didn't know what to say.

Mr Wilkie did, though. 'Don't answer that silly question, Charley,' he said. 'The inspector likes to play those little tricks, don't you, inspector? Why should Mrs French be called upon to help with the painting of a picture?'

Sesina looked at Mr Dickens. Time he put his oar in. Not slow to speak up in the usual way of things. Saying nothing, now. Just looking at poor Charley and then back at the inspector again.

'I just want to know the truth, Mr Collins,' said the inspector. 'I would like Mr Charles Collins to answer my questions.' The inspector tried to sound all reasonable. He pretended to face Mr Wilkie, but Sesina could see how his eyes slid sideways and how he kept close tabs on the poor young idiot. *Go on, tell some lie or other!* The words were shouting in her mind and she wished that she could pull a wire and ring a bell inside that noddle of his, put him on his guard.

The inspector looked around, beckoned and someone came forward from the shadow near to the window. The young policeman. Sesina's heart sank. He had a bag with him. Seemed to know what the inspector wanted. Bent down, pulled something out. The painting coat! Held it up. Covered in stains, smudges of paint of all colours: red, blue, yellow, green and all the other colours but Sesina's eyes went immediately to the large plaque of dark clotted blood.

'You recognize this painting coat, Mr Collins?' The inspector was speaking to Mr Wilkie now and Sesina could see how that comical round face of his with its little spectacles suddenly went a deadly white.

'It looks like my father's painting coat. I think I even recognize a scrap of blue paint from that seascape over there, behind your head, inspector.'

Good try, thought Sesina, but she knew that it wouldn't work.

'You don't paint pictures, yourself, Mr Collins, do you?'

The inspector was going on talking to Mr Wilkie, but he never took his eyes off poor Charley.

'No, I don't at the moment, inspector. Tried it, would do the odd picture for fun, perhaps.' Mr Wilkie took off his spectacles, wiped them, put them back again and reached across as if to take the coat. Sesina held her breath. Could he persuade the inspector that it was his, now?

'But this is not your coat, is it? I can see that it has two names on it, the one stitched under the other. The top one is William Collins, and the other, below it, is Charles Allston Collins. So this now, ever since the death of your father, has been the property of Mr Charles Collins, worn whenever you painted, isn't that right, Mr Collins?' Now he had turned away from Mr Wilkie and back to his brother.

'That's right!'

'And you had it with you when you went up into Mr Milton-Hayes' painting studio?'

The poor fellow gaped like a fish on the end of the hook.

'That is correct, is it not?' The inspector lifted his voice a little. Making it sound like a threat and poor Charley went all white and winced like someone had slapped him across the face.

'That is correct,' he said in a sort of strangled whisper.

'I wonder,' said the inspector, all polite now, 'whether I could trouble you to come down to the station with me, Mr Charles Collins. I would like you to make a statement. Perhaps your servant could fetch your coat and your hat.' He gave a nod in Sesina's direction, but still kept his eyes fixed on Mr Charles.

Sesina didn't move. Who was he to be throwing orders around? *Not my master. Don't pay me wages, do you, Mister?* And so she just looked down at the carpet. No one else moved or stirred neither.

And then the poor, silly clown had to do for himself. Put his hands over his face. Clapped them to his eyes just like he had a sudden terrible pain. Began to cry. Big, loud sobs. Just like a child. Bent his head down. His brother went over to him. Put an arm around his shoulders. No good. Should have put a hand in front of his silly mouth.

Sobs or no sobs, the words came out clear as a bell. 'All right, inspector. I killed him. Now stop torturing me.'

The inspector took a step forward. One step, two steps and then Mrs Collins spoke up. Not usually too gentile, used to be poor when she was young – she told Sesina that once – but this time she was more gentile than any of them.

'My son is just trying to protect me, inspector. I am the one who killed Mr Milton-Hayes. I am ready to make a full confession.'

NINE

Wilkie Collins, *Hide and Seek*, 1854:
The horror and misery of that moment is present to me
now, at this distance of time. The shock I then received
struck me down at once; I never have recovered from it,
and I never shall.

I didn't know what to do for a moment. My eyes seemed to
start from my head, my fingers trembled and an icy perspir-
ation poured from my forehead. For a few moments my
throat seemed to close over. I looked up at my father's portrait
above the mantelpiece. The steady brown eyes seemed to be
judging me, to be looking at me with an air of sorrow. *'Not
to be trusted to look after your mother and your little brother,
Willie; how can you let me down like this!'* The eyes sent
the message and I flinched. My father, unlike most fathers,
had never struck me, but there had been times when he had
wounded me to the core with his sorrowful appraisal of me.
*'Never amount to anything. Need to have courage. Need to be
a man, Willie.'*

I looked an appeal at Dickens, at the man who, though
there was a bare twelve years between us, had almost taken
the place of my dead father, a man who was my guide, my
mentor, my counsellor through the difficult path of life.

And Dickens did not fail me.

He smiled sympathetically at my mother. Not a broad smile,
more a warming of the face and a softening of the eyes. And
then turned back towards the policeman.

'Reminds you of your school days, eh, inspector. The
splendid mother of Zeus! What mothers won't do for their
sons! Brings tears to my eyes.'

I held my breath. Took off my spectacles, wiped them and
then replaced them. The moisture had gone and now the scene
was clearer. Charley sobbing, with his head in his hands, my

mother standing beside him, stroking that red hair which had betrayed him. The inspector, stolid, refusing to look at Dickens, but nevertheless conveying an air of uncertainty.

And then he seemed to make up his mind, seemed to decide to ignore my mother's words. He walked across to the picture on the chair, but Dickens was too quick for him.

'Come, come, my dear Mrs Collins! Inspector, I'm sure that you recognize the power of mother love. But this good lady, such a loving, such a good mother to her two sons, this lady cannot be allowed to incriminate herself in this way. You, like me, can, I'm sure, separate truth from a gallant lie.'

The inspector looked from him to my mother. I held my breath. I could see that this latest turn in events bothered the man immensely. He didn't mind arresting my young brother, but he couldn't easily drag a lady of my mother's age down to the police station and cast her into a cell.

'I have my duty to do, Mr Dickens,' he said, speaking like an automat, 'I have a duty to my employers and to the public. I have a dead man on my hands, his body down there in the station and another man who has confessed to the murder.' The inspector avoided my mother's eyes and looked uncomfortably at my friend.

Dickens nodded. 'Just so, just so,' he said. 'And I'm sure that we will all testify to the excellent way in which you have performed your duties. But, you see, inspector, the hour is very late. The young man is not well, in fact, I would not hesitate to say that I don't think that he is wholly in possession of his wits. I think a lawyer might make quite a good case against the police if he were arrested now, at a moment when it might be said that he was not responsible for what he was saying. God bless my soul, I know of many a lawyer who would make mincemeat of this case just on those grounds alone. He's not in a condition to be questioned. You know that, don't you, inspector?' Dickens, always quick and decisive in his thought processes, seemed to have decided that the inspector was not going to follow up on my mother's confession and so he confined his eloquence to pleading for Charley.

A slight glimmer of hope. I held my breath. My mother stayed very still, her hand on Charley's shoulder, her direct gaze on the inspector. I kept my eyes fixed on Dickens. His mobile, dark face was going through many changes of expression. It had now moved from confidence to pensiveness. He grimaced slightly, rubbed his chin like a man wrestling with a problem.

'Of course, I see your problem,' he said confidentially, speaking as though no one but he and his friend, Inspector Field, were in the room. 'Yes, I do see your problem. You fear that the young man might take himself off in the small hours of the morning, might not be available for questioning when you turn up tomorrow.' Dickens, an amateur actor to the bone, knit his heavy brows in a way that would signal to even the dullest audience that he was thinking hard. I held my breath.

'I'll tell you what I'll do, inspector,' he went on in his irresistible fashion, like a mountain stream in full flood, sweeping all before him, 'I'll solve your problem, and I know how to reassure you that all will be well.' He looked all around and I admired how assured he appeared. 'What I will do is that I will stay here tonight and if our hostess will permit, I will hold the keys to the young man's room.' He swept another look around at those who remained: my poor brother, sobbing helplessly; my gallant mother, white as the lace at her neck, her head held high; myself, uncertain, glancing up at my father's portrait, wondering what to do to keep my brother safe and to save my mother from her desire to sacrifice herself in order to keep her youngest child from prison. Dickens waited for a moment, waited until all eyes, including those of the inspector, had turned towards him with an expression of dawning hope. He nodded gravely. 'And if you are happy about this arrangement, inspector, then, in the morning, Mr Charles Collins will be himself and will be able to give a more coherent and plausible account of his day and of what he saw and what he found when he went to the Milton-Hayes residence. I'm sure that you'll find that I am right, inspector,' he went on with his usual air of quiet confidence. 'And, of course, once morning comes, we'll all have cooler heads and we can work out this question of who killed Milton-Hayes.' He looked along the row of pictures on the chairs and said with a touch of grimness in his voice, 'There may be about ten people here,

painted by that man, Milton-Hayes. Ten people whose reputations, liberty and lives have been threatened by these pictures.
It's important, is it not, inspector, important for everyone's
sake that the right person is arrested.'

I could see the inspector turning this over in his mind.
He had received great fame from Dickens' article about him
in the *Household Words* magazine. 'Shrewd'; 'sagacious';
'vigilant', the praise had flowed out and it had done, so the
rumour went, no end of good to Inspector Field; earned him
great respect both from his superiors and from the criminal
classes.

And now there had been a slight emphasis on the words,
'for everyone's sake,' in Dickens' voice and a raised index
finger lent extra weight to his warning. The inspector frowned
at his subordinate. The young policeman looked back at his
superior deferentially, but I thought, from his expression, he
knew that nothing was going to happen before the morning.
The inspector cast an appraising look at the sobbing figure
on the chair and then nodded his head.

'Very well, Mr Dickens,' he said. He hesitated for a moment,
looking back at the pictures still propped upon their chairs
and then at the artist's satchel standing by the curtain. Dickens'
eyes followed his.

'Thank you, inspector,' he said gravely. 'And to express our
gratitude, Mr Wilkie Collins and I will put our heads together
and endeavour to come up with a list of those who might be
portrayed in these abominable works.'

I stiffened. I had no desire to place some man, or worse,
some woman, in the noose, but then a quick glance at Charley,
and at my poor mother, made me hold my tongue. This murder
would be all over London soon. The newspapers and the
pamphlet writers would have a field day with it. Everyone in
the small world of the murdered artist and the Pre-Raphaelite
circle would fall under suspicion. Secrets would be uncovered.
Friend would betray friend; the whole matter would be
discussed in coffee houses, whispered about in studios and by
the end of it all, reputations would lie in the dust and perhaps
more deaths would occur in order to keep the matter a secret.
Yes, the sooner the guilty person was arrested, the sooner

that my young brother would be safe from arrest. I relaxed, nodded my head, and pulled the bell.

By the time that Dolly arrived, my mother was herself, directing the woman to fetch the house keys from her bedroom. When they were given to her, she, herself, took off the key and handed it over to Dickens with a calm and even slightly detached air. I smiled at her, doing my best to let her know how much I admired her courage. It was time, I thought, to get rid of the inspector and to allow my mother and my brother to get some sleep. I held out my hand and she placed the rest of the keys upon it.

'Sesina will show you out, inspector,' I said happily. 'You'll lock up then, Sesina, won't you? And bring the keys to me. My mother is unwell.' That was enough. The girl was clever enough to know what I meant. I wanted those two policemen out of the house, and wanted no chance of either of them coming back before morning.

And by morning, I tried to tell myself, Charley would be himself, would come up with some plausible explanation about the blood on his painting coat, and would, perhaps, even be tricked into telling the name of the true murderer, if he knew it – and I had begun to wonder whether he did. In the meantime, myself and Dickens would put our brains and our knowledge of human nature together and try to solve the problem of which of those invited guests might have murdered the man who had invited them to my mother's dinner party and who had planned to destroy their reputations.

'Come on, old chap,' I said to Charley, slipping an arm around his waist and hoisting him up and accepting the key from Dickens with the other hand. 'Let's get you to bed, Charley. You are not well, poor fellow.'

He came with me, docile as a child. He brought tears to my eyes and I swore that at all costs I would save him from the hangman's noose. I gave him another dose of laudanum and waited with him until it had taken effect. When I had him tucked into bed, blond eyelashes closing over his inflamed eyes, I began to draft, in my mind, a letter to my yachting friend, Pigott. When he was asleep, I quietly locked the door and slipped into my own room. The letter didn't take long. I had resolved on what to say. Pigott knew Charley; he was the one who, by writing the newspaper article, had started that joke about Charley, the artist who had spent the summer matching a set of eyelashes to the colour of a fly's eye.

Pigott would understand what Charley was like. And so not too many explanations of Charley's state of mind were necessary. Once I could get Charley onto that boat, then he would be out of harm's way until the real murderer was captured. 'All expenses will be borne by me,' I wrote. When I finished the letter I slipped a couple of five-pound notes into the envelope, wrote the address and after I had glued the queen's head to the envelope, I rang for Sesina.

'Slip out of the house first thing in the morning, Sesina,' I said, handing her half-a-crown. 'I want that letter to go in the post as soon as possible. Do it before you light the fires and before we have any early-morning callers.' I hesitated for a moment and then added, 'It's very important for my brother that this letter should reach my friend quickly, by tomorrow late morning, if possible.'

Sesina would know what I meant and she was fond of Charley, quite motherly towards him, I was always amused to see. She would understand that I would not want the police to lay their eyes on this letter or to delay it in any way. The half-a-crown would keep her sweet and give her a stake in this enterprise. I put in a request for a pot of tea for the two of us and she smiled happily. I winked at her and she returned the wink. And then, with a heavy heart, I went down to see Dickens and to hand over the key of Charley's door to him.

He pocketed it in an absent-minded way. He had coolly taken a sheet of my mother's writing paper from her writing table and had made a list in his decisive, strong handwriting. He held it up to me and I could see that the titles of the five pictures were listed and emphatically underscored. I scanned it while he took out a penknife and sharpened the quill to his satisfaction. Beneath each title was a space for names and already Dickens had filled in the names of the figures in *Taken in Adultery*. 'Charles Allston Collins, Mrs Molly French, Mr John French.' He read them aloud, dispassionately and without emphasis and then moved on to the next title on his list.

The Night Prowler, he said, rolling the 'r' and almost gloating over the picture. 'Now then Wilkie my boy, not too much doubt about the main character in this picture, is there. I've seen that ring, before, haven't you? Supposed to be part of the Irish inheritance of Lord Douglas. Indeed, I've heard it said that it's probably the most worthwhile part of it and that the family estate is nothing but boggy fields, filled with rushes. But the lady, old man, who is the lady? No face, of course, and nothing too distinguishing about her, is there? You don't recognize that purple dress, do you?'

'Not the dress,' I said, hesitating a little. 'But I have heard rumours, haven't you?'

'No, go on, tell me. You know I have no time to listen to gossip,' he said impatiently. I was not surprised. Dickens was the talker and I was the listener. When Dickens was surrounded by people they looked to him to entertain them, to flash out those jokes, to amaze them with his scintillating wit, to listen eagerly to his remarks about the book that he was writing, or the book that he had just finished writing, or the book that he intended writing when the present book was finished.

But it was different with me. People were comfortable with me, liked to tell me juicy pieces of gossip. 'Of course, it's mainly her mother's fault,' I began hesitantly. 'That poisonous woman is always fussing about the poor girl, trying to get her to marry rich old men, or even rich, though unpleasant, young men,' I added thinking about Milton-Hayes and all the trouble that he had caused.

'So, Florence Gummidge? That's who you think it is, don't you?' Dickens cocked an eyebrow at me and I nodded. He filled in the name of Lord Douglas as well and then sat back as a knock came to the door. I went across and opened it and stood back to allow Sesina to come in, her eyes bright with excitement.

I gave her a wink, half mechanically, and then went and pulled out a leaf of my mother's cherished Pembroke table and watched her place the tray carefully in the middle of its shining surface. 'Good girl,' I said. She had brought not just a large pot of tea, but some of Mrs Barnett's ginger biscuits, and I applauded her initiative. 'Sesina,' I said, 'will you just pop up to Mr Charles's painting room and bring me down his canvas knife from the drawer of the table. Don't cut yourself; it's very sharp.' I slipped a sixpence into her hand. She gave a grin and went off. I could hear her running lightly up the stairs. She was back into the drawing room a few minutes later. The knife was in her hand and she placed it in front of me, to the side of the tray. I looked down at it, but did not touch it.

'We'll serve ourselves, Sesina,' said Dickens and I could have sworn that the girl looked disappointed. He was right, of course. No sense in letting her get above herself, but I thought that if I had been on my own I might have weakly asked her opinion on who might have murdered Milton-Hayes. Maidservants, my mother always said, often know more about your friends and acquaintances than you do, yourself.

Absent-mindedly I filled the two cups and added milk. And some sugar into my cup. Dickens, I knew, never allowed himself sugar in either tea or coffee.

'I'll bear witness to that.' He had taken an eyeglass from his pocket and with the other eye closed, he was bending over the table, peering very closely at the knife.

'To what?' I felt slightly irritated by him and his calm air of being in charge.

'To the fact that you sent the maidservant for the knife and to the fact, as far as I can tell, that there is no stain of blood, not on the blade, nor on the sheath.'

I shrugged. I was not sure that fact was a cast iron piece of evidence that I had not interfered with the knife. I could, after all, have been up in Charley's room earlier and might have cleaned the knife then. On the other hand, Inspector Field was very influenced by Dickens and would take his word for evidence in a way that he might not if another man were involved.

'Let's get on with the list,' I said impatiently. 'I never did think that Charley was guilty, just wanted to remove that knife in case he got any ideas of ending his life. Luckily his religion might save him from that.'

Dickens said nothing in reply to this. He was, I knew, not particularly fond of Charley, considered him to be a weak character with dangerous leanings towards Roman Catholicism. He had, though, I knew from his expression, been immensely impressed by my mother's courage and display of love for her son. There was a determined look on his face as he looked back at the list.

'So we write down the name of Lord Douglas below the title *The Night Prowler*. I'm going to give my suspects marks out of ten. I'll give him eight. I think he has the nerve and the determination to do a deed like that.'

'And Florence Gummidge?'

Dickens pursed his lips and shook his head decidedly. 'One,' he said with authority. 'A girl like that wouldn't go in for murder. She might have allowed a lover to persuade her into some dangerous games after midnight in country houses, but murder, no. I don't believe that. She would leave it to the noble lord, himself. She's under her mother's thumb and that means she doesn't have much initiative of her own.'

'And her mother, Mrs Hermione Gummidge? Frantic to prevent a scandal. Distraught at the idea of her only daughter being pilloried, being exposed to the London world in an exhibition of paintings.'

Dickens nodded. 'You've got a point. A much more likely person. Five for her, then,' he said, 'but, mind you, I don't think this is a woman's crime. Women are more subtle than men. Mrs Hermione Gummidge is much more likely to have bought some arsenic, invited our friend Milton-Hayes to her house and handed him a cup of tea, with a smile on her face, of course.' There was a slightly abstracted look on his own face as though he had suddenly thought of an idea for a book and I made haste to recall him to my brother's plight.

'*Forbidden Fruit*,' I said, looking across to the picture of the man urging the young girl towards the church. 'Can't be quite sure, but I do think that is meant to be Walter Hamilton, the friend of my brother's. He sat opposite you at the table. Don't know whether you had any opportunity of exchanging words with him. He's very shy. He has a very promising pupil, a young girl, and I've met them together a few times. She seems to adore him, and he adores her, so I've heard. I have heard rumours about a marriage, a planned marriage. But she is a schoolgirl, only fourteen years old, I think.'

'Disgusting,' said Dickens. 'About the same age as my Mamey and Katey. The man should be horsewhipped. I'd do it with pleasure myself. Nine marks. I do believe that a villain like that would do anything, would commit any crime.'

'No, no,' I said soothingly, though I had to smother a laugh. 'No, Walter is a very nice fellow. And they are very romantic together. I'd say that talk of marriage is more on her part than on his. She adores him. And anyone in the art world seeing that picture would be more inclined to laugh than to condemn. No, I'd give him one mark, and one mark only. He's a dreamer. He wouldn't kill anyone. And, you know, it's only a civil offence, he'd just have to pay a fine to her parents. And even if they got married, well, I think that it would just be a secret marriage and no consummation.' I didn't like to tell Dickens that Walter had discussed the matter with me and that he and his lovely girl had decided that they might get married but would wait until she was sixteen before they lived together. 'The idea of marriage is definitely hers,' I said aloud. 'She's very romantic, you know.'

'Four marks, then,' said Dickens, but he still wore a scowl and glared back at the picture.

'*Taken in Adultery*,' I had summoned up my courage and named the picture. I looked at the three names. Molly French, John French and Charles Allston Collins. This, I knew, was a very different matter. If the elderly and very rich John French found out that his beautiful young wife was having an affair with my brother Charley then he would, almost undoubtedly, throw her out of the family home and immediately divorce her. Molly had no living parent, no brothers nor sisters. Her reputation would be in shreds, but worse than that, she would have no home, no money.

'You know that picture that Augustus Egg is planning, Dick,' I said soberly. 'He was telling us about it one night at Foster's party. How he was going to have the first picture of a sobbing wife lying on the floor while her children played at building houses with cards in the background. The husband sitting in judgement on her. And then in the second picture, the two girls, their daughters are older. Their father is now dead, their mother lost to them for ever. And then in the third picture he is going to paint Adelphi Arches by moonlight, the erring woman has sunk to the lowest echelons in society and is sleeping among the prostitutes under the archway near to Hungerford Stairs.'

'I remember,' said Dickens soberly. 'And you think that Molly – and yes, they were there that night. I can remember them. I was sitting beside Molly. I remember that she shivered and I called on Augustus Egg to cheer up and I sang my comic song about the Cats' Meat Man.' His face was sober. He heaved a sigh. 'So society would judge her, I'm afraid.'

'And I'm afraid that it looks bad for Charley,' I said steadily. 'He would risk anything rather than subject the woman he loves to a fate like the woman in the triptych that Augustus Egg is planning.' I reached over and wrote the figure eight beside my brother's name. I pondered about Molly, but did nothing, just thought sadly about my gentle, conscientious brother.

'This is just for ourselves, Wilkie,' said Dickens quietly. He gave me a worried look and, with a demonstrativeness unusual for him, he reached out and squeezed my arm. 'Don't worry, my dear friend. We'll arrive at the truth. Now what about the husband?' he asked more cheerfully. 'It seems to me that any husband seeing a picture of his wife in the arms of another man would want to revenge himself on the artist who painted that picture.'

I shook my head. It was kind of Dickens, but I didn't believe that John French would have taken that step. His first move would have been to interrogate his wife and his second would have been to come storming around to confront Charley.

'I'd give him one mark, only,' I said. 'He's an old man. His eyesight is poor. Don't you remember him peering through that eyeglass tonight? I wouldn't think he is too strong. I don't see Edwin Milton-Hayes standing there and allowing a frail old man like that to hack him to death. No, my friend, one has to say that Charley is a hundred times more likely to be the assassin than John French.'

'And Molly? Quite a tall girl, isn't she? And, of course, a

woman would have an advantage over a man because she
wouldn't be taken seriously. He may well just have laughed
when she snatched up a knife . . .'

'His knife, you mean Milton-Hayes' knife?' I asked quietly.

'Well, yes.'

'You remember that the inspector said that he had checked
that very carefully. He said that he hadn't found any signs of
blood upon it or on any others. I think he said Milton-Hayes
had a few knives.'

'Could have been cleaned.' Dickens watched me carefully.

I cast another glance at the knife that Sesina had brought
down from Charley's painting room. Yes, Charley's knife did
look perfectly clean. But perhaps the inspector might have
some way of finding out whether it had been contaminated by
bloodstains at an earlier stage. A proposal to test the Milton-
Hayes knife might prompt the police to test Charley's knife.
I compressed my lips and passed on from *Taken in Adultery*. I
hadn't really studied the next picture and so I endeavoured to
concentrate upon it now, walking across the room and peering
at it in my short-sighted way.

'*Den of Iniquity*,' I read out. This was a very crowded picture,
more like in the style of William Frith than Milton-Hayes' usual
paintings. One face, and one only was obliterated, but the other
faces were blurred and unimportant. No models, I guessed, had
been used for them. These were background fill-in and nothing
more. It was an opium den, a common subject among painters,
though not so common for the Pre-Raphaelites. I concentrated
on the central figure, a man, lying between two other figures,
slumped upon a bedstead that had given way under their weight.
Dickens peered over my shoulder.

'Middle-aged, heavily built, grey hair,' he said after a
minute. 'Now who were the middle-aged men at your mother's
dinner party this evening? So far, the guests have all been
proved to have been carefully selected by that enterprising
artist, Milton-Hayes.'

'No wonder that the inspector remarked upon his flour-
ishing bank account,' I said, thinking about my very talented
young brother who earned almost nothing and was dependent
on my mother for virtually every penny.

Dickens ignored this. Unlike myself whose attention was taken by every wandering thought, Dickens was a man with an enormous capacity to focus intently and grimly on one matter at a time. 'Middle-aged men,' he said. 'Let me see.' His eyes stared ahead and I knew that he was visualizing my mother's dining table. 'Not Lord Douglas,' he said decisively. 'Not young, but his hair is a glossy black. Not heavy, either, like this man. In fact, I wouldn't choose him in any case. I'd say that it would be most unlikely for an opium addict to have the nerve and the self-possession to creep around his host's house at night.'

'It will be someone that we haven't identified already,' I said. 'What about William Jordan, himself? The fact that the wife is a gambler doesn't preclude the husband from being an opium addict. What do you think?' I felt a rush of energy at the thought. I didn't like the man, I had decided.

Dickens made a face, pursing up his mouth and wagging his head from side to side. He said nothing but his feelings were obvious.

'Well, otherwise it has to be Molly's husband, John French, and I can't see him somehow. He's far too old and that figure here looks heavier, broader than he.' I was getting tired of the game. It all seemed very unreal. There were just two pictures that I felt warranted murder. One was *The Night Prowler*. That would not only ruin a man and his accomplice, but would land him in prison. And, I had to admit, that the picture *Taken in Adultery* would ruin Molly for ever, would cause her to be cast out from her husband's house. And that my brother was not a man to allow that to happen to a woman that he loved.

'No,' I said resolutely. 'That has to be William Jordan if it's anyone. And if it is him, it may well damage his business badly, might stop people buying pictures from him, I suppose. So I'll give him five and now let's finish with this business.'

Dickens nodded, but said nothing, just put a tick beside my figure. 'Let's look at the last picture,' he said.

'*The Root of All Evil*,' I read out. It was a gambling den, but only one figure was identifiable, an elegant lady, one hand was held to her heart in the age-old gesture of despair and the other hand loosely held, splayed out, a set of cards. The cards were immediately identifiable, a two of clubs, a six of diamonds and a three of hearts. A hand of cards that could bear no hope for its owner. The face, like all the other faces in these evil pictures, was unidentifiable, a blank oval of creamy-white, but the rich auburn curls piled on her head, the long slim neck with its close-fitting collar of pearls. All of these were unmistakable.

'Helen,' I breathed.

'Wife of our friend William Jordan, the art gallery owner, is she not?' Dickens asked the question but I knew that he was aware of the answer to it. He grimaced unhappily. I had seen him earlier in earnest conversation with Helen. Though he had only met her once before that very morning, they had been getting on like old friends. She was just the sort of woman that he liked. Discreet, well-mannered, calmly clever, humorous in a quiet sort of fashion. And beautifully dressed. He liked that in a woman. One thing had been missing. Helen, this evening, had not worn the collar of pearls. I had never seen her before without them at a dinner party or at the opera.

'Yes, Helen Jordan, that's Helen Jordan, I would lay a wager on that,' I said aloud. 'She wasn't wearing that collar of pearls tonight, but I have often seen her wear it.' Had she seen the picture, I wondered, seen the picture and wanted to lessen her resemblance to it by leaving her pearls at home on the night when she expected to meet Milton-Hayes?

And then as he still looked unsure, I said, 'Dick, she's a gambler. She cannot stop herself. She's a nice woman, an attractive woman, but she plays cards like a drunkard drinks, incessantly! She gambles. Gets into debt. And then plays again in order to pay off that debt. And then when that doesn't work, when she finds herself ever deeper in debt, why then she plays again, digs herself deeper and deeper into debt. And, of course, when her debtors find that she will be unable to pay, that she cannot pay, why then they go to her husband. After all, in law, he is responsible for his wife. And that is why he . . .'

'Did what?' Dickens, I thought, knew the answer to that question. I had seen a dawning look of remembrance on his face. Most people, I thought, might have seen or heard something about that notice in *The Times*, but what was a terrible tragedy for one man and his wife, was only a tiny item of news for those who hardly knew them both.

'Why he has repudiated his responsibility for her debts. Shamed them both with the notice in the newspaper. And I did hear that she has been threatened with divorce if she ever plays again.'

'And this diabolical picture is to inform her husband and to inform the world that she has been unable to refrain from the deadly temptation. Poor man,' said Dickens, always one to be sorry for husbands. 'Poor man,' he repeated. 'He is in a terrible quandary. And it is made no easier by being set out in front of the art lovers of London. Well, what do you think, Wilkie? They both have a motive, do they not?'

I thought about it for a moment or two. 'It's not a huge motive,' I said at last, speaking slowly. 'Half of London probably knew that she had gone back to gambling once again. I don't think, to be honest, that he had any motive. He made no secret of his feelings, would tell anyone about the quandary he was in – a matter of losing his wife, or losing his fortune was how he put it to me and I hardly knew him. He's bought quite a few of my father's pictures, but that's in the past. A couple of Charley's pictures, but I've had nothing to do with that. But it shows that he makes no secret of the matter. So I'd say that he has nothing to lose by the revelation in this picture. Most people were quite sorry for him and he lapped up the sympathy.'

'And she?'

'She's a different matter,' I said reluctantly. 'She had everything to lose if her husband knew that she was continuing to gamble his money away.' Sadly I wrote the figure five next to Helen's name, and then crossed it out and replaced it with a six. I felt very sorry for both husband and wife and a surge of anger against this fiend, Milton-Hayes, rose up within me.

'Why on earth did that wretched canon commission that man to do these pictures? Look at the trouble it has caused.' I banged a fist on the Pembroke table and the drop leaf bounced upon its support.

'I suppose,' said Dickens with an ironical twist to his lips, 'that he thought he would save people from sin by bringing to their notice the consequences of their wrongdoing.'

'And he ends up by being the cause of a murder, at least one murder; I feel that I could murder him myself, stupid old man,' I said savagely as a vision of the fat, self-satisfied face came to my mind's eye. I looked back at my list. 'I suppose that there is no doubt that Milton-Hayes was using these pictures to blackmail.'

'No doubt, I'd say. The inspector said that the housemaid had instructions to leave the door on the latch if she had to go out as he had a lot of visitors and he had even told her not to answer the door, that he would do it himself. Of course, she only works part-time for him. He and a house further down the road share her. And so the coast would be clear,' I said. 'He would bring them up to his studio, show them the picture *Winter of Despair*. That would have been on the easel. But what about the other pictures, Dickens? They were unmarked.'

Dickens thought about the matter for the moment. 'What about if he first showed *Winter of Despair* and then went off to fetch the companion piece. The two pictures, the diptych, would be overwhelming, would cause the victim to pay up instantly. That would have been the result in the case, probably, in most circumstances. But our murderer was a man, or woman, of instant decision, a person who immediately recognized the consequences that would ensue. And before the second picture could be produced, the artist and his *Winter of Despair* were both slashed. The man was killed and the picture was ruined. That's the only solution that I can see. How many pictures was Milton-Hayes going to bring to your mother's dinner, Wilkie?'

I shrugged. 'No idea. I don't know whether he would have given advance notice, or not. They were always fairly informal, these affairs. But, remember, Dick, we found just those five pictures packed in a bag. I'd say that was what he would have brought. Would have called a cab, put the bag on the seat beside him and set off for Hanover Terrace. No more pictures were intended, I'd say, Dick. You saw yourself that when the inspector had put in the mutilated picture of *Winter of Despair* that the bag looked over-full.'

'So, five pictures and we have identified . . . how many possibilities from each picture?' Dickens scanned the piece of paper in his hand. I noticed how he, normally the most decisive and fluent of men, had hesitated before choosing the neutral word 'possibilities' in preference to the word 'murderers'.

I felt like that myself. If it were not for the imperative necessity to clear my unfortunate and helpless brother from the charge, I would have had no interest in discovering the man or the woman who had put an end to Milton-Hayes and his blackmailing – would feel no imperative need to condemn. But Charley had to be extricated from the threat of prison and of the gallows and so I turned my attention back to our list.

Root of All Evil: Mrs Helen Jordan – a gambler, but could she be a murderer?

Den of Iniquity: her husband, William Jordan, was he an opium consumer?

Taken in Adultery: Charles Collins and Molly French. Charley, I had to admit to myself, was a strong candidate.

Forbidden Fruit: Walter Hamilton, but as far as I and Charley knew, he hadn't done anything towards an illegal marriage with a girl under sixteen and his pretty little admirer still lived with her parents and did her lessons like any other girl of her age.

The Night Prowler: now this was a different matter and I felt myself cheering up a little. 'Lord Douglas,' I said aloud – 'not Florence Gummidge; she's just a silly girl. And as for her mother – well, a woman of that age is unlikely to have taken a knife to a man. Don't see her murdering anyone, but Lord Douglas is a strong possibility. Would lose his place in society, his inheritance, his liberty and his life itself, perhaps. All of those jewellery thefts which have been happening over the last year or so have involved items of high value.'

I gazed at my list with a feeling of depression. I seemed to have come to the conclusion that Lord Douglas and my brother Charley were the most likely suspects. The one was guileless and ridden by nervous tensions. The other was cool-headed, fluent of speech and arrogant. I shuddered slightly and put some more coal upon the fire. Charley, I thought, despite my mother's gallant effort to save him and sacrifice herself, was in deadly danger.

TEN

*S**leeping like the dead.* Sesina said those words to herself as she unlocked the door and stole into Mr Charles's room the following morning. She smiled a little as she thought about Mr Dickens solemnly taking the key last night. As if the house was not full of keys. She wondered whether to wake Mr Charles up and show him that she had a key, but then she thought she'd allow him to sleep while she lit the fire and made everything comfortable for him.

She felt wide awake herself. The trip out through the empty streets to find a letter box had woken her up thoroughly. Just arrived when the postman was collecting the letters. Had a bit of fun with him. Cheeky lad. Pretending that he could fit her into his sack. She had wished that she had a job like that. Would have enjoyed going around the streets and knocking on doors. But girls didn't do things like that. Nothing but boring housework or stitching for girls, or else join the streetwalkers, and she didn't fancy that at all. No, delivering and collecting the post would be fun.

She tried to imagine what that postman was doing at the moment, bringing his bag down to the Regent's Park Post Office and then taking the sorted letters and going through the streets popping them into letter boxes – perhaps Mr Wilkie's letter would already have been delivered to that Mr Pigott. She imagined him going to that address and having a bit of backchat with the girl cleaning Mr Pigott's steps.

A bit dull, though, Regent's Park; she'd prefer to be around Covent Garden; it would be fun delivering letters there, she thought, imagining how lively the place would be even as early in the morning as this. Still, no good thinking like that. She riddled the range in the kitchen, made sure that it was burning brightly, then cleaned all of the downstairs grates; since she was early up, she would do them first, she decided and then she worked her way through the bedrooms, leaving, as always, Mr Charles to the last.

After two years of working in the household, after all the warnings that she should not wake anyone, she was expert at opening a door soundlessly, at emptying the ash into her bucket, black-leading the fireplace, then piling up the balls of crushed newspaper, placing the kindling on top, adding coal, piece by piece until the fire was glowing a bright red. Quite a task to do all that without waking the person sleeping in the bed, but she was an expert by now. She cast a glance through the hastily drawn bed-curtains. Still stretched out, but something strange about him. Mouth wide open. A strange noise. Snoring.

She began to brush the ash softly through the grate but then there was another loud noise. Not an ordinary snore. Sounded more like someone choking. She put down the hearth brush and went towards him, slipping soundlessly through the curtains.

And he lay there.

Mouth open.

Face bright red.

Not like him. Always so pale.

Sounded very strange. She went a bit nearer. There was a stain on his pillow. A bright red stain. Blood. Very, very bright red blood. It was dripping from the cut that she had noticed yesterday. The cut just under his ear that he had made when he was shaving. Something had made it bleed, and there was something strange about the blood. Very thin, and that strange colour. She had never seen blood look as red as that. Softly she took a linen handkerchief from on top of the commode cabinet beside his bed, folded it and placed it gently against the blood. In a second, the linen was stained a bright red. The blood was flowing very fast. She pressed it a bit harder. He didn't move. Didn't seem to notice. Just went on snoring in that strange fashion. She began to feel a little panic-stricken. There was something very odd about the way that the blood was flowing out of that tiny cut that had been almost healed yesterday and now that she was near to him she could see that the sheet and the pillow were both stained with that same bright red blood.

And now that she was so close to him she could see

something else. Foam in his mouth. Foam in his nostrils. Strange glistening foam. And clutched in his hand, an empty jewelled pill box.

'Oh, my God, you bitch!' said Sesina aloud. She dropped the handkerchief. She was doing no good. Already it was soaked through. In a second, she was through the door and running fast down the passageway. Didn't care how much noise she made. No time to knock. She burst through the door, flung back the curtains and shouted in his ear.

'Oh, Mr Wilkie, come quickly, Mr Charles 'as poisoned 'imself.'

He was awake in a moment. Out of bed. Pulling on a dressing gown. Grabbing his glasses. Blind as a bat without them. Out the door in his bare feet. She stopped to grab his slippers from under the bed and went after him as he went faster than she had ever seen him move, down to his brother's room. Hadn't exclaimed or questioned her, or even looked astonished.

He might have been expecting something like that.

She was right beside Mr Wilkie as soon as he reached the bed. He didn't touch his brother, didn't try to stop the bleeding; just stood looking down at him. Silently she handed him the empty pill box and he sniffed at it.

'What's he taken?'

'Prussic acid, I think. I hope. Get me some salt from the kitchen. Quick.'

She flew. Urgent. She knew that. You didn't have much time if someone took poison. Make them sick it up straight away. She was back with the salt and a large kitchen mug in seconds and she held the basin as he made his brother vomit. Still breathing badly, but the red colour under the white skin was fading a bit.

'More,' he said. And she filled the mug with a steady hand. Now it was only the water that was coming back up. And he did look a little better. Not breathing so badly now. She washed his face tenderly with a damp sponge. Still unconscious, poor fellow. Mr Wilkie had left him and was scribbling a note.

'Here you are, Sesina. Take this to Dr Beard. Go as fast as you can. Here's half a crown. Take a cab if you need to, but you may be as quick on foot. Go now. Quick!'

Sesina fled down the stairs. She would go as she was. Going to the basement would be dangerous. Cook and Dolly would be up by now and there would be questions to be answered and delays. If she ran fast she wouldn't be cold.

She had just reached the hall when the front door knocker sounded, softly, as though the visitor knew that it was a most unreasonable hour for a morning call.

She opened it impatiently. A young man, quite brown-skinned, blond hair.

'Mr Wilkie Collins in?' he enquired. 'I'm an old friend and he is expecting me. My name is Pigott. He wrote to me and I met the postman. Wonders of our mail service, don't you think? I'll go up. I know Wilkie. Even if you had the house on fire you wouldn't get him out of bed before eleven o'clock in the morning. Top floor. First bedroom, right-hand side. Don't worry. I'll find my way.'

He was gone before she could say a word and she shrugged her shoulders. She wasn't worried about him. She had more important things to think of.

ELEVEN

Wilkie Collins, *Hide and Seek*, 1854:
It is useless now to write about what I suffered from this
fresh blow, or to speak of the awful time I passed by his
bed-side in London. Let it be enough to say, that he
escaped out of the very jaws of death; and that it was
the end of February before he was well enough to be
taken home.

As soon as Sesina had gone, I began to feel that I had
done the wrong thing by sending her out. I should have
rung the bell and summoned Dolly and sent her for
the doctor. Dolly knew his address and she knew Frank Beard
very well. The physician had been one of two who had tended
to my father in his last days. Dolly would have known exactly
where to have gone and how to convince the doctor of the
urgency of the case.

And, also, Sesina had been a practical support to me during
the moments when we had worked together over my brother's
unconscious body. We had encouraged each other and I had
found comfort from her swiftness of thought and of movement and her words of encouragement. I missed her when I
was left alone in the room. My brother was now very pale.
I supposed that was better than the strange bright red of his
face previously, but he seemed lethargic, unable to keep
his eyes open and every breath he took seemed to be drawn
with intense difficulty, almost as if each inhalation might prove
to be his last.

'Charley,' I said urgently. 'Wake up, Charley. How are you,
my dear fellow?' I put my two arms around him and tried to
pull him up to a sitting position, but he flopped like a heavy
sack and I was forced to let him lie down again. I did not
like the sound of that breathing at all. Sesina had lit the fire
and the room was beginning to warm. I chafed his cold hands

and then berated myself for a useless gesture. Air. He needed
air. I went to the window and threw up the sash. The damp
fog streamed into the room and Charley coughed. Was that
good? Or not? I didn't know. My hands were shaking, my
forehead wet with sweat and time after time I had to remove
my spectacles to wipe the damp from them. I looked around
the room frantically and then grabbed a few overstuffed cushions from the sofa. Clumsily, I pulled him up and pushed
the cushions behind his shoulders. And still his breath came
in loud gasps, slow and painful. I rubbed his back between
his shoulder blades, feeling the harsh rattle beneath my
fingertips.

And then a sound from outside. Not Sesina or Dolly. They
wore felt-soled shoes. This was a man's footfall, treading
cautiously, but with a man's weight behind each step. It
couldn't be Frank Beard already, could it? Impossible. A glance
at the mantelpiece clock showed that. Barely five minutes
since Sesina had left.

And then a cough. An artificially loud cough. I knew that
cough. And a whisper, piercing enough to carry on a foggy
stretch of seawater.

'Ahoy, the house. Wakey, wakey, Wilkie!'

'Pigott!' In my excitement and relief at the prospect of
sharing my burden, the word burst out in a joyous shout.
An immensely practical fellow, Pigott. And not just with
boats, either. It suddenly rushed into my mind how I had seen
him once resuscitate a half-drowned sailor on the Norfolk
Broads. 'In here, Pigott,' I shouted. 'In here.'

He was unperturbed at the sight of the room. He came
through the door, shut it quietly behind him, looked straight
at Charley.

'What did he take?'

'Prussic acid, I think.' I showed him the jewelled box. He
took it from me and he raised his eyebrows.

'M,' he observed. And I saw his finger trace the pattern of
the sparkling diamonds.

I hardly listened. 'I've made him vomit. He was very
red-faced, but that's faded now. It's just his breathing. He
sounds . . .'

'Just build up that fire, Wilkie, like a good fellow.' His voice was soothing, but his eyes were anxious. He placed a large brown hand on my brother's chest and then pulled him into an upright position. I tried to build up the fire. My hands were trembling so much that the pieces of coal continuously escaped the tongs and clattered on to the tiles of the fireplace. In the end, I just picked them up with my fingers and dropped them on to the glowing embers and then dusted my fingers on my dressing gown.

'Anyone else in the house?' he asked. 'Not women or children. Need a strong man. He's a big fellow, this brother of yours.'

'There's Dickens,' I said. I didn't wait to ask him what he wanted a strong man for, but fled out of the room and down the stairs, glad that I just wore slippers. The last thing that we wanted now was my mother making a dramatic scene.

Dickens was already up and dressed. I supposed that Dolly must have brought him hot water because he was neatly shaved and his brushed-back hair looked damp. He looked mildly surprised when I burst in and then his eyes sharpened.

'Charley?' he queried.

I didn't hesitate. 'He's tried to commit suicide. Pigott is here. He wants you. He wants you to help him with Charley.'

'Edward Pigott. Good. Just the man we need.'

Dickens, of course, knew Pigott very well, we had both been on a cruise on his yacht to the Scilly Isles. He asked no questions about Charley, but followed me silently up the stairs to the top floor and went into Charley's bedroom with just a nod of acknowledgement to Pigott.

'We need to keep him walking as fast as we can, Dickens,' explained Pigott. 'The faster he goes the more he has to breathe. Want to get plenty of air into his lungs. Open that window a bit wider, Wilkie.'

I watched anxiously as they marched my poor brother up and down endlessly. Dickens tired eventually, though Pigott was still as energetic as ever. I took Dickens' place and did my best to support my brother, but I was too small, too unfit and Dickens took over again.

Was Charley any better for this treatment? He was still deadly pale, but perhaps that was good. I gazed anxiously into his face. We needed a doctor.

And then I started. Footsteps again. Coming up the stairs. Two sets of them. One heavy, the other one light and almost soundless to anyone who was not straining an ear. I went to the door instantly.

'Prussic acid, is that right?' Frank Beard was already opening his bag as he came into the room. 'Carry on, Mr Dickens,' he said and gave a nod at Edward Pigott.

'Smell it for yourself.' I held the jewelled box with the ornate initial 'M' under his nose.

'I'd guess anyway from what your girl here told me. Let's see if we can get this stuff into him. Sit him on the bed here.' Frank Beard took out a small bottle from his medical bag and removed the stopper.

'Now then, Wilkie, see if you can get his mouth open, tilt his head back, yes, that's the way. I think he is coming around. Now then, Charley, swallow this.'

'What is it?' I was watching anxiously as my brother obediently swallowed.

'Strychnine.' Frank Beard never liked explaining any medical mysteries so I said no more and hoped that the cure wouldn't be worse than the poison. Charley had already begun to look better under Edward Pigott's rough and ready treatment. He gulped violently and shuddered. His whole body was convulsed for a moment. Frank Beard watched him with satisfaction and Dickens with an air of quiet interest. Pigott and I exchanged alarmed glances but no one spoke. Charley convulsed again and then vomited. Sesina held the basin with a steady hand, but I felt myself tremble all over. Were we killing my brother? I dared not say anything. The case had to be left to the doctor. Sesina emptied the basin into the commode and shut the lid, though the room still smelled of vomit. She took a sponge and washed his face as tenderly as though he were a child. I saw Dickens look at her with interest and I wondered myself whether she was in love with my brother. It was, I thought, possible and I wondered how a story might go about a servant girl in love with a visitor in a house. At the back of my mind I had the germ of a story about a fabulous Indian precious stone called a moonstone and I wondered about introducing this servant girl with her doomed love into the thread of my narrative.

'You should have left me to die.' Amazingly, it was my brother's voice, hoarse, but perfectly understandable. I felt tears come to my eyes. Frank Beard looked from one brother to the other and I could not control my voice enough to explain. Amazingly, though, Charley was cool and collected.

'Better a death by prussic acid than by hanging from a noose,' he said huskily.

Frank Beard turned an enquiring eye upon me.

'Edwin Milton-Hayes has been killed,' I explained. 'His throat was cut, probably with his own knife. He had painted some scurrilous pictures of nine or ten people that he knew and was demanding money for them. The police think that Charley might have been the one who killed him. He's worried about it. That's right, isn't it, Charley?'

My brother gave a weary sigh and bowed his head into his hands. Sesina brushed the hair from his forehead with a gentle hand and I felt tears come into my eyes. I took off my spectacles and wiped them carefully on my pocket handkerchief.

'But you're not guilty, are you, Charley? That's what you need to keep in your mind. You must not despair, no matter how dark is the hour,' said Dickens. His voice was cool, quiet and authoritative. I saw Sesina look at him with attention and I myself was conscious of a ray of hope.

'And so, therefore,' he continued after a few moments, 'I think we'd better get you out of the way until the truth has been found out. Your brother and I are working on it, Charley, and no doubt with the combined power of two such great intellects we will soon have the matter solved.' Dickens laughed lightly at his own joke. No one else smiled, though I was amused to see Sesina give him a scornful look.

'But,' he resumed, holding out an index finger, 'but we must get you into safe keeping, while we are working on the case. I propose, now you are feeling better, that we pop you into a cab and Dr Beard will undertake the nursing of you in his

own home. I can guarantee that you will be well looked after.
At least,' he continued, 'that is what Sesina will tell Inspector
Field, won't you, Sesina?'

Sesina looked at him with some surprise, but I wasn't
surprised when Dickens added, 'but in reality, I think that
Frank, here, would prescribe some sea air. That's right, isn't
it, Frank? What about a little trip to the Norfolk Broads, or
the Scilly Isles, what do you think, Pigott?'

'You'll need a crew,' I said, taking some notes from out my
pocket book. 'Charley won't be up to much for a while.' Pigott
pocketed the notes with a grateful nod. There were three
muscular brothers who crewed for him from time to time and
the money I had given him should be enough to secure their
services. Pigott was sailing mad – never happier than when
poring over maps and making adjustments to sails. Charley
would be distracted from his woes by constant appeals to do
the hundred and one little tasks with which sailors occupied
themselves.

'Let's get you dressed, old man,' I said with an eye on the
clock. 'Sesina, will you go and tell my mother that Charley
has gone off with my friend Mr Pigott. But wait until we're
gone, Sesina, won't you.' I wondered whether Charley would
make a fuss about this; he was very much a mother's boy, but
he was too weak, too exhausted from his treatment to say
anything. With the help of Frank Beard I got him dressed.
Very pale, very weak, but he was himself again.

Dickens, I noticed, was holding a low-voiced conversation
with Sesina and I saw his hand go to his pocket and then place
a coin in hers. Then he turned to me.

'Now Wilkie, I don't think Sesina is the one to tell your
mother about all of this. Let's leave Charley to the care of
his doctor and his friend; I think you must be the one to stay
here and to reassure your mother. And . . .' He hesitated a
little and I could see that he was thinking of a way to put the
matter. 'Let everything appear natural,' he said in the end,
looking directly at me and then giving a sidelong glance at
Sesina.

Solemnly and ceremonially, he placed within the safekeeping of his waistcoat pocket the keys to Charley's bedroom,

the keys that he had promised Inspector Field to keep in safekeeping and which he now held in his hand. He cast a quick glance at the housekeeping keys that Sesina had left in the door and then said, authoritatively, 'Now I will leave all in your hands.'

I understood him well. He would like to help Charley, to back me up in my effort to save him, but something within him, something that was allied to his public persona, would not allow him to take any part, whatsoever, in the early-morning disappearance of my unfortunate younger brother. Dickens would have to be on the side of the law. I watched him go with understanding and felt a great sense of gratitude to him that, despite his misgivings and his strong principles, he would turn a blind eye towards the planned escape of my young brother. But it was only after he had left us that I suddenly thought of what Pigott had said, a few weeks earlier. I left my younger brother to Sesina's ministrations and turned to Pigott.

'My dear fellow, there is something I need to ask you, something that needs to be cleared up before you go. Do you remember saying something to me about Milton-Hayes? You said, didn't you, that Milton-Hayes was an assumed name.'

He was amused by that. A very easy-going fellow. Always saw the humorous side of everything.

'Well, come on, Wilkie,' he said with a smile on his lips. 'Have you ever heard a more fake name in your life? "Milton" – well the country is full of Milton Manors. And then Hayes. Well, it was Norman aristocracy, wasn't it? Such a good name for an artist, don't you think?'

'But what was his real name?' I said impatiently. 'Think hard, Pigott. You must remember. What was his real name?'

He thought for a moment and then shook his head.

'Sorry, old boy,' he said. 'Gone right out of my mind. Have a feeling that it was something to do with dogs, to do with terriers. That's what is at the back of my head.' He thought hard for a moment and then said pensively, 'It couldn't be anything to do with Jack Russell terriers, could it? That's sticking in my memory. Jack Russell terriers. Jolly little fellows. Very tenacious, stick on to anything.'

'Jack Russell,' I said aloud. I couldn't see too much wrong with it. Would a man really go to the trouble of changing his name just in order to get rid of a perfectly respectable, old English name like 'Jack Russell'?

TWELVE

Sesina was puzzled; puzzled and worried. She had thought that today, after all the fuss yesterday, would be a quiet day. Mr Charles was off, supposedly in Dr Beard's house, doing well, according to Mr Wilkie, though he had a twinkle in his eye. Inspector Field was keeping out of the way for the moment. Busy with another crime, she hoped. She seemed to remember Mr Dickens saying that there were only about ten detective policemen like Inspector Field so he must be busy, she thought. Anyway, it was good to be without him in the house.

But things weren't settled yet. There was another policeman in the house and he seemed to be watching her all the time. Not fooling. Not trying to mess about with her. Not trying to snatch a kiss or anything like that. No, he seemed to be just following her everywhere, peeping around corners, asking her questions about the artists that came to the house. And about the dead one. That Mr Milton-Hayes. Had he ever used her as a model? Did she go to his house? Every time he laid eyes on her the young man came up with a new question.

Something was going on. It had started with Dolly. She had been a long time up in her mistress's room, even longer than usual. Perhaps there was nothing too strange in that fact of itself. Everyone in the kitchen understood that this was a time when the two women had long chats. The cook often tossed her head and made spiteful remarks about it to Sesina and when Dolly came back, Sesina would tease her and try to needle her into revealing what the conversation had been all about. But Dolly never would say. Would give a little smile and look smug.

But this morning it had been an extra-long time and when she had come back Dolly was looking quite different from her usual self-satisfied smugness. The woman had been looking very worried. And she had avoided Sesina's eye, flushing up

and looking away when the second housemaid had caught her
eye. Almost as though she were afraid that a secret would leak
out if she didn't take care to keep her mouth shut.

And then the bell had gone. All three women had looked
up at the wall of bells. The main bedroom.

'For you,' said Dolly to Sesina. She had expected the
summons: that was plain.

'How do you know? She usually wants you. Anyway it was
just one bell.' Sesina knew that she was being stubborn. It
was obvious that Dolly knew that Sesina was going to be
summoned. Still, thought Sesina, let's hear it. She was a fluent
and imaginative liar, but it was always best to know in advance
what the accusation was going to be. She ran through various
scenarios in her mind. If it was anything about going out early
in the morning, well, then, she would just tell Mrs Collins
that she had been sent by Mr Wilkie. It had to be that. And
yet, Sesina could have sworn that there had not been a curtain
moved or a soul around when she had stolen out through the
back door before six o'clock this morning. As for the day
before, well she hardly liked to think about that. And after
all the distress about Mr Charles, she would have thought
that there would not be any fuss about that. Something was
up, though. Dolly had a very uneasy look on her face.

'Well, you can expect trouble, Dolly, if you've been telling
lies about me,' she hissed and was glad to see how Dolly
flinched.

'That's the line to take,' she muttered to herself as she
bounced up the stairs. No slinking in through the door in a
shamefaced fashion for her. She gave a sharp rap and then
turned the knob and was inside the room before Mrs Collins
could say a word.

'You want me, ma'am. Dolly says that it's me that you want.'
She made her voice sound tough and aggressive. *Always
attack before they attack you*: Isabella used to say that when
they were both together in Urania Cottage, Mr Dickens' home
for homeless girls.

It worked, too. Mrs Collins was looking at bit taken aback,
caught on the wrong foot, Sesina told herself. She moved
uneasily, looked down at her desk as though looking for

inspiration and then looked up again. Sesina stood up very straight and looked her mistress in the eye.

'Well, Sesina, I've just had a most distressing letter.'

'I'm sorry to hear that, ma'am.' Sesina twitched her morning apron into place and folded her hands in front of her. What was a letter to do with her?

'It just came about twenty minutes ago. Dolly met the delivery boy when she was doing the doorstep. It was sent around by hand.'

'Yes, ma'am.' *Come on, spit it out.*

'It was enclosing a letter about you. A letter that came from a highly respected person, Sesina.'

'Yes, ma'am.'

'And I'm sure that this person is not the kind to make a mistake, or to take away a girl's character lightly. In fact, Sesina, I would trust this person to judge a situation.'

'Yes, ma'am.' *What was all this leading to?*

'I'm sure that you want to know what is said in the letter.' Mrs Collins reached over and took an envelope from her small lamp table.

Sesina waited. *Save your fire until the old woman comes to the point,* she told herself.

'It says . . .' A pause while Mrs Collins hunted for her spectacles. *By the mirror, you silly old fool!* Sesina waited, her hands folded across her apron and her eyes looking at the toe of her boot.

'Well,' said Mrs Collins, at last. She left a pause, but Sesina did not move nor even look at her. 'Well,' continued Mrs Collins, holding the letter very close to her face, 'this is what the letter says:

Dear Mrs Collins, I am sorry to send such disagreeable news so early in the morning, but I thought that you should know as soon as possible. A friend was returning late in the night before last and saw a young maidservant from your household steal out, surreptitiously, from your house. My friend is sure that it was number 17 Hanover Terrace and the gas lamp gave a clear sight of the young person, very small, almost child-like in size. In view of

the recent murder and the connection to that household, I do wonder whether the housemaid might have
some connection with housebreakers. It's impossible, I'm
sure, for us all to know whether any money was stolen
before the murder of Mr Edwin Milton-Hayes was
committed. Heaven forbid that this young girl could have
had anything to do with the murder! However, I feel
bound to mention that I have notified Inspector Field that
she was seen out there on a road . . .

Mrs Collins stopped and looked across at Sesina and Sesina
looked steadily back. Mrs Collins, she was glad to see, looked
a bit disconcerted by her firm gaze.

'And what have you to say, Sesina?' she enquired. *Giving
up hope of tricking me into saying anything*, Sesina thought
to herself as she frowned. She was a bit bewildered by this
sudden accusation, but resolved to say nothing until she thought
about the matter for a few more minutes and so she remained
silent. It was a puzzle. Why was someone trying to get her into
trouble? And who was this person. Writing to the police
inspector. Making the suggestion that she was part of a housebreaking gang. Why should he or she do that? Only one reason,
thought Sesina, her mind working rapidly. Whoever wrote that
letter is the one who murdered Mr Milton-Hayes. That made
sense. Getting worried. Wanted to move the police suspicions
on to someone else. A housemaid was a good idea. So that
was why the policeman was asking her if she had ever acted
as a model for the artist.

'You, of course, would have no business to be out late at
night,' stated Mrs Collins.

'No, ma'am,' said Sesina calmly, but her mind was working
fast as she recalled the streets that she had gone through on
her way to and from the house in Dorset Square. And, of
course, Church Street. Could this letter have come from the
canon? She thought about the canon, rapidly ran her mind
over him. Fat, grey-haired, seemed like the usual clergyman.
No vail, when he left, of course, but she hadn't expected one
from a clergyman and was certain that she had shown no
annoyance. Why would he have it in for her? He had to have

a guilty secret. Had he thought she spotted him in the picture? No, it had been later on that she had seen that possibility. And Mrs Gummidge? Well, that was different. Sesina had called attention to her daughter when everyone was gawping at the pictures, had suggested that Florence might have been a model for the girl in *The Night Prowler* picture. Nothing like diverting attention to another suspect, she had thought at the time. Everyone knew that the police were dead stupid. Easy to fool them.

She'd have to watch her step, though. Didn't want to end up in prison.

'No, ma'am,' she said aloud. 'No, of course not, ma'am. I'd never go out at night, ma'am. Myself and Dolly are always off to our beds once we got the kitchen cleaned up.' Not quite true, but true enough for the purpose. She didn't want to bring Mr Wilkie into the conversation unless she really had to. Still, she would have a word with him afterwards. Tell him about the canon. Might give him some ideas. He and Mr Dickens had been talking it over, were making lists. She didn't think that they had got anywhere, and then this morning there was all the fuss about poor Mr Charles. Still, he was taken care of now. Now she waited calmly and allowed Mrs Collins time to look back over the letter.

'Late at night. Out at night!' Mrs Collins was still stuck on that. Reading it out from the letter.

Sesina shrugged her shoulders. This was a good house with plenty of room for the servants. She and Dolly each had their own bedroom. There was no way of proving that she hadn't gone out in the middle of the night. She'd say nothing about the letter until she had a chance to talk with Mr Wilkie. He mightn't mind telling his mother about how he had summoned his friend and how Mr Charles was now on a yacht. Probably had told her. It wasn't like Mrs Collins not to be rushing off to visit her darling boy if she really believed that he was in the doctor's house. She'd lay a bet, though, that Mr Wilkie wouldn't want that police inspector to know anything about that letter he had sent to his friend with the yacht. And certainly not about how Mr Charles, instead of lying in his doctor's house, dying of an overdose of prussic acid, was now, in fact,

on the high seas in that very yacht. An idea came to her and
she smiled a little.

Mrs Collins looked at her suspiciously and Sesina put a
hand across her mouth to half-hide the way that her smile had
broadened.

'Excuse me, ma'am . . .' She felt her throat move with a
suppressed giggle. She kept it down for a few moments and
then allowed it to escape. She clapped her hand in front of
her mouth but allowed the sounds to last for a few seconds.

'I beg your pardon, ma'am,' she said then. 'I was just
thinking about that morning when I came out to whiten
the doorstep and this drunk man came along and said to me:
"What's a little girl like you doing out in the middle of the
night by yourself?"' She allowed another giggle to escape and
then said, 'Of course, ma'am, it was November, just like now
and daylight wouldn't come until about eight o'clock in the
morning. So you see, it was dark night for him and the morning
for me.'

Mrs Collins' frown cleared as by magic. 'Why, of course,
what a clever little thing you are, Sesina. Of course, this person
must have made a mistake. Thought that it was still night, but
really it was morning. Hand me my pen case and the writing
pad, Sesina, and I'll write a note about it. And I can explain
to the inspector. Don't know why he had to be involved in the
first place. Strange! Still, some of those people do think they
are up there with God Almighty.'

Sesina didn't move. 'Don't worry, ma'am, don't waste your
money on stamps. You know what it's like. People don't like
to be found in the wrong. And it doesn't matter to me, ma'am,
as long as you are satisfied and as long as you mention to the
inspector that it was all a mistake. Now, if you'll excuse me,
I'll go and see about breakfast for the gentlemen. I thought I
heard Mr Dickens go downstairs a little while ago. The main
thing is that Mr Charles is being well looked after, isn't it,
ma'am. Mr Wilkie will make sure about that. Didn't look at
all well yesterday, ma'am, did he? We were all worried about
him in the kitchen.' *Say nothing about suicide to my mother*;
that had been Mr Wilkie's instructions. *I'm just going to tell
her that he is unwell.*

'Oh, Sesina, poor boy, my poor, poor boy!' Mrs Collins' face crumpled up like she was going to burst out sobbing. She shook her head violently and sucked in a few deep breaths. No more talk about going out in the night. Sesina's business now was to comfort her mistress and console her. Silently, she tiptoed over to the breakfast tray. Still some tea left. And the hot water. She poured out a cupful and added a generous spoon of sugar.

'Drink that down, ma'am. That will do you good. And don't you worry. Mr Wilkie and Mr Dickens will be working away at trying to sort things out and in the meantime, Mr Charles will be safe with his doctor.' Sesina thought of the piece of paper, rescued from the wastepaper basket and now hidden in her apron pocket. She would go over that list herself. Have twice the brains of them men, she said to herself. 'And Mr Dickens will sort out the policeman if there is any trouble, don't you worry, ma'am,' she continued. 'The woman in my last place; just a housekeeper she was, but she knew what is what; and she made remarks on how the police obey Mr Dickens, just like he was the prime minister of the whole country. That's what she said, ma'am, and she said it like she knew the truth.' Sesina paused. What would Dolly do now for her mistress? She looked at the sobbing woman. She was trying to drink the tea but she was failing miserably. The tears were coursing down her cheeks, one drop following another like raindrops on the window glass. 'Why don't you go back to bed for an hour or so, ma'am?' she said. 'Have a little sleep. I'll send Dolly to see to you.'

Sesina picked up the breakfast tray. A nice amount left on it. She'd take a few bites on her way down the stairs and finish it off when Dolly was safely despatched to her mistress's side.

And then she would take out that list and have a good look at those names that she had glimpsed, scribbled on the piece of paper, each one of them bearing a figure after it.

When she brought the news back to the kitchen, Dolly went flying up the stairs, in a state of mad fury that Sesina had interfered between her and her mistress, probably giving her cups of tea and comforting her, when everyone knew that Dolly was the only one that the mistress trusted.

The cook went off into the pantry to make a list of meals in the coming week. Mrs Barnett always liked to do this well ahead of the moment when Mrs Collins, full of bright ideas, would descend the stairs into the kitchen and try to disrupt all of the arrangements already made.

Sesina sat down at the table, popped a hot scone into her mouth, took out the list and read down through the list of the pictures and the guests' names after them. Well, well, Mrs Molly French. And Mrs Hermione Gummidge. Mrs Collins would be glad to have her suspected of murder. That woman had got on her nerves, coming in like that and trying to upset her arrangements. And now, Sesina would take a bet on it, trying to involve the housemaid in the murder.

And that fellow, Lord Douglas! So he was a suspect. She was pleased about that. Tried to pinch her bottom once, but didn't do it again as Sesina had jumped in a spectacular fashion and managed to spill some hot soup down the front of his trousers. Never said a word, either, did he, just dabbed at it with his napkin. Doesn't want to attract attention to himself, she thought afterwards and did wonder why. She would love him to be accused of the murder. She had felt like murdering him that day. How did he dare! And just when she was in the middle of serving the soup.

Well, she thought, time to see what the clever Mr Dickens was up to. Sesina picked up the few remaining scones from the table, still hot from the oven, arranged them neatly on a plate and carried them into the dining room.

'Your scones, sir,' she said politely and placed the dish in front of Mr Dickens.

He looked a little surprised, but obligingly popped one into his mouth as he chewed upon it rapidly.

'I must say that you kept your head well, there, Sesina,' he said with his mouth full. 'Mr Charles might owe his life to you. A good job that you noticed him. And that you noticed that pill box. Say nothing for the moment, though, will you? Mum's the word, Sesina.'

'Yes, sir,' she said demurely. She wouldn't tell him about the letter, either from the canon, or from Mrs Gummidge, she decided. She would think about the woman and the canon herself. Funny fellow, that canon. His name wasn't on their list, not on the list that Mr Dickens and Mr Collins had written out, and yet most of the others were. Some crossed out, of course, but they had been thought of. But why not the canon? Could he, not Mrs Gummidge, have been the one who wrote that letter to Mrs Collins? She'd have to go and have a look at those pictures in the drawing room, volunteer to be the one to clean it today. See if she could spot the canon in one of them. She suppressed a giggle as she added more hot water to the teapot. She knew how to manage it so that she would be the one to do the drawing room, though Dolly liked to do it herself, usually. Loved dusting all those old paintings. She knew what she would say and she practised it silently. *You're too busy, Dolly, what with the mistress being unwell and taking up so much of your time.*

So why should the canon try to get her into trouble with the police? Sesina puzzled over it after she had examined the pictures as carefully as she could. No, no canon in them, she thought. Would be easy to recognize his clerical outfit.

She hadn't been out at midnight, or after midnight. Had he seen her the morning she went to fetch Mr Charles's painting coat? Or had he seen her when she had gone to post a letter to Mr Piggott early yesterday morning?

Dark, yes. The middle of the night, no. The skivvies in the clerical houses would get up at that hour, or shortly afterwards, just in the same way as they did in ordinary households. A drunk might think it was the middle of the night, but a sober churchman would have a watch or see a church tower clock.

No, it was more likely to be Mrs Gummidge. That letter, the reporting of her name to Mrs Collins, had to be a deliberate attempt to make the police suspicious of her, to make her sound like someone who was in with a housebreaking gang. Sesina thought about the names on the list that she had picked out of the basket. She thought about Lord Douglas, about Mrs Gummidge and Molly French. And Charles Allston Collins. One of them was guilty and she was sure that it wasn't poor Charley. His brother, ever so fond of him, couldn't think that.

Perhaps the list was meant to be a list of all those suspected
by the police. And one of those people had gone to the canon
and he had tried to get her into trouble.

So who could have written that letter? Sesina thought about
her route in the early hours of the morning. Unusual for anyone,
except a worker, to be out at that hour of the morning. The
only one she had seen was an old gentleman in ragged old
clothes. Not a beggar, though he was dressed like one. Had
tripped over the pavement edge and had sworn like a gentleman.

Perhaps it could have been Mrs Gummidge who saw her,
thought Sesina. Mrs Gummidge lived somewhere around there.
Yes, she remembered now, Balcombe Street. Might have just
looked out of the window. So she wrote the letter or else got
someone else to do it. Just the type to sneak around to the
canon and get him to talk to the police. Mrs Gummidge was
good friends with the canon, had been deep in chat with him,
had gone across to greet him when he arrived. She had been
talking about her daughter to him, and about the dangers of
London. And, yes, there had been something about housebreakers. And about being burned in one's bed. Silly old cow,
Sesina had said at the time, but now she did not feel like
laughing. It was clever of Mrs Gummidge, and by now she
was sure that it was Mrs Gummidge. And the canon was in on
it, also. Yes, it would be clever of Mrs Gummidge to bring the
canon into it, perhaps suggesting that an eye should be kept
upon the house.

A deliberate attempt by either the canon, or else Mrs
Gummidge, to make the police suspicious of her, to make her
sound like someone who was in the pay of a housebreaking
gang. Sesina felt her mouth go dry. She had been in and out
of courts since she was a small child and she knew well how
quickly a verdict was brought against someone who had no
lawyer to represent her. No one to speak up for her in court.

Her only hope was to avoid arrest. And the only way to do
that was to pin the crime onto someone else.

The murder of Edwin Milton-Hayes was not like the murder
of a dock worker or a homeless man of the street. This was
a rich man. If his murderer was not found, the newspapers
would start asking questions. And the police would not want

that to happen. They would find a name, find someone to pin it on if one was not found for them. And that person would be taken to court, would be convicted. The judge would put on the black cap and pass sentence. And then they would be hanged by the neck until they choked to death. Sesina shuddered. She had been about ten years old when she had witnessed a woman hanged at Horsemonger Lane Gaol. She still could see the woman's face – Maria Manning had been her name and she had worn a black silk satin dress. Sesina still had bad dreams about the howls and screams, and the laughter of the crowd as the woman swung slowly around, her face convulsed and her neck broken. Whatever happened, she had to avoid that fate.

Sesina decided that she needed some time for thinking. Unfortunately time for thinking was difficult to come by in this busy kitchen, with Mrs Barnett and Dolly chattering at the tops of their voices and clattering dishes. Only one thing for it. Drown it all out.

With a busy and preoccupied look, Sesina sorted out the knives from their drawer, arranging them into groups of nine. She climbed on the wooden steps, took down the Kent Knife Cleaning Drum, found the emery powder and then she inserted the first bundle into the slots on the top of the wooden drum and poured the emery powder into the centre opening. Once she had started to crank the cast-iron winch handle, there was such a din from the noise of the wooden discs with their rows of bristles scraping against the knives that no one could even think of addressing a question to her or of asking her what she was thinking about. And, while she was thinking, the emery power was polishing the steel cutlery so no one could accusing her of being idle.

No good protesting. Even Mrs Collins, normally a fairly decent employer, would not hesitate to sacrifice a housemaid if her son could be saved. Mrs Collins didn't know that Mr Charles was not at the doctor's house, but hopefully now safely out on a yacht, going up towards Norfolk. If only she knew!

Sesina nibbled her bottom lip as she tried to think about what to do.

The first step would be to talk to Mrs Collins. In fact, a

summons would be coming soon, probably as soon as the woman was dressed. Sesina took out the shiningly clean knives and slotted in another nine. While she was pouring in the second lot of emery powder, her mind was active. A bit of acting. That was what was needed. And then her own quick wits and the skills that she had perfected when she had been part of Mrs Jerrryman's gang.

'Going to be all day at them knives!' yelled Mrs Barnett at the top of her voice and Sesina slowed down the cranking handle and looked at her innocently.

'Did you want me, missus?'

'Just hurry up, won't you. Some of us have to get the lunch.'

Well, go on, then, get it! Don't need to gossip while you are making it, do you? Sesina turned the handle as fast as she could, making, to her satisfaction, an even greater noise. The cook and Dolly put their hands over their ears and turned their heads away, hunching up their shoulders.

Good as a play to see them, thought Sesina and then got an idea. She stopped the handle abruptly.

'That was the mistress's bell,' she said, fixing her eyes on the row of bells that hung above the range. 'That'll be for me, Dolly, won't it?' Without waiting for a reply, she went instantly towards the kitchen door, saying, over her shoulder. 'You can finish off the knives, Dolly. I'll be busy with the mistress.'

Before leaving the basement, though, she slipped into the laundry. Very nice laundry place in this house, she had often thought. A wash room, a drying room and an ironing room. From the ironing room, she took a handkerchief and examined it on the way up the stairs. That was the one that she had noticed, the initials, H.G., were stitched into the corner. Mrs Collins had been Harriet Geddes before she was married and some of her handkerchiefs still had the old initials H.G. on them. Mrs Collins wasn't a woman who was too interested in things like embroidery and certainly not in unpicking initials, she thought. When she was married she must have got a new set of handkerchiefs and underclothes that were marked with her new initials, but from time to time a few of the old ones surfaced.

If she was challenged it would be easy enough for Sesina

to pretend that she had thought the handkerchief belonged to Mrs Hermione Gummidge. But probably she wouldn't be challenged. Mrs Collins wasn't the sort of woman to worry too much about small things. She was busy writing the story of her life. Wanted to be a novelist like her eldest son, most like. Sesina practised her opening line before she knocked on the door.

Oh, Mrs Collins, I've just found this. It's belonging to Mrs Gummidge. It got caught up in a cushion in the dining room. Should I pop around and give it back to her?

Mrs Collins lifted her head from her slip of paper as Sesina entered the room, not waiting for Mrs Collins to invite her in. Mrs Collins' first finger was steeped in ink and she had a spot of ink on her chin. Sesina smiled and tried to make her voice apologetic.

'Oh, ma'am, I've interrupted you in your book. I'm sorry for that. What page are you on now?'

It worked. She knew that it would.

'Page twenty,' said Mrs Collins proudly. 'It's all true, you know, Sesina. Well, most of it anyway. Don't want to make it too dull.'

'I bet everyone will be queuing up to buy it, ma'am. I would, I know. You've had such an interesting life. You'll sell as much as Mr Dickens when *Bleak House* came out.' Sesina thought for a moment. She had been at Urania Cottage when that had come out and she remembered all the fuss that was made about it and how Mrs Morson organized the girls to make a banner with the words 'Bleak House' and the number thirty-four thousand embroidered upon it. That had been just the first week, of course. Better beef it up a bit.

'Bet you sell a hundred thousand copies,' she said encouragingly and Mrs Collins beamed and pretended to laugh.

'Oh, Sesina!' She held her two hands framing her face as though to hide her blushes. Such an actress, thought Sesina. You had to like her sometimes. She grudged the thought. Made her seem soft. *'Don't get soft and don't let the bastards get you down'*; her friend Isabella used to say that and it was probably good advice.

In any case she was doing Mrs Collins and all the Collins

family a favour if she managed to pin the murder on Mrs Hermione Gummidge, so quickly she said, 'Dolly says that you want to speak to me, ma'am.'

'Did I?' Mrs Collins was startled enough to knock her pen from the inkwell. Sesina rushed forward and grabbed a piece of blotting paper.

'There now, ma'am, as good as new. Hardly a mark to be seen. Would have been terrible if it went over your words, wouldn't it? You mightn't be able to find them again, might you?'

'You're quite right, Sesina. And especially words that I've written first thing in the morning. They're often the best that I write even if I spend a whole day writing.'

'It's my fault,' said Sesina with a catch in her voice that sounded rather good, she thought. 'I startled you. I didn't mean to startle you. Oh, and ma'am,' she said, quickly moving on while Mrs Collins was still a bit embarrassed about the mistake, 'I found Mrs Gummidge's handkerchief under the cushion of the chair where she was sitting. It's got her initials on it. Should I ask Dolly to take it around to her house?'

That was a good move. Dolly was always complaining about her fallen arches and how much her feet ached. Any errands that needed to be run would usually be handed over to Sesina. Mrs Collins didn't hesitate. She had already picked up her pen and was forming an elaborate letter 'I' and following it with 'loved'. Over her shoulder, she said casually, 'Just take it around yourself, Sesina. Your young legs will enjoy the exercise. Tell Cook that I sent you, won't you?'

Won't I just? Sesina giggled to herself as she went quickly and lightly down the stairs to the basement.

'Going out, Mrs Barnett, off on an errand for Mrs Collins,' she said, opening the door and calling the message across to where the cook stood sieving flour for the pastry.

'Where are you off to?' Mrs Barnett didn't sound pleased. She had a large bowl of plums sitting on the table waiting for Sesina to slice and remove stones.

'Just going around to Mrs Gummidge's place; got a message for her.' Sesina enjoyed the look on both women's faces. A message meant a tip in all probability and Dolly would have put up with her fallen arches in order to get one of those. Sesina gave a wink.

'Be good while I'm out, both of you,' she said daringly and fled before the cook could explode.

It would have been Mrs Gummidge who had tried to get her into trouble. The more she thought about it, the more she felt convinced. After all, why should the canon bother? No one suspected him. It would definitely have been Mrs Gummidge. She was probably terrified that the police had recognized the portrait of her daughter in *The Night Prowler* and she wanted someone else to be arrested for the murder before any questions were asked.

THIRTEEN

It didn't take Sesina long to pop around to Balcombe Street. The door was opened to her, not promptly and not by a well-dressed housemaid or parlour maid, but by a slovenly-looking kitchen maid. Looked exhausted, poor thing, and there was a pail and a mop dumped in the middle of the hall and a deck scrubber leaning against the wall. She had been interrupted in a scrubbing session and the hall certainly needed it. The floor was filthy, the stair carpet had a dark track in the centre of each step, the hall table had a layer of dust and Sesina could see ancient stains on the wallpaper. The hall certainly needed sorting out and this girl didn't look up to doing it on her own. Exhausted, she seemed. She stared dubiously at Sesina and looked as if she didn't know what to do.

But then a door at the side of the hall opened and Mrs Hermione Gummidge herself came out of what looked like a dining room. The girl, her daughter Florence, was inside, piling plates and cups onto a tray. One servant only, probably, guessed Sesina and she was interested in this. Perhaps it was of vital importance to Mrs Gummidge to marry her daughter, Florence, off to a rich man. That was why she came around and disrupted the dinner arrangements at the Collins' household.

Hard luck for her that Mr Milton-Hayes got himself murdered, thought Sesina. But perhaps good luck for the daughter. She shot a quick glance through the dining-room door before it was shut in her face. Had Florence wanted to marry this man, Milton-Hayes, or was it just her mother's idea? Perhaps she was having fun stealing jewellery with his daring lordship, the heir to the Earl of Ennis. Sesina imagined that it might be an interesting way of making a living, especially if your name was Lord Douglas. And, of course, if Florence married him, why then she would be Lady Douglas and the two of them could get themselves asked to all of the smart house parties in London or in the country. Mr Wilkie

was always going off to these Friday to Monday affairs. She
must ask him about them. Pretend to be writing a book. That
always worked with Mr Wilkie. He'd talk for ever about making
money from writing stories. 'No reason why you shouldn't
make a fortune, Sesina, as long as you stick to writing what
you know about. I'll give you a few tips if you like. Write it
about a housemaid who is having a lot of fun, fooling her
employer,' he had said to her once and then he had winked
at her.

'Mrs Collins from Hanover Terrace sent me around, ma'am.
Sent me with a message for you.' Sesina was determined
not to waste her time talking to the woman in this hall and in
front of the servant. That would give her no opportunity to
carry out her plan.

'Yes,' said Mrs Gummidge impatiently. She looked around
at the mess in the hall and then jerked her head impatiently as
some water was sent flying from the bucket.

'Shall I come back later, ma'am?' It was taking a chance
and she might be reported to Mrs Collins for impudence, but
Sesina thought that she could talk Mrs Collins around easily.
For a moment, though, she held her breath. Mrs Gummidge
was hesitating. Probably curious as to what the message was.
Could be another invitation to a dinner party for all she knew.

'You'd better come upstairs,' she said then and Sesina
picked her way through the drier parts of the hall and followed
the woman up the stairs. Take a fortnight to get this place
properly cleaned up, she thought. Even the balustrade bars
were coated thick with dust. To her satisfaction they went up
two flights of stairs, up to the bedrooms.

At least this place is a bit better. Probably keeps it clean
and tidy herself. Sesina followed Mrs Gummidge in and
then took the package from her basket. She had purposely
wrapped it in several layers of tissue paper and had tied up
the whole thing with several knots in the twine. While Mrs
Gummidge was struggling to open it, she had a quick look
around. A breakfast tray on the small table by the bed. And
a spoon on the edge of the saucer. Sesina's eye went to it
and then she relaxed.

Not much of a breakfast. Tea and toast. A teapot, a plate

with toast crumbs, a butter dish with a slab of butter, unevenly cut. No refinements of butter balls or butter curls. Wouldn't suit Mrs Collins. But then Mrs Collins had a decent, hard-working husband who had left her a fine sum of money, if the cook was to be believed. Mrs Gummidge seemed to have only her wits and her ambitions for her moon-faced daughter. Sesina waited for the cry for assistance.

'I can't open these knots; haven't you ever been shown how to tie up a parcel properly?'

In a bit of a state, that woman. Voice very high and a bit cracked. Hands shaking. Worried about the picture that seemed to show her daughter working hand and glove with a night prowler. Worried about this death. Worried for herself, perhaps? Or was she worried about her daughter?

'Sorry, ma'am.' Sesina undid the knots and held out the handkerchief, obligingly unfolding it and displaying the corner where the initials H and G had been embroidered in a distinctive dark brown thread. 'Mrs Collins thought that it might be your handkerchief, ma'am. She said that them were your initials.'

Mrs Gummidge gave it an indifferent glance. 'Not mine,' she said firmly. 'I've always embroidered mine in love knots.' And with an air more for displaying her superior taste than for convincing Sesina she took from her pocket a delicate piece of lawn and displayed it to her.

'Yes, of course, ma'am, it's quite different, isn't it? Looks pretty, doesn't it? Ever so nice with the letters stitched like that in blue and pink.' So these were love knots, were they? Well, no chance of her not owning up to that handkerchief. She'd never be believed for one minute if she said that it wasn't hers.

Sesina's heart fluttered slightly with excitement. There was no doubt but that the handkerchief was distinctive. She watched the woman replace it into her pocket. Immediately she turned the focus.

'You've dropped a spoon, ma'am,' she said, bending down and poking under the small lamp table and then moving slightly aside.

It always worked. It was human nature to bend down when

told that you've dropped something. Sesina waited that fraction of a second while the woman lowered her bulk. Easy then to take a spoon from the tray.

'Got it,' she said and proffered the spoon to Mrs Gummidge.

Already the handkerchief with its distinctive initials was deep in her pocket. 'I'd better be off, ma'am,' she said. 'We're busy this morning. We've a couple of women in to do the washing and they always slow the rest of the work up. You know what they are like! Want this and want that.'

Mrs Gummidge, she guessed, never employed washer-women, but a flow of conversation always made an easy way out of a house and gave no chance for someone to look around and miss that object which was now snugly hidden in a pocket. Sesina walked briskly down the stairs, trod her way through the puddles in the hallway. Once outside she made her way towards the nearest butcher shop. She spent only a few minutes there, hovering between a tray of chops and a tray of beefsteaks and then left with the air of one who is in a hurry.

When she came to Hanover Terrace, she mounted the steps and rang the front door bell. She could always pretend that she had forgotten her key to the basement, but, as it happened, Dolly was so pleased to see her back, that she didn't even mention the matter. Just opened the door and ushered her in with the air of someone who is bursting to tell the latest news.

As she had guessed, the police were in the house. The inspector, according to Dolly, was in the painting room with Mr Wilkie and Mr Dickens had insisted on staying with him. Made a big fuss about Mr Charles not being available for questioning, according to Dolly, and Mr Dickens had calmed him down. Mr Wilkie had ordered a tray of tea and biscuits for the three of them and since that had been brought in, not a sound had been heard from the room. The other two policemen were sitting by the kitchen fire and waiting for orders. According to them, they were waiting to search the house and look for clues. Very puffed up with themselves, they were.

The mistress, said Dolly, was in a terrible state. Ever so upset and worried.

Sesina nodded. The bloodstained handkerchief was still in her pocket and she needed to get rid of it quickly before there was a search of the house.

'That's never a smell of burning coming up there, is it?' she asked, pointing her nose in the direction of the back stairs and puckering her nostrils.

Dolly fled. Sesina half-smiled. Poor old Doll. Easy as anything to trick.

With a quick glance around she went across the hall to the dining room. All in perfect order after the dinner party. The family took meals in the small parlour when there were no guests. The dining-room chairs were still in the positions where she had placed them when she and Mrs Collins prepared for the dinner reception. Three chairs across the top of the table. Three down at the bottom and four on either side. She remembered very clearly where everyone had sat. She had placed the name cards before the meal and then served them from all of the dishes during that eight-course dinner.

Mrs Hermione Gummidge had been at the bottom of the table on the right-hand side of Mr Wilkie, in between him and his brother, Mr Charles. Sesina went straight down. The cushions had all been shaken up and dusted earlier that next day, of course, but luckily, she herself was the one who had been given that task. She would plead feeling unwell, no, better still, being called away at that very moment. She didn't care really. It wasn't a hanging offence to forget to shake up every single one of the cushions. Nothing to do with the police, anyway, and they would never get it out of her that she was telling a lie. Quickly she lifted the cushion on that chair at the bottom of the table; squeezed up the bloodstained handkerchief; dug it in between the wooden edge of the chair and its removable seat. And then she replaced the cushion. Now it would be up to the police to find it. And, of course, if they didn't, well then she would have to point them in that direction. Have a little word with the youngest policeman. He looked easy to fool, she thought.

She was just about to leave the room when she heard them in the hall outside. Instantly she went to the sideboard and took out the silver, and was busy polishing the knives with a soft duster when they came into the room. They were pleased to see her. Getting bored with searching. She could see that immediately. It's a boring and frustrating job to be searching for something, but not know what that something was. Something, anything suspicious. That would have been their orders.

'Give us a kiss,' said the older of the two.

Sesina gave him a scornful glance. 'You'd be better off finding who murdered that poor man, wouldn't you, instead of being cheeky. You watch your step, young man, or I'll be having a word with Inspector Field.'

'Oh, so that's how you spend your free time, a nice little girl like you. Having words with Inspector Field. An old man like that, ugly too.' The policeman laughed uproariously at his own joke. Sesina gave him a scornful glance.

'Why don't you search the room? See if you can find anything. They was all sitting here, you know, sitting in this very room and the body lying cold just where they left it.'

'Well, actually, by the time that they were all sitting in here in this dining room, the body was in the police mortuary. We'd found it hours before.'

That was a bit of a set-back. Sesina hadn't known that it had been found as early as that. Still, didn't make too much of a difference.

'Well, go on then, why don't you have a good search of this room?' she asked innocently. 'They all came in and sat around this table. I can tell you where everyone sat.'

'And if I sat on one of the chairs, would you sit on my knee?' This was the younger one. Getting brave.

Sesina gave a sigh. It was a nuisance for someone like herself to have to deal with such stupid fellows.

'Where did Mr Charles Collins sit?' The older fellow started to look behind the curtains, but he gave her a quick, shrewd look.

'Over there, just near the bottom of the table.' Sesina saw her opportunity. She walked across and indicated the chair and then she picked up the cushion, shook it; looked under the chair, tilting it onto its back legs. She moved the chair and indicated the space of clean carpet beneath it.

'Nothing there,' she announced.

'Wants to join the force,' said the older policeman with a wink at the other fellow.

'And Mrs Molly French sat here, on the left-hand side of Mr Charles.' Sesina went through the same procedure with this chair, shaking the cushion thoroughly, tilting the chair and then spinning it around on one of its back legs. I should be on the stage; still better get on with it, she told herself. Any minute now they'll get bored and be off.

'And Mrs Hermione Gummidge sat here on Mr Charles's right,' she said, 'in between him and Mr Wilkie.' She picked up the cushion with a flourish and then stopped with it held mid-air.

'Blimey!' she said dramatically. 'Look at that.' She clapped her hand to her mouth. 'Is that . . .?' She gulped hard.

'Looks like blood on that there wipe, don't it, Tim?' He was getting excited.

'Call the inspector.' And the other one all excited, too. The blood really did look good. A nice dark red colour. Sesina hoped that it would impress the inspector. She took her hand away from her mouth.

'That was where Mrs Hermione Gummidge was sitting. She's the mother of Miss Florence. You know the one that is in the picture of *The Night Prowler*, the lady who is peeping in the door.'

No harm in spelling it out a bit for them. In any case, Mrs Gummidge was a good choice. She was a tough-looking woman. She hoped that the inspector would think the same as she did. Where was he, anyway?

He couldn't be far away. Sesina had heard him a couple of minutes ago. Talking to Mrs Collins on the landing above. She stayed very still as though frozen to the spot, holding up the cushion and staring down at the bloodstained handkerchief as they came into the room.

'Goodness me,' said Mrs Collins. Sesina heard her voice, but didn't turn her head. Best to stay where she was. The inspector was coming over now. Tim was muttering to him, saying something that she couldn't hear. She strained her ears. Was he pretending that he was the one who found it? The cheek of him.

'I found that handkerchief, ma'am.' She addressed Mrs Collins.

'Really!' Mrs Collins had taken a box of matches from the drawer of the sideboard and had gone over to a candelabra on the table. In a moment, a glow of light illuminated the blood-stained handkerchief, lying in the middle of the chair. Sesina still held the cushion in her hand, but now she put it aside, placed it upon one of the other chairs and watched while Mrs Collins picked up the candelabra and bent over the chair, looking intently down upon the handkerchief.

'You were shaking up the cushions, were you, Sesina?' Mrs Collins' voice sounded a bit odd, but she did not look around.

Sesina took a second to think about this. It might not be a good idea to annoy the police by pretending that she was doing their business for them. She should, she thought now, have got one of the two policemen to pick up the cushions.

'That's right, ma'am.'

'I wonder why you went straight into the dining room on your way back from delivering your message.' There was a funny sound from Mrs Collins' voice. Made the inspector look at her. Sesina did not quite know what to say in answer to that.

Wonder on, she said to herself, but aloud she said nothing, just bowed her head. Never hurt to look like you've done something wrong. Never answer back. Mrs Morson of Urania Cottage used to say that to the girls when she was training them to work as maidservants. '"The Mistress knows best", say that to yourself a hundred times a day, and keep your temper. No good ever came to a girl who loses her temper. Instant dismissal. That's the reward for an outburst. So swallow your pride, girls and think of the future.'

The words came back to Sesina now and she decided to act upon them. She hung her head a little lower. 'Sorry, ma'am,' she said.

'And you delivered the handkerchief that you said you found. The handkerchief that was belonging to Mrs Gummidge?'

Nothing for it. Would have to tell the truth. Perhaps Mrs Gummidge noticed the missing handkerchief, sent a message. 'It didn't belong to her, ma'am. She said it was not the way that she marked her things.' And if, thought Sesina, there had been a message about a missing handkerchief, well, then she would just have to deny everything. Nothing like sticking to a lie. Never confess, never let them get you down: that was her motto.

'And as soon as you came back into the house, you went straight into the dining room and found Mrs Gummidge's handkerchief, concealed under a cushion, on the chair where she sat during dinner, is that right?'

'Yes, ma'am. I was just shaking up the cushions, ma'am. I picked up the cushion and I saw it there and I saw . . .' Sesina heard her voice tail out. There was an odd expression upon Mrs Collins' face. It disconcerted her and she felt disinclined to say anything else until she had decided what the woman was doing.

'Of course, the cushions should have been shaken when the room was cleaned and tidied, by you and Dolly.' Although she said 'you', Mrs Collins didn't look at Sesina, but looked at the inspector when she said this. And he looked across at Sesina, looked at her with pursed lips and narrowed eyes.

'Yes, ma'am.' Best to keep on saying that. What had got into the woman?

'But I must tell you, inspector, that I myself, personally, inspected the dining room after the guests had left that night. It's my invariable habit, something that my mother had taught me to do. It causes such unpleasantness in a household if a guest finds something missing on arrival home, mislays something and then accuses the staff of the household of pocketing the article and so I always check the rooms as soon as the guests have departed.'

Did she really do that? Sesina had never heard any hint of it. Never seen her do it. Would have thought that Mrs Barnett or Dolly would have mentioned that little habit. There was very little that the mistress did which that pair didn't know about. Didn't seem like her, somehow, either. There was something odd about the woman's expression, looking at Sesina just like she was trying to send a message. Looking at Sesina and then blinking and slanting her eyes at the inspector.

'Come on, now, admit it, girl, admit you stole the hand-kerchief and tried to make mischief when you saw it was so badly stained that it would be of no use to you.' Was Mrs Collins trying to send a message? Or was she deliberately trying to get her into trouble.

'I never!'

'Yes, you did. Don't contradict me.'

Sesina hung her head and said nothing more. The inspector, she saw, was looking at her with interest so while she hung her head she tried to keep an eye on him surreptitiously.

'Let the girl speak, Mrs Collins. Come on, now, Sesina. Tell the truth. Where did you find that bloodstained handkerchief?'

Sesina thought hard. There was something going on here. What was she supposed to bloody well say?

And then she got an inspiration. Now had a much better story.

'I found it in Mr Charles's room, Mrs Collins.' For a moment she enjoyed the shock in the woman's eyes before she added with an innocent air, 'Mrs Gummidge must have dropped it when she returned Mr Charles's painting coat. It was all wrapped up in the coat. Stained it too, it did.' Sesina folded her hands in front of her and waited for a response, facing her mistress, but keeping a sharp eye on the inspector.

'Returned Mr Charles's painting coat!'

'That's right, ma'am. Becky saw her. She was the one that opened the door to her. Don't you remember, ma'am. It was when you were here in the dining room, ma'am. When we was putting out the cards on the table.'

'And then she came in here and upset my arrangements.' Mrs Collins sounded stupefied.

'No, that was afterwards, ma'am. She went upstairs first. Told Becky she had Mr Charles's painting coat.'

'Why was I not told about this sooner?'

'Didn't know myself, ma'am. Becky wasn't to know any better, ma'am. Dolly usually opens the door, but she must have been busy.' And if that got Dolly into trouble, then that would serve her right.

'And who's Becky?' The inspector was looking a bit puzzled.

'She's a scullery maid, inspector. Comes in two or three

times a week to help with the scrubbing and on washing day. But Sesina is right. Dolly should have opened the door. The child wasn't to know any better. How very, very extraordinary! How on earth did Mrs Gummidge come to have my son's painting coat?'

Mrs C. was getting into her stride now. Beginning to get the plot, thought Sesina. They could carry the story between the two of them.

'Seems strange, doesn't it, ma'am, that there was blood on the painting coat and blood on the handkerchief. You see the handkerchief was wrapped in the coat. It soaked into it, do you think, ma'am?' That could be the heading for a new part of the story.

'No one could understand why there was blood on that coat.' Mrs Collins was looking at Sesina when she said that and Sesina knew that it was her turn.

'Wonder was it the same blood?' she asked innocently, addressing her question to a space midway between the inspector and her mistress. She waited for a moment to give them the chance to exchange glances. Things were going much better than she could have dreamed of. Now a whole new story was opening up and she would enjoy guiding the inspector through it.

'I wonder . . .' The mistress put the edge of her first finger to her mouth and looked across the room at the window, giving a very good impression of someone who is struck by a new thought.

'So why did you slip Mrs Gummidge's handkerchief under the cushion of that chair, Sesina?' The inspector asked that question and his two underlings looked at him respectfully.

Sesina suppressed a smile. She had been waiting for that. 'I didn't think it was right that a married woman would visit a young man's bedroom,' she said softly and hesitantly. 'Even if she is a widow, she's too old for him. She's far older than his own mother.' Sesina slipped a surreptitious gaze at Mrs Collins and saw that had gone down well. 'I didn't like to say anything about it, but I didn't want to leave her handkerchief there,' she continued. 'And so I brought it back to her today and she said that it wasn't hers. Struck me all in a heap, that did!'

'Said it wasn't hers,' echoed the inspector. Sesina saw that he looked at the handkerchief with renewed interest. Encouraged by that, she went on, 'So I didn't know what to do. I knew it was hers. And so I slipped it under the cushion where she had been sitting that evening. Just so as the mistress could find it and deal with the matter,' she ended humbly, wondering whether to dab her eyes with her apron. She rejected that though in favour of the honest, straightforward gaze of a conscientious and troubled servant.

'I see.' The inspector was so excited that he couldn't help exchanging a glance with Mrs Collins. Mrs Collins widened her eyes and bit her lower lip. A good actress; there was no doubt about that. Should definitely have gone on the stage, thought Sesina, wondering how to get out of the room. Best to leave them now. Let them talk it over. She glanced towards the door and Mrs Collins did not fail her.

'That's all, Sesina, unless the inspector wants you for anything else.' She cast an enquiring look at him and he gave a slight shake of his head. 'Oh, and Sesina, you will have a word with little Becky about not answering the front door bell, won't you? I don't want to upset the little girl, but really she mustn't take it upon herself to do things like that. I'm sure that I can rely on you to explain matters to her, can't I?' She had a meaningful look in her eyes and Sesina had to bite back a grin.

'Yes, ma'am,' she said humbly. 'You can rely on me, ma'am. She's a very good girl, Becky, just wants to please. Loves coming here. She's ever so useful, ma'am.' No harm in putting this in. Mrs Collins must know that silence came with a price. No harm in giving Becky a leg up.

'You're right. She is a good girl. I'll have a word with the cook about giving her an extra day's work. But I'll leave that other matter to you, Sesina. You will explain to her, won't you?'

Don't overdo it: I'm not stupid and nobody ever thought that I was. Sesina got herself out of the room as quickly as she could before all this insistence about Becky might wake a suspicion in the dull mind of the inspector. As she went down the stairs to the basement, she went over the next part she had to play. Just had to get it firmly into Becky's mind. She had a quick look into the kitchen. Dolly and Mrs Barnett, heads together, happily gossiping while chopping hazelnuts. She shut the door quietly. No point in disturbing them.

Becky was in the washhouse, pounding the dolly up and down on the table napkins that were steeping in a mixture of lye soap and water. Poor little scrap, looked exhausted.

'Give yourself a rest, Becky,' said Sesina. Becky always did what she was told and so she stopped instantly and gazed at Sesina with her frightened large eyes. A bit 'wanting' at times, thought Sesina and wondered how to put it to the girl. No point in too many explanations.

'You opened the door to Mrs Gummidge, Mrs Hermione Gummidge, didn't you, Becky?' And then when Becky continued to stare, Sesina gave her a nod and then added a wink.

'Yes,' said Becky, with an uneasy look.

'That's right.' Sesina nodded enthusiastically. 'That's right. You opened the door to Mrs Gummidge and she asked you where Mr Charles's painting room was. And you showed her up.'

This was going a little too fast for Becky. Her eyes widened even more and she stared at Sesina with an expression of bewilderment.

'Just say it, Becky.' Sesina was beginning to lose patience. Any minute now, that inspector might ask to speak to the girl who admitted Mrs Gummidge to the painting room. Slowly and carefully, enunciating the words with great care, Sesina said, 'I opened the door to Mrs Gummidge. She asked for Mr Charles. I showed her into the painting room. Now you say that, Becky.'

With a relieved expression, Becky repeated the words without the slightest mistake. Not stupid then; just frightened out of her wits half the time. Sesina rewarded her with an enthusiastic grin and another wink.

'Say it again, Becky.'

This time it came out in a more natural-sounding manner.

'Good girl, Becky.' Sesina made her voice sound excited. She seized the dolly and pounded the napkins with immense vigour. She was fizzing over with enjoyment. This was brightening up a dull day. 'Say it again!'

Becky was getting into the spirit of things and now the words were coming out in a more and more natural fashion. Wouldn't matter if she sounded a bit frightened. The inspector was the sort of man who would expect a kitchen maid to be frightened of a great man like himself.

'And now one more bit, Becky.' Sesina gave the girl a wide smile. 'Say this: "She asked me where Mr Charles's bedroom was and I told her it was next door".'

'Mrs Gummidge asked me 'bout Mr Charles's painting room. Showed her in.'

Even better, thought Sesina. Sounded more like the way that Becky would speak normally. She gave the girl a hug and then in an excess of generosity, she fished out a sweet from her pocket. Mr Wilkie was mad on sweets and always kept a pile of them by his bed. Would offer her one if she came in while he was there. 'Help yourself, Sesina,' he'd say and so she did, whether he was there or not. Bless him; he wouldn't mind. And it was worth it to see the look on little Becky's half-starved face. Probably the first time she had ever tasted a sweet. Didn't have the nerve to pinch one from the stalls in Covent Garden. Amazing that the girl was still alive. Didn't seem to have no idea of how to look after herself.

'Say it again, Becky,' said Sesina and Becky shifted the sweet to the inside of her cheek and said it all again, changing the first bit, just as she had changed the last bit. Didn't matter as long as she got the three things right: Mrs Gummidge. Mr Charles. The painting room. Sesina gave a few more vigorous blows of the dolly on top of the load of table napkins and then left the girl with instructions to keep saying the words to herself until she was sure that she wouldn't forget them. She wouldn't mention the possibility of another day's work for Becky until she was sure that it was going to happen. Mrs Collins had a habit of saying things and then of forgetting all about them unless reminded at frequent intervals. But she was mad about her two sons and anyone that helped one of them would be rewarded by her.

Let's get this affair of Mr Charles over and done with first, thought Sesina. She must make sure that there were plenty of other people for the inspector to suspect. She hesitated for a moment outside the kitchen, but Dolly and Mrs B. were happily chattering, at least Mrs B. was telling Dolly some lies about her family and how well-off they had been and Dolly was saying, 'Well, I never! Well, it must have been a great shock for you to have to go into service!'

Sesina grabbed a tin of polish and some polishing rags from the cupboard outside the kitchen door and made her way upstairs in search of Mr Wilkie. There was always some piece of furniture in the house which needed polishing so nobody could accuse her of being idle. Mrs Collins was busy with the inspector, Mrs Barnett was busy with her imaginary tales from the past and so Sesina might be able to have an uninterrupted chat with Mr Wilkie. She wondered how he and his friend Mr Dickens were getting on with discovering the real murderer. He would never believe that his brother had killed the man. Knew better – well, he must have done. After all he knew him since he was born and I bet, Sesina thought, that while little Wilkie was getting up to mischief, little Charley was a good little boy. The older boy had the gift of the gab and might have managed to make his way even if he were born in Monmouth Street and had to make his way among the swarming inhabitants of the streets around the Seven Dials.

But little Charley Collins, without a rich father and an easy life, would, like many that she had known, have faded away at an early age. Had eaten nothing this morning. That was always his way when he was upset. Needs someone to look after him, she muttered and though she told herself that she was being soft, she swore that she would do her best to get him out of this terrible mess. But she could do with some help. This was a murder committed by one of the toffs; she was sure of that. And to get into their world she needed to link up with one of their own kind.

She would have to talk with his brother, Mr Wilkie, as soon as she could.

FOURTEEN

Wilkie Collins, *Hide and Seek*, 1854:
Now, the parlour of Mr Thorpe's house was neat, clean,
comfortably and sensibly furnished. It was of the average
size. It had the usual side-board, dining-table, looking-
glass, scroll fender, marble chimney-piece with a clock
on it, carpet with a drugget over it, and wire window-
blinds to keep people from looking in, characteristic of
all respectable London parlours of the middle class.

I finished the last rapid sketch. 'I'm no artist,' I said, pinning
the slip of paper beside the other four. I stood back and
looked at them – five sketches and one of them bore the
shape of a murderer. 'But I am a competent draughtsman,' I
added. 'Even my father used to admit that.'

Dickens and I were hard at work, sitting cosily beside the
fire in the small downstairs parlour. The inspector had taken
the pictures away, but I felt that I had produced a reasonable
facsimile of each one of the five intact pictures. I felt a driving
need to discover who had murdered Edwin Milton-Hayes.
Charley was safe for the moment, but he couldn't spend the
rest of his life on a yacht. Knowing Charley, he was probably
homesick already, might even insist, in his oddly obstinate
way, of coming back and of endeavouring by means of logical
argument to convince Inspector Field of his innocence.

Dickens looked up from his notebook. He seemed interested
in my last statement. 'Did you ever mind, Wilkie, that your
father thought so highly of Charley, believed that he had infinite
promise and yet dismissed your skills?'

I thought about that for a moment, but for no longer.
'No,' I said and I hoped that he could hear a note of sincerity
in my voice. 'No, I didn't. To be honest, I thought that I had
something superior. I—'

'And so you had,' interrupted Dickens. 'You have the ability to take pains, the courage to try and fail and then get up and try again. Charley has none of that. If I hadn't known your father, didn't know your mother, I would imagine that he had his spirit broken at an early age. But I know that there is no truth in that. He was truly loved and given everything that a boy could ask for, education, training, praise. Perhaps, though, he got too much praise and too easily. He sticks at nothing, Wilkie. Doesn't even know what style of painting that he wants to adopt. And he's no boy; not any longer. When was he born? Four years after you, wasn't it? 1826, is that right? No child, Wilkie; he's a man. I was a husband and father at that age. And earning a good living. Time he got to his feet, shook himself and became a man.'

I bowed my head. He was right, of course. And yet, he wasn't. 'You forget, Dick,' I said. 'You forget that heaven tempers the wind for the shorn lamb. Charley isn't like you, strong and self-reliant. He's not even like me. I'm like my mother. I have a happy temperament. Charley is like my father, a man who worried over everything. My father was lucky, or perhaps wise. Or you might say that marriage forced him in one direction, but he decided early on what he could do well and that was to paint landscapes and seascapes. The sort of paintings that people wanted upon their walls; that they liked to look upon. And he worked hard at these, studied the market and studied his craft.'

'And he made a success, Wilkie. Someone told me that he made more money than Constable, who would be the critics' favourite. Your father didn't hang around sighing and doctoring himself, he went out there into the market place. He perfected his craft and he sold his pictures. You and your brother profited from that. Neither of you was deprived of anything. You were both sent to school, your wishes for the future were consulted; you were supported and housed. And when he died, so you told me, your father left the enormous sum of eleven thousand pounds which meant that you and your brother had no pressure on you to earn money. Eleven thousand – why that is a fortune indeed. What a provident father you had!'

Dickens' voice had an unusual note in it. A note of slight bitterness. I said nothing. It was not for me to probe, but he had said, almost as clearly as though he had put it into words, that we, my brother and I, had had an easy life and had everything done for us. I knew from a few remarks that he had let fall, that he was not treated like that. I knew that from an early age, sometimes he hinted at a very early age, but certainly by the time that he was sixteen he had been his own breadwinner, that he had married at the age of twenty-four and was a father when he was far younger than Charley was now. And yet, something in me protested. Something cried out that it was different; that not all are born alike and that Charley needed care and protection.

'I have to look after my brother, Dick,' I said stubbornly. 'Charley is incapable of murder, but he is very likely to drift into trouble and to find himself in court facing judge and jury, just because he did not take care in time, just because he allowed matters to drift. I am sure he is innocent; as sure as I am that you and I are discussing this matter, I do fully believe that someone, some guilty person, is trying to shift the consequences of their own crime onto my brother's shoulders.'

Dickens said nothing. He just stood there contemplating me with an unusual degree of attentiveness. I almost expected him to make a note, as he often did whenever he came across an interesting character or an interesting turn of phrase, something which would fuel his imagination in his new book.

'Very well, then,' he said, quite cool and quite self-possessed. 'Very well, then. So who is this person, this guilty person?'

'I don't know,' I said, conscious of a slight drop in the intensity of my voice. Would Dickens think that I, like my brother, was a dilettante, someone who was incapable of pursuing an idea, of accomplishing a task? But, no, he had praised my working ability, my perseverance in accomplishing my novel *Basil* and now he was also approving of the present work on *Hide and Seek*. I strove for his good opinion and wanted to show myself as a man who valued method, order and logical thinking.

'Let's begin at the beginning,' I said, trying to inject a note of authority into my voice. 'Weak but amiable' I had heard someone describe me. At the time, I had been amused. Had raised an eyebrow, cleaned my glasses with a deprecating air, but now I wanted a different description. I wanted Dickens to think highly of me, to esteem me for the qualities of order and method.

'Let's begin with the canon,' I said. 'Now Milton-Hayes wouldn't have embarked on those five pictures unless he had some buyer in mind. I'd like to know whether it was he or the canon who came up with the titles for the pictures.'

'The canon, I suppose,' said Dickens, but he had a slight frown between his bushy eyebrows. 'After all, you know the old proverb. He who pays the piper . . .'

'No, I don't think so, though,' I said eagerly. 'After all, if it were the canon, one would expect a more conventional, churchman's list, the seven deadly sins; that's what I'm thinking of. What are they, those seven deadly sins? I'm sure that I should remember them from all the church-going that I was subjected to when I was young. My father was fanatical about church on Sunday. I hated it and Charley, poor fellow, loved it. Always very devout, is Charley.'

'Nothing wrong with that,' said Dickens and the frown deepened. 'One can be devout, render onto God on a Sunday and get on with life on the other days of the week.'

'Yes,' I said hurriedly. I didn't want to start him on Charley again and on his lack of moral fibre. 'Yes, I remember them now; the seven deadly sins: pride; greed; lust; envy; gluttony; wrath; and sloth. That's what you would expect the canon to have requested. So was it Milton-Hayes that came up with *The Night Prowler* and *Den of Iniquity* not to mention *Root of All Evil*? Not very biblical terms, are they? I do believe that it was Milton-Hayes himself and that he meant it for blackmail. I mean to find out whether Milton-Hayes had been trying that on before. And *Winter of Despair*. If only we could see the face on that drowned body. There must have been a face. And other faces. Otherwise, why did the murderer hack this one to pieces? I think we must find out more about the canon and where the notion came from. Perhaps we'll go and see him, take him a letter, even a little present from my mother, say how sorry she was about the murder. How about that? Let's go and see her now.'

I bustled him out of the room. I didn't want to listen to

any more criticism about my brother. He would say no more in the presence of my mother. He knew how much Charley meant to my mother and he was too sensitive a man and too chivalrous to upset her by making any criticism about her youngest son.

We found my mother active in the small sitting room, beside her bedroom. Duster in hand, she was busy sorting out the contents of her cabinet. I caught a glimpse of all of the relics that she had preserved after my father's death, sketchpad, his paints, his brushes, sketching pens and graphite pencils, knives and even his sticks of charcoal. For a moment her hand caressed the wooden paint palette which he used for outdoor work, but then she hastily replaced that, also, within the drawers which held her treasures and I saw how, surreptitiously, she mopped a few tears from her eyes.

Dickens, who at times could be as perceptive as any woman, took up a framed painting of myself and my brother when we were young. 'Two lovely little boys,' he said admiringly. 'Look at the pair of them! Look at Charley. Look at those freckles and the curls. A little angel straight out of paradise. Don't you wish that they never had to grow up, Mrs Collins? I do with mine.'

My mother was herself again and prepared to entertain the guest that I had thrust upon her so heedlessly. She made polite enquiries about the Dickens children, exclaimed with amazement at the news that there were now nine of them. Dickens led neatly up to the subject of the canon by telling a funny anecdote about the christening of the latest arrival. 'I wanted the canon of Rochester to do it,' he said blandly, 'but when he heard the likelihood of the other eight little angels attending the ceremony, why he backed out and I couldn't,' said Dickens with an earnest face, 'really blame him as I felt like backing out myself. But I'm sure that the charming man I met at your dinner table would have been more accommodating.'

'We were thinking of going to see him, Mamma.' I had a better knowledge than my friend of my mother's sharp brain. It would be no good trying to fool her. We might as well come straight out with it. I had caught the glance that she had given to Charley in that painting of us two when we were young

boys and I knew that mentally she was promising our father
that she would do all in her power to safeguard his youngest
son. 'I was wondering, Mamma, about whose idea it was to
do those pictures and so I thought that Dickens and myself
could go and have a word with the canon. But I don't want
to be too obvious, so we thought that I could be a bearer of
a letter from you . . .'

I said no more. She had understood instantly. In a moment,
she had crossed to her desk, had taken out a piece of writing
paper and now began to write the note.

> My dear Canon Rutter,
> So, so kind of you to send a note thanking me for the
> evening. I will say no more about the terrible tragedy,
> but I do hope that when all is well again that I may be
> so blessed as to receive you again on a happier occa-
> sion. In the meantime, I send my best regards and
> implore your prayers that this unhappy affair will shortly
> be settled.
>   Yours respectfully,
>   Harriet Collins.

My mother ended the note with a flourish beneath her name,
rather like the one that Dickens himself used to decorate his
correspondence. She sprinkled the letter with the pounce jar
and turned back to me.

'Will that do?' she asked. There was a question in her
eyes which I knew had nothing whatsoever to do with the
note which she had just scrawled.

'I'll do my best,' I said, answering the unspoken question.
She bowed her head. I had an impression that she was thinking
hard.

'Wilkie, when you are out could you pop into dear John
Millais and tell him to come and see us some time. I'm sure
he won't mind. He would cheer up Charley. Oh, what it is to
have the artistic temperament. Just like his father; always up
in the skies or down in the dumps!' She smiled bravely. She
had said the last words with a touch of her usual spirits and
I pressed her hand in admiration for her courage.

'A bunch of flowers for the canon?' I suggested and added, 'Dickens and I feel that would be a good touch. I fear that I will be the one saddled with carrying them, though.'

'Yes, indeed.' Her response came automatically, but she hesitated for a moment with her hand on the bell pull. In the end, she pulled three times. So Sesina was being called. That was unusual. My mother and Dolly were very close: Dolly had been in her service for as long as I could remember. After my father's death, my mother in her grief clung to Dolly and became quite dependent upon her for a month or two. And even now, Dolly was always called in when my mother wanted to discuss something. I would have thought that the two of them would have mulled over the question of suitable flowers for a canon – something that he might like to have in his room, or, alternatively, be suitable to be placed on an altar in the church.

But no, she had summoned Sesina and as soon as the girl appeared at the door I knew that there was some sort of secret between them.

'Sesina, did you do as I asked you?'

'Yes, ma'am.'

There was something rather stagey about the question and the answer. And the way in which my mother seemed to relax and then to put in the request for a bunch of flowers from the conservatory.

'Not too big,' I warned. 'We don't want to be walking through the streets behind a moving flower bush. On second thoughts, I'd better come with you and make sure that they are suitable. I'll just be a minute, Dickens. You can entertain my mother with an account of that play we went to see the other night. The one where I fell asleep. She keeps pestering me about it.' I pocketed the letter and rose to my feet. There was something going on and I was determined to get it out of Sesina.

'So what's the big secret, then, Sesina?' I queried as we went into the conservatory. I could see her thinking about her response as she made a fuss about a chair being in the wrong place and ostentatiously picked up a dead leaf which had blown in.

'Secret, Mr Collins?' Her voice held a question, but I was not fooled, nor was I impressed by the title of Mr Collins. Although my father had died over six years ago, I was always known as 'Mr Wilkie' in my mother's household.

'Oh, come on, Sesina, we're friends, aren't we? Tell me what this is all about. You and my mother are up to something.'

'Up to something, Mr Collins? What would I be up to?'

'You're not going to tell me, then, are you? Don't suppose it's all that interesting, is it? Women's secrets,' I added teasingly, but she was unmoved. She gave me a quick glance and it puzzled me. Almost a glance of exasperation, as though I were being very slow to take a hint. She turned her back on me, took the flower-cutting scissors from the shelf and began to snip. A bright girl, I thought. Quick and competent, snipping off bright red flowers with small heads and short stems. She said no more and I said no more. I had an uneasy feeling that I might just, in a male, blundering fashion, put my foot in it, if I pressed for an answer.

I waited in silence; then, waited while she completed the modest bunch of flowers, waited while she wound the stems with a strand of raffia. 'Thank you, Sesina,' I said coldly.

She said nothing to that, just gave a quick bob. Not at all like Sesina, just as though she were acting a part. I went back up to my mother's sitting room feeling rather puzzled. I could hear Dickens' voice as I went up the stairs. Just his voice. My mother, normally the most talkative of women, did not seem to be saying a word. I didn't bother going in, just opened the door, said goodbye to my mother, while observing that Dickens was quite glad to get away and that he had run out of subjects that might be supposed to interest my mother.

We went down the stairs together, took our coats from the hallstand. I was just extricating my umbrella from the over-full umbrella stand when Dolly appeared. But it was not to minister to us, but in answer to the doorbell.

'Oh, Mr Wilkie,' she said, sounding somewhat flustered. 'I didn't know that you were going. The mistress didn't ring.' And then she went to the door and opened it to Inspector Field.

'Come in, sir,' she said and bobbed to him as though he

were a frequent guest. 'The mistress is expecting you. She's up in her sitting room.'

He had looked slightly surprised to see us, slightly taken aback, but he said nothing beyond a greeting and did not propose that we accompany him. I picked up the bunch of scarlet geraniums and feeling rather a fool, as though I was off to court a young lady, I followed Dickens down the steps.

Once I reached the pavement, though, I stopped abruptly. 'You don't think that he has tracked down Charley, do you, Dick?' I asked anxiously. I would never forgive myself if I just walked off and allowed poor Charley, my very vulnerable young brother, to face up to matters on his own.

Dickens shook his head. 'No,' he said decisively. 'Didn't you hear the servant? She said, "The mistress is expecting you", no, Wilkie, your mother sent for him. I wonder why. And I wonder why she didn't mention it when we were there. I could have given her some advice. I would have told her to be careful. Inspector Field is a very clever and subtle man, but he is also a most ambitious man and he wants an arrest as soon as possible. I passed by St Paul's yesterday afternoon and those pamphlet sellers were all shouting about the murder – "Painter's Painful End", "The Colour of Blood", "A Picture of Death" – all that sort of thing. Quite soon even the respectable newspapers will be demanding an arrest and there will be questions in Parliament. I hope your mother is not doing anything dramatic again, trying to pretend that she did the murder herself or anything like that. A mother sacrificing herself for her son. I think I managed to convince the inspector that it was maternal love, but if she goes on asserting this, he might just decide to take her seriously.'

I made an impatient swipe at a lamp post with my bunch of geraniums and Dickens took them carefully from me. 'My favourite flower,' he said reproachfully and buried his nose in the scarlet cluster.

'They don't smell,' I said impatiently. I suspected him of trying to change the subject. I was regretting bitterly that I had not taken off my hat and my coat and accompanied the inspector to my mother's room. My mother was a creature of impulse. I bitterly regretted my father's death. He was always wary of my mother's impulses, always talked sense to her. He was the artist, but she was the one who had the artistic temperament. I saw Dickens look at me curiously and so I voiced the thought aloud.

'I'm worried about my mother as well as about Charley. I'm afraid of her starting some sort of wild goose chase. She is a very impulsive and imaginative person. She wanted to be an actress, but her family wouldn't allow her,' I explained. 'They persuaded her into being a governess instead and she hated that.'

'Your grandparents were wise,' said Dickens grimly. 'Your mother makes enough drama in her private life without ever needing to go on the stage.'

I laughed and began to feel a little better. My mother had probably had one of her, so-called, good ideas. My poor father used to clasp his head in despair when she made the familiar announcement: 'I've got a good idea.' However, Charley and I used to love her 'good ideas'. They always led to something interesting and exciting. She was the one who had got the idea, when a welcome legacy had come to my father, that the whole family should decamp and go to Italy so that my father could study the great Italian art works and could paint the wonderful Mediterranean beautiful scenery in his own particularly English style. It had proved to be a 'good idea' as my father had made quite a lot of money from these works of art and I had had a wonderful time. Came back brown as a sailor, speaking fluent Italian and having learned to get on really well with those of the opposite sex. I decided to stop worrying about my mother's vagaries and to concentrate on solving the problem of that guest list that the murdered man had drawn up so carefully.

'Why do you think that Milton-Hayes wanted to invite the canon to the dinner, Dick?' I asked.

He took my question seriously, looking straight ahead, frowning brows pulling his hat down close to those brilliant dark eyes. 'I suppose that you could say that the canon was the buyer, the man who was going to have first pick from those rather arresting pictures,' he said, but there was a hesitant note in his voice which invited me to disagree.

'But the dinner, we now know, was not really an occasion to debate artistry, as Millais and Holman Hunt and even Ruskin had asked my mother to host. No,' I said emphatically, 'this dinner was the work of a devil. Milton-Hayes was showing his power over his poor victims. If they paid up, ahead of time, well he might have withdrawn the picture, but if they refused, they would have had a taste of what was to come when they witnessed friends and acquaintances speculating in whispers about the inspiration behind those diabolical pictures.'

'I wonder whether some had paid up,' said Dickens. He nodded amiably at the amazed and excited face of a bookseller who had come out of his shop to inspect his display of *Bleak House* and who was stunned to see the man himself glance at the shop window.

'Perhaps,' I said.

'Because you wouldn't have expected him to carry all five pictures, six if you include *Winter of Despair*, into your mother's drawing room.'

'I suppose not,' I said. I had never taken too much interest in Charley's friends and their concerns. 'I usually steal off and smoke a pipe,' I admitted.

Dickens gave me a censorious look. He would insist on believing that, as a man, I would have influence over my mother. I, however, knew, for many a year, that I had none and I had never wanted any. As long as she was happy and I was happy and poor Charley was as happy as his temperament and training at that Jesuit school would allow him to be – well, as long as all that came to pass, I would never have dreamed of having the slightest say in my mother's dinner parties. After all, it was her house and her money. I endeavoured to be helpful, though. Dickens' good opinion was very important to me.

'I remember that we had a dinner to look at Holman Hunt's picture *The Awakening Conscience*. I thought the girl didn't look animated enough, didn't look as if much was troubling her, to be honest, but everyone else disagreed with me, so I took myself down to the kitchen and had a second helping of Mrs Barnett's apple charlotte pudding.'

Dickens was satisfied with this. 'I thought so,' he said in his definite way. 'Holman Hunt brings one picture and that probably would have been the norm. Milton-Hayes might have planned to bring just one or two. The threat might have been enough to make most of his victims pay up hastily and then Milton-Hayes might have brought something different to your mother's dinner. If, for instance, your brother Charley had not managed to get hold of a slice of that money that your provident father left, then Milton-Hayes might have moved on to the husband of the lady. No man likes to be shown up in public as a cuckold and an old fool. Or else, perhaps he would have tried to milk Lord Douglas or his father. There must be money in that family and if his father, the Earl of Ennis, was unable to pay, why then a cousin or two might have been persuaded to cough up the necessary sum. Clever fellow, that Milton-Hayes, wasn't he?' added Dickens with a reflective expression on his face as though he were auditioning the artistic Milton-Hayes for a part in one of his novels.

'Came from Essex, I think. Perhaps he'll tell your mother.' Inspector Field's visit to my mother was still intriguing him; I could tell that.

I myself was interested. It seemed undoubted that my mother had summoned the policeman. Probably sent Dolly with a message. Or was it Sesina? That might have been the answer to her little air of self-consequence. She might be pleased to be a messenger, might have made the most of her previous contact with Inspector Field. I hoped that there would be no more dramatic confessions on my mother's part. The uneasy spectre of my father hovered around me. '*Willie*,' I seemed to hear his solemn and reproachful voice in my ear using the old, childhood name which I had long swapped for my more adult second name, '*Willie, I've left your mother and your brother in your care. What are you doing to safeguard them?*' The words rang through my mind incessantly. It was a relief when Dickens began speaking again, his decisive quick voice breaking up the ghostly echoes in my mind.

'I was talking to Augustus Egg about Milton-Hayes, and he had a few interesting things to say.'

I was immediately intrigued. Augustus Egg, for an artist, was a very sensible fellow and had a greater hold on reality than most of the Pre-Raphaelite brethren.

'What did he think of him?'

'Of Milton-Hayes? Didn't care for him much, I had the impression, but that's not the interesting bit. He said . . .' Dickens paused with his eye on me before continuing. 'He said that he thought the name was assumed. He remembered once that the man was writing a note. He was drinking in an inn with some of the others and he scribbled a note and gave a boy a few pennies to take it to his house. And,' said Dickens with emphasis, 'he put his name at the bottom of the page and then crossed it out, violently, according to Egg and then wrote "Milton-Hayes". Now a man doesn't make a mistake with his own name. Any other word in the English language can be misspelt by a man in his cups, but I venture to assert, though I don't, as you know, like to be too dogmatic, but I'm sure that you will agree with me that one's signature is almost a reflex action, as part of one's self as it is to put one foot in front of another.'

It would be for Dickens who once told me that he never wrote less than a dozen letters a day, but perhaps not quite so much for others. Still, every painting that the man did was signed by the ornate flourish of his double-barrelled name. Aloud I said, 'I'm not surprised if it's an assumed name. Did Augustus manage to see the first name before it was scribbled out?'

'He thought it began with an R. I went around to see him last night and I tried to get some more out of him. The man is so indecisive.' Dickens began to walk fast with a frown that lowered his eyebrows down over his eyes. He was fond of Augustus Egg, I knew, but if there was anything that Dickens could not abide, it was being indecisive. Often I found myself trapped into a hasty decision in order to avoid the charge. I felt rather sorry for poor old Egg, a man who liked to smoke peacefully until inspiration struck and then to work at a very leisurely pace. I controlled my thoughts though and turned an interested face towards Dickens.

'I sat him down at the table, mended a few pens for him, took out a fresh slip of paper and said to him, "Now then, Egg, don't think of anything except that day in the inn. You are watching a word being written at the end of a note. Milton-Hayes is holding the pen and the pen is travelling over the page. Now write that word, write it again and again until you are satisfied."' Dickens smiled grimly to himself.

'And did it work?' Myself, I would have given the man a dose of laudanum, but Dickens was a puritan and any mention of laudanum caused him to frown. He regarded the taking of opiates as a sign of weakness and so I avoided letting him know of my own usage. There was many a time that I resorted to them, however, in order to get a story moving and was often amazed how my pen seemed to scrawl across the paper almost as though under its own steam.

'I said to him, "Keep going, Egg; keep going. Don't stop to think, just keep writing until you think that you have it." He filled half a page and then he sat back, well, you know Egg. He can never make up his mind about anything. He stared at the scrawls on the page as if he wasn't sure how they got there. I didn't rush him or anything. I just waited. I know how to deal with people like Egg and so I gave him lots of time. In the end, very quietly, I just told him to point to the one that looked the most like it. Unfortunately,' said Dickens, neatly sidestepping a drunken man, 'unfortunately, the one that he pointed to was the most incomprehensible of the lot. I could only be sure of the letter R and it was probably the letter A or else U after it. Egg, of course, God bless him, was very cheerful about it all and left all the guesswork in my hands. He thought that he had done his bit when he had ruined one of my pens, dropped some ink on my rug and used up a whole slip of expensive paper.'

That acerbic note was unlike Dickens who was generally the most generous of men and was unsparing in pressing friends to partake of his hospitality. I took it as a measure of his friendship to me and his determination to solve this murder and to free my brother from his state of despair.

'It's useful, though, isn't it?' I said in his ear as we crossed St Mark's Square. 'He might have been named Raymond, or

Ransley, or Raeburn, or even Russell,' I ended, thinking back on what Piggott had said about Jack Russell dogs.

'Or a million others,' said Dickens. 'Anyway, let's see whether the canon knows any more. All we need is just a hint of a murky past. Just something that would give Inspector Field an excuse to shift the focus from your brother and move it onto someone else. He's under pressure from his superiors at the moment, you know.'

It was my first hint that Dickens had been talking with Inspector Field in private and I felt very grateful for his interest. He was an extremely busy man, writing every morning, writing to a deadline, month by the month, the next episode in *Hard Times*, his novel about the industrial north.

The canon was pleased to see us. A newly promoted man, I sensed that he had not quite fitted himself into his new role. Perhaps my mother was right. The move from the docks on the east side of London to the leafy precincts of Regent's Park had made him feel rather self-conscious and he wasn't yet comfortable in his new role. He was effusive in his praise about my mother, in the role that she played in charitable works, in her interest in the church and in her support for new ideas and new methods. A woman, he said solemnly, who had a great love for God. He rapturously inhaled the scarlet flowers before laying them reverentially on the windowsill. I could have told him that the flowers of geraniums had no scent. I, also, could have told him that my mother's religious instincts were purely a matter of boredom. She had worked hard at my father's career, had been responsible for dealing with art galleries and arranging exhibitions and her suggestions of subjects to paint often turned out to be his most successful works. Since his death she had been at a loss. If Charley had the self-confidence to accept her help, she might have been the making of him, but he shunned her counsels, rejected her suggestions, exclaimed with horror at the idea of making use of her influence and seemed to glory in going contrary to her ideas. Poor fellow. His own worst enemy, I thought and wondered how this affair of the murdered artist was going to turn out and if we could ever find the real murderer and rescue my poor brother.

Winter of Despair. I thought of Milton-Hayes and his
picture and of his diabolical way of blackmailing those who
had welcomed him into their fellowship. He had misused
whatever gifts that he had, had employed them in blackmail,
had enriched himself and had misused the art of picture
making.

However, this canon was friendly and perhaps as much a
victim of a plausible tongue as some others. I smiled at him
in a friendly fashion and accepted his tributes to my mother
and then looked across at Dickens. He immediately took up
the bat and carried on the conversation.

'Yes, a remarkable lady, this mother of our friend, here;
I've seldom admired a woman more than when she dealt so
calmly with all of the sad events on the night of what should
have been one of her pleasant little dinner parties,' he said
promptly. 'A shocking business. Shocking to me and I hardly
knew the man. And, of course, the report of Mr Milton-Hayes'
death must have been a great shock to you, also. I understand
that you knew him well.'

'Oh, no, not well.' The canon seemed somewhat taken
aback at that. 'No, not well at all. Good heavens, no. I barely
met him on a few occasions. But it was a relationship that I
felt should be encouraged by me. I had hoped that good things
would come of it: this alliance between the man of God and
the man of Art. Our medieval church made great use of art in
order to explain religion to the people and that was my connection with Mr Milton-Hayes; that was my sole contact with
him. I commissioned him to paint some pictures for me. We
are opening a new hall for the use of the laity and it seemed
appropriate to decorate it with paintings which would be beautiful in themselves, but which would also open minds to think
upon religious matter.' The canon folded his arms across his
plump stomach and smiled tentatively at us.

'And so Milton-Hayes did his version of the seven deadly
sins,' I said.

'An interesting idea. Was it yours or was it Mr Milton-Hayes'
concept?' asked Dickens with one of his keen looks.

The canon hesitated and I felt rather sorry for him. Those
pictures, I was pretty sure, were not at all what a dignitary of

the church would actually want on the walls of a room meant for the pious laity. Surely children would be admitted to these rooms and no one would want their innocent child speculating on the meaning of *Den of Iniquity* or *Taken in Adultery* and certainly not *Forbidden Fruit*, or any of the other pictures. I looked at the canon dubiously. It seemed impossible that a man such as this, hesitant, hide-bound within the constraints of conventional morality, would have really wanted pictures like these.

'Well, the original inspiration was mine, but . . .' He hesitated and looked at me for help.

'But you had to leave the execution to the artist,' I said, encouragingly. 'I know that my brother and his friends talk a lot about this. They feel that an artist, unlike an artisan, cannot be tied down to a particular subject or particular way of working.'

The canon smiled at me benignly and I thought I could read a touch of thankfulness in his face. 'You're quite right, Mr Collins. In fact, I felt a bit of a fool as I was trying to explain, but Mr Milton-Hayes seemed to brush aside what I said and kept on assuring me that he perfectly understood what I wanted and that I would be delighted at the result.'

There was a short silence after he said that and then it was broken as Dickens, always courageous, said, 'And were you? Were you delighted at the result?'

The canon's eyes fell before his and he chewed upon his rather full lips. And then he looked up and said, '*De mortius* . . .' He left a silence and we both knew what he meant by this Latin tag – but neither of us felt like commentating. No, no one wanted to criticize the dead and yet it was the living who matter. I thought of trying to say something about that, but again it was Dickens who took the initiative.

'And so you were deeply appalled at the use which Milton-Hayes made of your commission. And the choice of subjects, *The Night Prowler*, *Taken in Adultery* etc. It was the artist who chose the subjects.'

'I tried to make some suggestions, brought along a few prayer books, an illustrated version of the "Sermon on the Mount" but, as I said, he didn't want to be hampered.' The canon wiped some sweat from his brow and I began to feel very sorry for him.

'But the church was paying for these pictures, is that not so?'

'That was so,' said the canon. I could still see a sheen of sweat on his forehead and his eyes had a deeply troubled look. 'You'll have to excuse me, gentlemen, but the diocesan lawyer is due here at three and I see that it is past that hour now. Will you please give my most sincere thanks to your mother, Mr Collins?' He shook hands energetically with us both and expressed himself overwhelmed to have had another opportunity to meet with the famous Mr Dickens, rang his bell for an attendant cleric, and then we found ourselves out on St Mark's Square once more.

'I wonder whether he will have to pay for those pictures,' I said.

'Not if the diocesan lawyer knows his job,' said Dickens cynically. 'That is what diocesan lawyers are for. Anyway, technically speaking they are unfinished, though I suppose any competent artist could supply the missing faces. Nice job for Charley, wouldn't it be?'

I shuddered at the idea. Charley was in a bad enough state. I began to feel uneasy about him again. Goodness knows what was happening while I was out of the house.

'I'd better be getting back, Dick,' I said. 'My mother is very worried and I should be with her.'

FIFTEEN

Sesina was in the hall when Mr Wilkie came in. He had a way of running up the steps, rattling his umbrella against the area railings and he could always be heard in the kitchen if you were anywhere near to the window.

'Better give that hall table a rub; the mistress was having a bit of a look at it this morning,' she said blandly to Dolly. Not waiting for a reply, she seized the cloths and the tin of polish that she had left near to hand upon the dresser and went straight through the door and up the stairs to the hall.

Mr Wilkie was just taking his key from the front door when she came into the hall. He didn't look too worried, just thoughtful.

'Just going upstairs to give your tables a bit of a polish, Mr Wilkie,' said Sesina. 'Do you want me to come back later?'

He looked at her with a twinkle in his eye. Could read her easily. Knew that she wanted to be in on this affair. He gave her a wink and she bit her lips, though she knew that she was only half-concealing the smile.

'I was, so!' she asserted, but then she allowed the smile to come.

'Go on, then, up you go,' he said. 'Mrs Collins in her sitting room?'

'Yes, sir,' she said. He had something in his mind; she could see that by his eyes. Trying to be the same as usual, but there was an air of suppressed excitement about him. Just like he was, sometimes, when he was writing his book. He would be down-hearted for a while, sighing heavily, kicking at the wall under his desk, scratching his head and rubbing his eyes. And then, suddenly, he would say, 'Don't utter a word, Sesina. I've got an idea!' And then his quill pen would dip in and out of the inkwell as fast as a bird pecking at the crumbs on the lawn. And he would tell her again and again, 'Don't speak, Sesina, don't say a word, I have an idea.'

And that was the way he was tonight. Not writing, but gazing across the room, not seeing anything, she would have taken a bet on that, but gazing through the window and out into the dismal mists that hung over Regent's Park. Sesina held her breath, but she did not leave the room. In a few minutes, he might well want to talk about things and so, hoping that no one would come in through the door, she sat down on the rug beside the fire and waited for him to notice her. As long as Mr Charles was safe. That was the main thing. Otherwise, who cared?

Eventually, he gave a sigh. And then he spoke, not to her, but to himself. 'That might be it,' he said. And then he seemed to notice her.

'Sesina, give me a hand, will you?' he said and she rose to her feet instantly. 'Come down to the parlour with me,' he said and so she followed him. He knew what he wanted now, going down the stairs, two at a time, just like a young fellow and then he was switching on the gas lamps and searching behind the curtains for something. He had it in under a minute, a large leather bag and then he opened it and handed it to her.

'Keep it open, like a good girl,' he said while, one by one, he took the paintings from the stack on the table and put them into the bag. 'Five pictures,' he said, after he had finished. 'Five pictures without faces. One of those hidden faces, Sesina, might show the face of a murderer.'

'And then there is the sixth one,' she reminded him. 'The one that is on the table in your bedroom. The one that is called *Winter of Despair*, the one that has been slashed.'

He stopped and stared at her, his eyes large behind his spectacles. He stood so very still that she thought for a few moments that she had gone too far, had stepped out of her role as servant girl. And then he gave a deep sigh and beamed his nice smile at her.

'What a clever little thing you are, Sesina! Do you know, I'd almost forgotten about that picture, but you know, now that you remind me of it, something odd has just occurred to me.'

He perched on the edge of the table, the bag dangling from his hand. And then he put the bag on the floor and took off his glasses and wiped them carefully and meticulously with his clean pocket handkerchief. *He always does that when he's thinking hard.* The words were in Sesina's head, but she made no move and asked no questions.

'You see, Sesina; it's a bit odd; let me explain it to you,' he said after a minute. He bent over the bag and took out *The Night Prowler.* 'These pictures, see the holes in the frame, well they are meant to be clipped onto that picture in my room, *Winter of Despair*, and the two together make a little story.'

Sesina nodded. 'So it's like the Bible, ain't it, sir? You go stealing and then you end up in the river with everyone gawping down at you.' Don't always work like that, though, she thought to herself.

'That's the idea, anyway,' he said as though he had read her thoughts. 'But you see, Sesina, when the body of the late departed Mr Milton-Hayes was found, well then only the one picture was in the room and that's a bit odd. Say what you like about our late departed friend, Sesina, but he was no fool. The picture of *Winter of Despair* with no faces shown, well that wouldn't drive anyone to murder. Strange, isn't it, Sesina?'

Perhaps not, thought Sesina. An idea had suddenly come to her, but she moved it to the back of her mind until she would have time to think about it. She opened the door for him, but said nothing. There was such a palpable degree of excitement about him that she did not want to interrupt him. She just closed the door quietly and went to follow him back up the stairs to his study. As she came to the landing, the doorbell rang. She hesitated for a minute looking down into the hall. It was not her business normally to answer the doorbell, but she knew that Dolly was busy in the kitchen, helping Mrs Barnett with the dinner.

After another minute of hesitation, she went back down the stairs. After all, officially, she was supposed to be polishing the hall table. Mr Wilkie had disappeared up the next flight of stairs towards his study.

Feeling irritated and disappointed, she went down the stairs and opened the hall door. And then, when she saw who was standing there, her irritation turned to fear. Inspector Field was standing there and there was a very grim look on his face, and when he saw Sesina it became even grimmer.

'Ah, so there you are,' he said and then he gave a grunt. An unpleasant sound. Just as though he were saying, Now I have you. 'So there you are, young lady,' he said in that same unpleasant fashion. 'Take me up to your mistress.'

Sesina bobbed an acknowledgement, but she felt quite uneasy. She led the way up the stairs, though she thought that he could have found his way easily by himself. She was halfway up, when she thought that she should have left him in the downstairs parlour and then gone to see whether Mrs Collins was at home and willing to receive him. It was too late to change her mind, though. He had said, 'Take me to your mistress' and she had done what she was told. You have to obey the police, she told herself silently, but she was uneasy about the whole business.

When they reached Mrs Collins' sitting room, Sesina knocked and then instantly went in, shutting the door behind her and leaving the policeman standing on the landing.

'I'm sorry, ma'am,' she said in a low voice, crossing the room and standing beside Mrs Collins' chair. 'That policeman followed me up the stairs. I couldn't stop him.' She spoke in a low voice and she knew that he wouldn't be able to hear her. Might as well tell a lie. Nearly the truth anyway.

Mrs Collins looked quite startled. She had been sitting, looking into the fire, her handkerchief in her hand and when she jumped to her feet, a book slid off her knees. She hadn't been reading it, although it was open, and she looked quite surprised when it fell on to the floor. Sesina picked it up. She knew it well. It usually reposed on Mrs Collins' bedside table; it was the life of her husband written by her son Wilkie and it almost always made his widow cry. Worse than ever today when she was so worried about Mr Charles.

'I'm sorry, ma'am,' she repeated and this time she meant it. That inspector was a nuisance, tormenting the poor woman.

He had the brass nerve to follow her in. Just opened the door and strode in. Sesina bobbed and made for the door, but he put his back to it.

'Stay where you are, my girl,' he said in an unpleasant way. 'I'd like to have a word with you, if you please.'

There was something about the way that he said it, that made her stiffen. She thought that she might be able to guess what was coming, but she straightened her spine. *Stick to a lie to the bitter end*; her friend Isabella used to say that. Isabella was dead now, poor thing, but she hadn't deserved that death. No one deserved death before their time. God sent enough deaths from disease and from hunger without people lending a hand with murders and hangings.

'Yes, sir.' She said the words very quietly and stood with her hands folded in front of her and her eyes fixed upon him. *Look innocent and sound innocent, sound all shocked and surprised.* Another one of Isabella's sayings. Though she had to admit that Isabella would have been a bit scornful to know that Sesina was taking a chance, not for her own benefit, but just for the son of her employer. Still, poor fellow, he wasn't able to look after himself. In any case, he didn't do it. Sesina was sure of that and a little giggle surfaced as she imagined how shocked the policeman would be if he knew what she was thinking. It wasn't in Mr Charley to murder someone. She didn't think so, anyway. Not unless he was driven to despair. She did her best to keep her mind on him, on his red-gold curls and his sky-blue eyes. Perhaps if she saved his life he might marry her and she could become a lady. Worth a little dream, wasn't it? Marrying her would be better for him than getting himself hanged, in any case. She took the policeman's hat as he dumped it on the table and held it in her hand. She'd toss it to the back of the hat stand as soon as she escaped, she thought viciously.

'Now, then, young lady, what do you mean by telling me that Mrs Gummidge came here and that she went into Mr Charles Collins' painting studio?'

Sesina widened her eyes at him. 'What do I mean by . . .?' She stared at him with as stupid an expression as she could manage.

'You were telling lies, weren't you?'

'No, sir.' Just as well that it wasn't poor little Becky. She herself could happily spend half an hour like this if he wanted to waste his time, but Becky would go to pieces. Still, thought Sesina, Becky would go to pieces anyway, lie or no lie. There were people like that. Would swear black was white as soon as they got frightened. The police didn't like people like that. So Old Mikey had told her once. Said he always pretended to be half-witted if the police picked him up. Said the police didn't like half-wits. Always afraid that a judge might interfere, might ask a question, or might start listening to the evidence, might suddenly wake up and take notice, ask a question and then might get another answer out of them. Make everything start all over again when that happened, according to Old Mikey.

'And so, Mrs Gummidge came in and went into that painting room belonging to Mr Charles Collins.'

'That's right, sir.' Sesina did her best to sound a bit half-witted, but, in reality, she was bewildered. Had he forgotten that it was Becky who was supposed to have admitted the woman? She stayed very still though, and stared at him with her wide-eyed stare of innocence.

He stared back. And then he looked across at Mrs Collins.

'Could you send for the other girl, Mrs Collins?'

'Certainly, inspector. Fetch her, Sesina.'

Yes, thought Sesina as she rapidly slipped from the room before the inspector could insist on the bell being rung, or even on fetching Becky himself. Yes, Mrs Collins had realized that this story accounted for the blood on Mr Charles's painting coat. She knew that she had to back it up. The woman, thought Sesina admiringly, would have been good on the stage. Said that in just the right way. A bit offended, like. A hint of the *all my servants can be trusted, sir* and a slight suggestion that he was taking up a lot of her time over a matter that was really nothing to do with the household in Hanover Terrace. And it was clever to allow Sesina to have an opportunity of reminding Becky what to say.

There was a sound of a scrubbing brush coming up the basement stairs from the scullery and Sesina avoided the kitchen and went past the door as quietly as she could. No sense in involving Mrs B. or that nosy Dolly. This was something that she had to manage on her own.

Becky was washing the floor of the scullery. She had forgotten the goose grease again and her hands were bright red from the harsh lye in the kitchen soap. Her apron was filthy and there was a smear of something across one cheek bone. Sesina surveyed her. She looked a poor little scrap. Just right. Leave the dirty apron on, she decided. It gave just the right impression.

'Got some good news for you, Becky,' she said. 'The mistress is going to give you some more work here. Bit more money for you, Becky, but first you must tell about opening the door to Mrs Gummidge and about her going into Mr Charles's bedroom and all that.' She ran through the words, whispering them in Becky's ear as they went rapidly up the stairs.

'Here's Becky, ma'am.' Sesina gave a perfunctory knock, opened the door almost immediately, took the girl by the wrist and led her into the room. Mrs Collins, she noticed with admiration, had picked up her book and seemed to be immersed in it, while the inspector was reduced to gazing out of the window at the miserably dripping bare-branched trees in the park beyond. 'Here's Becky, ma'am,' she repeated as her mistress had not raised her eyes from her book.

Mrs Collins said nothing in reply, but she placed a book-mark on the open book in front of her, taking great care to line up the leather marker with the direct centre of the page. And then slowly and gravely she looked towards the policeman.

Inspector Field looked taken aback. Not used to being frozen out like this. Not sure about Becky, either. That was good. She did look a bit half-witted. He wasn't sure whether she would be much good as a witness. Sesina kept a smile off her face with difficulty.

'Will I ask her, sir?' she said humbly and saw him nod with relief.

'Now, Becky, listen to me very carefully. Did you open the door to Mrs Gummidge and take her upstairs to Mr Charles's painting room?' Sesina spoke loudly and very clearly, spacing her words out in order to make her question as easily understood as possible.

'No, I never!' The words spurted out of the girl's mouth and then she started to cry, giving terrified looks across at Mrs Collins.

Sesina was taken aback for the moment, but then she rallied.

'Don't cry, Becky. It doesn't matter,' she said compassion-
ately as Becky smeared her face even more atrociously with
the back of her filthy hand. She flicked a quick glance at her
mistress. 'She's worried because she's not supposed to open
the door,' she said to the policeman in a piercing whisper.

'Don't be upset, Becky,' said Mrs Collins. 'Dry your eyes
and answer the question.'

Becky mopped her face with her sacking apron and looked
at Sesina. Sesina gave her an encouraging nod.

'You opened the door because you were cleaning the hall
and you were just right next to the door, didn't you, Becky?'

A nod. Sesina persevered.

'And there was a lady standing there, wasn't there, Becky?'

Another nod. Sesina began to despair. This was no good.
He wasn't going to believe this. She threw caution to the winds
and staked all on a final throw.

'Tell's about it, Becky,' she said.

A blank stare.

Sesina put her hand in her apron pocket. One of Mr Wilkie's
sweets. She fumbled with finger and thumb, managed to get
it out. And, by some miracle, it was a peppermint candy. Great
smell, peppermint! Sesina rolled it in her hot hand and the
gorgeous sharp perfume came out and across to poor hungry
little Becky. She sniffed. Her face brightened.

'I 'member,' she said. 'Missus Gummidge.'

'That's right, Becky.' Sesina spoke loudly and clearly,
spacing out her words as though speaking to a half-wit.
Becky, she knew, was not a half-wit, but terror could make her
seem like one. She cursed herself that she had ever involved
the girl. At the time it had seemed like a good idea. She and
Isabella had always called on the other to back up a lie.

'That's right, Becky, you remember Mrs Gummidge, don't
you? What did she ask you?' That was about as far as she
could go. She rubbed the sweet again trying to subdue her
tension and once again the flavour of mint and of cinnamon
spice flooded out.

And it worked! Becky's dirty little face brightened, again.
'I 'member,' she said. 'Mrs Gummidge.' Another long pause,

but then Becky found her wits. 'Mrs Gummidge ask me 'bout Mr Charles's painting room. Took her in.'

'And so she went into the painting room. What was she doing there, Becky?'

That was a bit too much for Becky. There was another silence and Sesina trembled. But in desperation she continued to roll the sweet in her hand and to release the fragrance into the air.

'Puttin' back the painting coat – all rolled up.' Becky had said it. The words were out now and Sesina breathed a silent prayer that no further questions would be put. She scanned the inspector's face. It bore a look of confusion. He was wondering whether to interrogate the witness. He had lifted his chin, looking alertly across the room and then he dropped his chin again, took out his notebook and his pencil, licked the pencil, scribbled in the notebook for a moment and then put both of them away. Even the suspicious Inspector Field seemed to recognize that Becky was not the kind to tell a lie easily. Sesina swallowed a sigh of relief and glanced at her mistress.

'Take Becky back to the kitchen, now, Sesina,' said Mrs Collins. 'Thank you, Becky.'

'Thank you, ma'am,' said Sesina. She nudged Becky and the girl came out with a perfect imitation of Sesina's tones. 'Thank you, ma'am,' she said.

As soon as they were outside of the door, Sesina gave her a hug, popped the sweet into her mouth, shut the basement door upon her and then went back upstairs to find Mr Wilkie.

He was in his study and he had lined two of the walls with the five pictures and was sitting and staring at them. He showed no surprise at seeing her come in again.

'Can you read, Sesina?' he asked.

'Yes, of course I can.' Sesina was indignant at the question. *And I can write a better hand than you can, sir*, but these words were only uttered within her mind. He'd probably laugh, but then, again, he mightn't. No point in trusting the gentry-folk too far.

'Who taught you?' He seemed genuinely interested.

'I learnt a bit at the working house, but really it was Mrs

Morson, sir, when I was in Urania Cottage. She taught all of the girls to read and to write. Me and Isabella learnt ever so quick. We could even do a good match for her handwriting.'

'Yes, I remember the handwriting. And I remember Isabella.' He was silent after he said that.

But, of course, he didn't remember Isabella. A dead body tells you nothing about a person, tells no secrets. Still Sesina didn't want to contradict him. Pointless, anyway, thinking about Isabella. Wouldn't bring her back. What Mr Wilkie needed to do was to concentrate on his brother, make him pull himself together. Deny everything. She might have delayed matters a bit with that lie about Mrs Gummidge, but it wouldn't last. The woman would probably find a witness. Someone who would swear that she had not gone out that morning, something like that. It was always easy to find a witness if you had a bit of money.

Mr Wilkie had plumped himself down on his chair, taken off his glasses and put a hand over his eyes. Suffered with his eyes, he did. Used to take laudanum to ease the pain of them.

'Now, Sesina, read me out the name of each of these six pictures and I'll do my best to tell you what I know of them. We'll be two detectives on the case of the murdered artist. What do you think, Sesina? Do you think that we could crack open this murder between us? Now read me the first one.'

'*The Night Prowler*,' she said instantly. Might as well give him an easy one for a start.

'Well, I do believe, my fellow detective, that the prowling gentleman, candle in hand, is, in all probability, the noble lord, Lord Douglas, son of the Earl of Ennis. And that the lady, standing on guard, is probably dear little Florence Gummidge. What say you?'

'The picture could be of them all right,' said Sesina thoughtfully. 'But do you think that they would have done that, really done it? It'd be a norful risk, wouldn't it? Anybody could have spotted them creeping around in the dark. Not as if they was married, is it?'

'My dear little Sesina, much as I hate to disturb your sweet innocence, I have to tell you that in these country house affairs, men and women do, often, creep around in the middle of the night, and, no, they are seldom or ever married to each other. Married, yes! Married to each other, no!'

Sesina smiled. Mr Wilkie was fun when he was in that sort of mood.

'So no one would take any notice if they saw them,' she said, nodding her head to show that she understood the rules that these gentry played by.

'Precisely. The sport of creeping around corridors at night is about the only thing that makes these country house week-ends seem endurable. Though I have to hand it to Lord Douglas. He seems to have been somewhat more enterprising, if our late lamented friend, Edwin Milton-Hayes, is correct. He turned what was a sport for the rest of us, into a lucrative way of life. Made a good living out of it, Sesina!'

Sesina brooded for a moment. She didn't quite understand all of the long words that he used, but she could see the sense of this. Lord Douglas and Florence Gummidge were making a nice little heap of money for themselves by stealing jewellery, instead of just getting up to whatever hanky panky the rest of them got up to.

'Clever,' she said admiringly. 'I suppose all the ladies bring their best jewels to these affairs.'

'And their ugliest heirlooms, handed down to them by long dead grandmothers and great-grandmothers. On the whole, the size of the diamond and the quality of the cut means more than any mere decorative value, Sesina, so if ever you go in for stealing diamonds, remember that the necklace or the brooch or the tiara will have to be taken to pieces and so it's not a question of how pretty the whole thing looks, but how big the rocks, the diamonds, I mean, or sapphires or emeralds. All of them worth stealing, Sesina. And let me give you another piece of advice. If you see a string of pearls just test it before you steal it. And this is how to find out if a pearl is real, just lightly rub it against the front of your tooth – not against the edge of your tooth, Sesina, you don't want to scratch the pearl. Now if it's the real thing the pearl should feel gritty to your tooth.'

Sesina thought about this. He seemed to know plenty about stealing diamonds and pearls. A little thrill ran through her.

Perhaps Mr Wilkie was thinking of going in for something like that. He might get her a position in a rich person's house in the country, a place that had lots of visitors with jewels.

'But Mr Milton-Hayes' painting would put a stop to this game,' he went on. 'And so he, Mr M-H had to be wiped out of the picture, to coin a phrase. Makes sense, doesn't it, Sesina? Good pun, too, isn't it?'

She nodded. 'It makes sense, sir.'

'Good,' he said. 'Let's hope that I can gently lead our good friend, the inspector, to consider that money is the root of all evil. Now, speaking of that, what about that painting, *Root of All Evil*, what do you make of that, Sesina?'

Sesina considered the painting. Not as interesting as *The Night Prowler*, she thought. That had been a very exciting picture to think about. 'It's just a woman playing cards, sir,' she explained, noting that he had shut his eyes again. His spectacles were dangling from his waistcoat pocket, held only by one arm of the frame. Gently she removed them and placed them on his table. 'She's betting, sir, on the cards.' And then when he made no answer, she glanced away from the picture and at him. There was a smile curving his lips. He was getting stout. His stomach was beginning to stick out like that of an old man. Didn't keep himself nice and slim like his brother. Little fellow, too. Not like her Charley. He still said nothing so she looked back at the picture again. 'I think it looks like it could be Mrs Jordan. She was sitting next to you at the table, sir. She does her hair that way. I noticed it when I was serving.' And then, when he still said nothing, she said decisively, 'I don't think it would be her, do you, Mr Wilkie?'

'Could be.' He pursed up his lips.

'I don't think so. It's a mug's game, this betting,' she said, 'but it's her own business. Her own money, unless she stole it.'

'Ah but she did, Sesina, she did. She's a married woman. Her money belongs to her husband and he will divorce her if she spends it without his permission. He'll go to court and ask the court for a divorce and then she won't be a married woman anymore. And she won't have any money at all then, perhaps just enough to keep her from starvation. He's threatened it. So I have heard.'

'She might be better off without him,' said Sesina. 'It wouldn't be much fun being married to a man who didn't want you to have a bit of excitement. If I was her, I'd empty the house first and then clear off myself. Hire a van and take away all of the stuff. Start up again somewhere new. Go to another city. That's what I'd do.' She giggled a little as she remembered the time that she had stolen a bed, wheeled it down Ludgate Hill. 'She'd get plenty of money if the furniture is good stuff and her husband sells paintings, don't he? Well, then she could grab a few of them and sell them on the quiet. The carpets, too. I bet they are worth a lot. And the curtains, probably pure velvet. She'd get a nice sum for the whole lot. And who knows, she might get lucky at the cards. Someone has to win, don't they, sir?'

'Well, then, Sesina, we cross Mrs Helen Jordan off from our list, do we?'

He was looking amused and interested, she was glad to see. He needed stirring up, too sleepy half the time. They had to save Mr Charles. Wouldn't cross anyone off, if I was him, she thought, but then she moved on to the next picture.

'What about this *Forbidden Fruit*, sir? Don't make sense to me.'

'I think that the gentleman you see here wants to marry that very young lady and her parents say no. She's too young to get married without her parents' consent.'

People who have plenty of money worry about the most stupid things, thought Sesina. Aloud, she said, 'That's Mr Hamilton, ain't it? Nothing to stop him and her telling a few lies to a parson and getting married. Or else go off together and then the parents will come around quick, I can tell you that.'

'So you won't put your sixpence on Mr Hamilton, then, will you, Sesina.'

She shook her head vigorously. She knew where that sixpence should go, but she didn't want to say it, even to Mr Wilkie.

'Den of In . . . what's that word, sir?'

'In-i-qui-ty; that's the way to pronounce it, I think,' he said and she was pleased that he didn't make a game of her, but said it very seriously, just like he was working it out for himself. 'Just a long word that stands for good, old-fashioned wickedness. Do you recognize the man there, Sesina? Does it look like anyone who was at the dinner?'

Sesina gazed at the picture. Her first instinct was to say no, but then an idea came to her. She walked a bit nearer to the picture and inspected it carefully.

'Not so easy, is it, Sesina, to identify the man.' He sounded as though he knew and Sesina felt annoyed. Her mind went over the guests at Mrs Collins' dinner party. And then, suddenly, the solution flashed into her mind.

'It's the clothes, innit? He changed his clothes.'

'Not surprising, is it? Not the sort of clothes he wears every day, are they?' He laughed a little to himself.

Sesina felt annoyed. So he had guessed before she had. And she prided herself on her quick wits and there he was, half asleep, peering across the room with his little watery, screwed-up eyes. But the man in the picture did look so different. The clothes were that of a dock worker. He even wore a cap on his head, just half hiding the grey hair. Painted well that hair. She had stood behind him at dinner and had noticed the hair as he grabbed at the brandy. And there he was lying on that broken old bed. Filthy place! Smoke everywhere, almost hiding the figures sprawled on the beds. It was a very murky picture. The lamps, the pipes, the glass tubes, they stood out almost more than the customers. She had to say that the artist, that man Mr Milton-Hayes, was a good painter. He had just the right shade of grey on the bedsheets. A few stains, here and there, too. She knew what they were. She could almost smell the place!

'Wonder how he got hold of the clothes?' Mr Wilkie had got up and was staring at the picture, standing beside her.

'That's easy,' she said, glad of the opportunity to sound scornful. 'Bought them up Monmouth Street way. Wouldn't cost much, not old rags like them.' Rapidly she worked out how he would have managed it. Easy enough, she thought, picturing the scene. 'Wouldn't need to disguise himself, neither, could pretend that they were for charity,' she said aloud and saw from the twinkle in his eye that he had guessed her meaning. And then a memory dawned. 'Saw an old geezer like that near Dorset Square on the day that Mr Milton-Hayes was croaked,' she said. She was wondering whether to mention a name or to keep it to herself when the sound of a bell came through the doorway.

'Three bells, that's for you, Sesina. Well, you're in favour with my mother these days, aren't you? Better watch out or else Dolly will be poisoning you.'

In good form now, she thought as she went towards the door. She didn't bother laughing at his little joke. 'I'll put my sixpence on *Den of Iniquity* and the man dressed up in the old clothes, Mr Wilkie,' she said as she went out. She looked back at him and saw him turn his eyes from her. By the time that she closed the door, he was up close to the picture, scrutinizing it intently. Should keep him occupied for a while, she thought as she went down the stairs as quietly as she could.

SIXTEEN

Wilkie Collins, *Hide and Seek*:
. . . the smoke from the chimney-pots was lost mysteriously in deepening superincumbent fog; the muddy gutters gurgled; the heavy rain-drops dripped into empty areas audibly. No object great or small, no out-of-door litter whatever appeared anywhere, to break the dismal uniformity of line and substance in the perspective of the square. No living being moved over the watery pavement . . .

I thought about Milton-Hayes, and his change of name, during my walk that evening. It had begun to rain and I put up my umbrella, and then smiled to myself as I remembered Dickens looking at the name of the maker and berating me for not buying it in Burlington Arcade. The canon, I was sure, would not make a mistake like that. All of his clerical clothes, his umbrella, his stick, his top hat, all seemed to say 'money' and 'upper class'. But there was one thing that was not so easy to purchase and that he had perhaps retained from a former life.

It had not been a very useful interview. We had got very little out of the canon. He had appeared to be slightly offended by our questions, inclined to dismiss the whole matter as not having much to do with him. Had been certain that the choice of subject matter was left to the artist. Would never dream of telling a man how to do his own business. Had just stipulated that the subject matter should be instructive and moralistic. Pure chance had led him to the artist. Had heard his name mentioned. Had heard good reports of him. Could not remember now who had mentioned the name Milton-Hayes. 'But,' said the canon blandly, 'it was not a name to be forgotten.' Had there been a slight note of amusement in his voice when he said that?

That accent. Carefully enunciated as most of his words were, from time to time, the accent slipped. Rutter was his name. Canon Rutter. I had a feeling that I had come across that name before now, and I remembered that it was in a law case that I had been reading up when I was studying at Lincoln's Inn. Yes, it had been a dispute over an inheritance in the county of Essex. 'Rutter' I seemed to remember had been a popular name in Essex and there was an ambiguity about the will which left a substantial sum to a Tom Rutter and did not mention an address, thereby leaving the field open to a considerable number of Tom Rutters and of Thomas Rutters and even, I seemed to remember, a Thomasina Rutter. Yes, an Essex name. And someone had said that name to me recently and it was not in conjunction with the canon. I searched my mind for that elusive memory while repeating the name 'Rutter' over and over again to myself.

Strange name, I thought. Just as well that the good canon was not a schoolmaster. Even so, I could imagine that the small boys of his parish would have a lot of fun with a name like Rutter which could so easily have been turned into 'Ratter'.

Enough to make any man change his name! Still deep in thought, I emerged from under my umbrella to check on the sky.

And then I had an inspiration. It was Piggott, my yachting friend, who had mentioned that he thought Milton-Hayes was an assumed name, something to do with 'Jack Russell' . . . A Jack Russell is a game little dog who loved to hunt rats. Ratter/Rutter. Had Milton-Hayes, who was from Essex, originally borne the name of 'Rutter'?

And had there been an uneasiness in the canon's manner when we had asked him about when he first met Milton-Hayes? I resolved to think hard and to have a credible hypothesis by the time that I met my friend.

Dickens and I were going to the theatre and we were to meet at Drury Lane. I knew all of those streets below Regent's Park, to the north of Oxford Street and to the east towards Bloomsbury very well and could steer a course through small streets and terraces towards St Giles, taking short cuts where another man might not have ventured.

Nevertheless, since the rain was really quite heavy, I hailed a cab when I came out of the gate to my mother's house. It was vile and smelly, full of dirty straw and so once we reached Tottenham Court Road and I saw how the rain faded into the normal sheets of fog I rapped on the roof of the cab and took out my purse. I would, I decided, be as quick walking as sitting in that evil-smelling darkness with the horse proceeding at a slow walking pace. I would enjoy the walk and I would use the time to ponder over the possibility of Milton-Hayes having a connection to Canon Rutter.

And yet as I went along the foggy street, I was uneasy. There had been a cab behind mine and it had stopped when my man had stopped. I had looked at it idly, as I paid the man, but no one had descended from it. Nevertheless, I thought from time to time that I heard some people behind me. But every time that I stopped to listen, I could hear no sound; the heavy silent blanket of the fog drowned all sounds. I would stop and then walk on, feeling as though I were enveloped in an enormous cloud and totally cut off from the rest of mankind.

It was, I realized soon, an exceptionally severe fog and it seemed to have driven others off the street. Occasionally a cab passed me, going very slowly, bearing passengers, no doubt, as the driver did not respond to the signal from my raised umbrella. Or perhaps, an empty cab whose driver had decided to make for his home and his fire and was resolute that he would take no more passengers. And so I walked on, alone in a mist-enclosed silence.

But not complete silence. My ears, straining for sound, seemed to hear something now, the sound of something coming nearer. I was hearing footsteps coming steadily behind me, stopping occasionally – stopping, I thought, when I had turned to face them, but then proceeding on in a cautious manner. I dawdled on purpose, and then I, too, stopped. I stepped into a doorway and waited. There was a slight diminution in the density of the fog, sounds were clearer in the still air and now I could definitely hear footsteps. I waited, standing concealed in the deep doorway and waited for the footsteps to come nearer and nearer. Definitely more than one person.

I peered anxiously out into the white mist. I was no hero

and would always prefer to avoid trouble than to meet it bravely. I resolved that if they wanted my purse I would hand it over instantly and allow them to go on their way.

But when they came into view, I could see nothing to disturb my equanimity and so I walked on briskly. Two young gentlemen, rather the worse for wear, probably after a bottle of wine too much, wobbled into sight a few times and then fell behind again. Faint sounds of drunken laughter came to me as I walked on hastily. From time to time, I heard a few lines of a ribald song, intoned in a tuneless fashion. And then sudden silences, dissolving eventually into a fit of drunken laughter. Nothing to worry about, I told myself. I had been like that when I was a young student and I could remember the hilarity when a well-dressed, middle-aged gentleman, as I must now appear, turned around to face us.

Nevertheless, I quickened my step, walking smartly and quickly, swinging my umbrella and keeping a sharp look-out for another cab. The fog was now nothing but a damp inconvenience and soon the cabs should be out again. I should have kept that man, though his vehicle did smell so vile.

No cab came my way, however, and I decided to take a short cut through one of the alleyways, a narrow, filthy place, lined with decaying, crumbling buildings. I had shown this place to Dickens lately and he had exclaimed, telling me that he wanted to use it in his writing, saying that it was ideal for a scene that he had in mind for his next story. I thought now of my own book, of the background of one of the characters and of how he had fought the natives out in the wilds of America. The terror and uneasiness I had gone through during the last ten minutes should help me to experience his feelings while he was being stealthily tracked by revenge-filled men. I smiled a little to myself at the idea of equating an evening walk in the familiar streets of north London with the stealing through wilderness with a gang of cut-throat savages wishing to take my scalp. Still, I had learned that when writing the smallest of experiences were like gold in the safe. They could be drawn upon whenever the writer chose to dip into these hidden resources.

However, I seemed to have lost my followers in the fog and

I would now have to do my best to recollect my feelings of apprehension, of strained ears and of widened apprehensive eyes that could see nothing; of the sensation that every fibre in my body was awake, ears listening, legs slightly weak, lips dry and eyes trying to penetrate the gloom around me. Yes, that had been the way that I had felt. I felt pleased with myself as words and sentences flooded into my mind. I walked on, rapidly, my boots ringing on the broken paving slabs, trying as hard as I could to relive my earlier feelings so that when I sat down to work in the dark hours of the night, I would have a storage chest of sensations to call upon. Dickens had praised the descriptive passages in my published novel, *Basil*, but I had an uneasy feeling that *Hide and Seek* was not going to be as good, not going to garner as much praise from the critics. I needed to feel it more intensely as I was scribbling the words on the slip of paper, to experience it and I needed to live through it as I had lived through the agonies of mind and body when I was writing *Basil*. I walked a little faster and tried to summon those feelings of terror, the panic felt by the hunted as his pursuers gained upon him.

For a moment I thought that my imagination had begun to work overtime. But no. Surely these were actual footsteps behind me. Surely a muted whisper was carried upon the still air.

And then I realized that the footsteps and the whisper were real. Not the sound of drunken carousers, now, but the stealthy cautious movements of a pursuer. Not out in the wilds of America, but walking through the streets of north London. Quickly I began to run, stumbling along, one hand holding my hat to my head, the other holding out the fragile umbrella like a weapon. I cast a terrified look over my shoulder. They were behind me, had cast all caution to the winds now. They had lulled me into a false sense of security, but now that I had chosen a deserted alleyway, they had no fear now of bystanders. Both were undoubtedly following me, running with the long steps of fit and athletic young men. We were less than halfway down the small deserted alleyway and I knew that there was little hope of any help from those unfortunate creatures who might be sheltering within the broken

walls and gaping roofs of the buildings on either side of me.
It took a brave and confident man to come between a pursuer
and his prey on a night like this.

Nevertheless, I shouted 'help' as loudly as I could. Another
glance over my shoulder confirmed that they were almost on
top of me. One of them flashed a light from a bullseye lantern
which he wore at his waist. Not drunk, certainly not drunk,
not some poor wretches who would be satisfied with a few
coins from my purse. These men were dressed in respectable
ulsters, capes draped over shoulders and silk scarves tucked
in around their necks. But chillingly illuminated by the lantern,
both had fixed smiles upon their faces.

And before I could shout again, one of them was beside
me, his hand over my mouth. I did not struggle, but stood
very still. He flicked the silk scarf from the folds of his ulster
and slipped it around my neck. I choked as the noose tightened,
dropped my umbrella and tried to work my fingers inside the
smooth silk, struggled as hard as I could, but to no avail. My
throat hurt and I could hardly draw a breath. I remembered
reading once that silk is the strongest of all materials and now
I found it impossible to tear it from my neck. I heard one say
something about teaching him a lesson and the other said the
one word 'careful'. And then I felt my senses begin to ebb
and I knew that I was on the point of death. I began to sag.
The smooth feeling of the silk was now beneath my chin and
I drew in a deep breath and hung there, dizzy and almost
unconscious. They were laughing about something. My hands.

'Dinky little hands,' said one.

And the other said fiercely, 'Shut up, Toby.'

I made no move. My life, I knew, hung on a thread. The
strong silk scarf tightened a little around my neck, but then it
was loosened.

'Listen to me, little gentleman.' The voice in my ear was
rough, uncultured and did not appear to fit well with the silk
scarf and the respectable tweed ulster. I made no move and
resisted the impulse to raise my hands in order to release
the choking grip around my neck.

'Shine that glim over here, Toby,' said the man and the
bullseye lantern flashed its light. My captor was still holding

the scarf, drawn tightly around my neck, but with his other hand he reached into the pocket of his ulster and drew something out. He held it to the beam from the lantern. I blinked the moisture from my eyes and then, very gingerly, I reached up and took off my spectacles. My hands were free and I was able to rub the glass clean on the smooth silk of the noose that had been drawn around my neck. I replaced them.

'That's better,' I said and I forced a note of insouciance into my voice.

My captor gave a quick chuckle.

'Game little cock bird, ain't you?' he said.

I drew in a short breath through my aching throat and hoped that the worst might be over. Now let them search my pockets, take all of my money and release me.

They didn't though. There was more to come. Once more the silken noose was drawn up to the height of the man's head. I rose as high as I could, standing on the tips of my toes until the calves of my legs ached and my eyes once again wept tears of agony. I swayed there for a moment and then, just as I felt that I was losing consciousness, he loosened his grip and allowed me to sink back upon my feet again. I stood very still and did not attempt this time to wipe my eyes, just blinked, squeezed them tightly and allowed the water to trickle down past my cheek bones. I stood as quietly as I could and thought about my mother and about Charley.

The bullseye lantern still seared through the fog and lit up the blue and green threads on the second man's ulster. He, too, wore a silk scarf. I looked up at my captor. His hand was in his pocket now. He brought it out and displayed a short, stout stick.

'See here, see this cudgel,' he said hoarsely. 'Just you look at that, my little man. See the horseshoe nails hammered into the top of it. Now if I was to tap you on that great big head of yours, just a couple of good bangs, well, you know what would happen to them horseshoe nails?'

He didn't wait for an answer and I had none to give him, just stood there, feeling the sick dizziness getting worse and trying hard not to vomit.

'Not so talkative now, is he, Toby? Well, I'll tell you what would happen. They're short, little nails, you see and if I hit that bonze of yours well and hard, right against that big bulging forehead, well, these little nails would pop out with the force of the blow, go right into your head and they would go straight into your brain. And what sort of a state would you be in, then? What do you think?'

I made no answer. There was something horrible, something deeply frightening about his words and as I visualized the short, sharp little horseshoe nails shooting forth from the blunt-ended cudgel, and killing my brain, I felt my head almost split open with the force of my revulsion.

'What do you want from me?' I was conscious of how my voice shook with sheer terror and how the question came out in a high squeaky tone. But I did not care. All I could think of now was to get away from these well-dressed creatures of horror and to give them what they wanted.

'We wants you to keep your trap shut. You've been sticking your nose into matters that don't concern you,' said the man with the lantern.

'And now we're telling you to stop, to stop if you know what's good for you.' The second man swung the small stout cudgel in his hand and made a quick strike with it in mid-air. I flinched, jerked back, felt the silk scarf tighten around my neck and then stood very still. They both laughed, rough chuckles, and I felt ashamed of my cowardice. It was no good, though. I could not be what I never had been. There were two of them and each was almost a foot higher than I was. I looked down at my small, ladylike hands.

'Very well, then,' I said mildly.

That seemed to take them aback. They had expected questions, perhaps even some bravado and now they were at a loss for words.

'Very well,' I said. 'I'll do whatever you tell me. Tell me what I have to do.'

'Stop goin' around an' asking questions,' said Toby.

'Very well,' I said for the third time. And as they were still nonplussed, I said, rather daringly, 'May I go now?'

They were looking at each other. Unsure. Paid men; I had no doubt. Not too certain about their instructions. Violence and threats came easily, but now they didn't know what the next step should be.

And then all doubts were resolved. The still air that descends on the city with the advent of fog now seemed to be fragmented. A sharp, ear-splitting, high-pitched note from a police whistle rent the air. Quite a distance away, I guessed, but I didn't hesitate, but put two fingers to my lips. When I was twelve years old, an Italian boy had taken me in hand and taught me all the tricks that he and his friends had learnt. And one of them was to imitate a police whistle.

And the response came instantly. A perfect chorus of whistles. The police, and I blessed their benign presence, were out in force that night.

'Croak him, croak him quick!' hissed Toby, but his friend was more circumspect. He didn't reply. He snatched the silk scarf from my neck and took to his heels, sliding through a gap between the crumbling buildings, like a rat escaping from a pack of terriers. Toby followed him.

But I did not. I was no hero and so I once again put my fingers to my lips and blew the shrill note as loudly as I could possibly manage. My legs trembled and I felt that if I ran I would fall down, but leaning upon my umbrella I did my best to walk steadily. I was determined only to get out of this pestilent alleyway and never again would I walk in such places, alone and late at night. I stumbled along but fear drove my unsteady legs and eventually I was out in the main street. Once again I blew hard upon my fingers and then I waited for my rescuers.

Never was a sight more welcome than when they rounded the corner and advanced towards me, cudgels at the ready. Inspector Field and men. I hadn't ever cared very much for the man, and during these last days I had feared and hated him as a possible destroyer of my brother's liberty and life, but now when I saw Inspector Field I greeted him with great relief.

'Mr Collins, what's the matter, sir? Have you been attacked?' His concern seemed genuine and I realized that I was of importance as the friend of the famous Mr Dickens, a man whose name was on all lips and who, above all, had

written an article about Inspector Field and about the great
work that he was doing in the slums of London.

'I've been attacked,' I said, with my hand to my throat.
'Almost strangled, in fact.'

'Strangled!' He seized upon the word and I was reminded
of the image of a rat escaping from a terrier. Inspector Field
had barked out that word as though he were a pugnacious
dog.

'That's right. With a silk scarf, of all things.' I tried to laugh.
It was almost laughable, but my voice broke. The feeling of
the blood singing in my ears had been too recent for me to
dismiss the experience in an airy fashion.

Inspector Field did not laugh at the choice of weapon. 'A
silk scarf,' he said and there was a note of intense interest in
his voice. 'Did you hear that, sergeant,' he said and turned his
bullseye lantern upon one of the other policemen.

The sergeant's eyes, illuminated by a blaze of light, widened.
'Silken Sam's lot, were you thinking, inspector,' he said.

'And the other man, a man called Toby, he had a silk scarf,
too.'

Both men looked at each other and one whistled. They
looked all around, but I did not point them in the direction
where my tormentors had disappeared. I was far too shaken
to even think about doing without my protectors for even a
few minutes while they pursued the scoundrels.

Inspector Field, however, had my safety in his mind. 'We've
just passed Mr Dickens, sir. He was walking just by Shorts
Garden. We'll walk back there with you, sir.'

He said no more about Silken Sam and his strange choice
of murder weapon. Inspector Field had never got over
featuring in the daily newspapers as a guardian of the peace
in stories written by the foremost novelist of the day and he
was always eager to supply Mr Dickens with new material
in case he would be at a loss for something to write about. I
said no more, but walked by his side, gingerly feeling my
throat from time to time but relieved and happy to have such
a formidable guard to escort me to Shorts Garden.

Dickens was pacing up and down at the entrance to Shorts
Garden when we arrived. Inspector Field handed me over to

my friend with the air of a mother bringing her son to his first
school.

'Mr Collins has had a shock, sir,' he said solicitously. 'A
very nasty shock. Got held up by a brace of criminals.'

'Silken Sam,' said the sergeant and Inspector Field frowned
heavily at him.

'Don't know if you've heered of Silken Sam, sir, have you?
Gentleman Sam, some calls him, but mostly he's known as
Silken Sam. I'd say that you have heered tell of him, haven't
you, Mr Dickens,' he enquired.

Dickens' eyes burned with interest. 'Silken Sam' sounded
as though he could have stepped out from the pages of one
of his novels. He stopped beneath the gas lamp and took
out his notebook. Then he hastily shoved it back into his coat
pocket and turned to me.

'My poor friend,' he said. 'You must have a brandy. You
look shocked, doesn't he, inspector. Let's all adjourn to my
favourite hostelry. You know the Lamb and Flag, Wilkie.'

I said that I did. I had never heard of it as being a favourite
of Dickens', but he was like that. He had almost an owner-
ship of so many places, so many buildings in London that to
go around with him was to have the sensation of accom-
panying a man through a room full of friends. I listened to the
inspector agreeing that he and the sergeant could spare a few
moments and would be glad to assure themselves that Mr Collins
was no worse for the experience that he had undergone.

'It's the wish of the Metropolitan Police that all citizens can
walk the streets in safety,' he said with a flourish and Dickens
bowed gravely. His face, though, when he looked at me, was
full of curiosity and now that I had recovered from my fright,
I began to feel rather curious myself. My mind was busy as I
followed my friend and the inspector in the direction of the
Lamb and Flag. I noticed that the sergeant walked by my side,
matching his long stride to my short steps. His face, beneath
the brim of his hat, was filled with interest as, from time to
time, he glanced surreptitiously at me. 'Who are you to have
had such an interesting experience?' he seemed to be saying.

The Lamb and Flag was a good choice. A fire blazed with
that good clear red that can only be given by top quality sea

coal. It was too early to have many people there. One of the window tables was occupied, but Dickens, of course, was immediately recognized by the host and was ushered to a table by the fire. He instantly took the seat with its back to the wall. He always did that, I noticed. Seated thus he could see the whole room, watch who came in, inspect interesting faces, overhear scraps of conversation.

I took the seat beside him, leaving the two opposing seats for the inspector and his sergeant. Even so, I noticed, the inspector, under the pretext that his chair wobbled, managed to shift his position so that he, too, could at least keep an eye on the door. The sergeant got up and warmed his hands by the fire, rubbing them hard and casting sharp glances around the room and towards the curtained doorway that led to the kitchen.

However, when the steaming jugum of purl arrived and the landlord filled the four tankards, the sergeant came back and held the fragrant mixture to his nose and though still turning his head from time to time and scrutinizing the room with sharp glances, he gradually relaxed and took part in relating the litany of atrocities committed by my late acquaintance, Silken Sam and his gang.

'Yes, got a whole gang of them, Mr Collins. You was lucky, you know. They reckoned that you would be a soft touch. That would be the way of it. Silken Sam just brought Toby along. Toby is a new boy and he'd be training him, like. Didn't think they'd have any trouble.'

'So why is this ruffian called Silken Sam?' enquired Dickens while I hid a slight annoyance by swallowing a large gulp of the hot ale.

'It's the scarves, you see,' explained the inspector. 'He got a load of them silk scarves once from off a ship at the docks and he didn't sell them all. So every gang member gets to wear one when he goes out on a job.'

'Gives them a classy look,' inserted the sergeant.

'And he dresses them up, smart-like, good coats, hats, fancy sticks, just as though they were a few gentlemen out for a stroll in the evening, just like yourself and Mr Collins, Mr Dickens, sir.'

Dickens gave me a half grin. He had often laughed at me for my untidy and shabby appearance. But he was too interested in Silken Sam to tease me now. In any case, I was interested in the remark about the fancy stick.

'He threatened me. He told me to stop going around and asking questions. He took something out of that stick of his,' I said to the inspector. 'He unscrewed the brass ring on the bottom of the stick and then he took out a small cudgel.'

'Heavy?' asked the inspector with a knowing look. 'It would be that cudgel of his, the one with the nails in it,' he informed the sergeant and then looked across at Dickens to see whether he was impressed.

I shuddered. 'I didn't feel it,' I answered shortly and then took another swig of the ale. I wished that I had some laudanum powder in my pocket. Laudanum and purl made a very soothing beverage, I thought, as I listened to Inspector Field stimulate Dickens' imagination with intriguing details about the life and misdeeds of the individual known to all as 'Silken Sam'. He seemed to have forgotten all about the warning that I had received, perhaps did not quite believe me. I drank some more purl and then some more and felt that the hot ale was dissolving my troubles, clearing my brain of shadowy figures and bringing forth one figure so that he stood out against the background of indistinct figures clustered together in my mother's drawing room.

SEVENTEEN

Wilkie Collins, *Hide and Seek*:
In what precise number of preliminary mental entangle-
ments he involved himself, before arriving at the desired
solution, it would not be very easy to say. As usual, his
thoughts wandered every now and then from his subject
in the most irregular manner;

'Wilkie, wake up, wake up, old fellow. Time for us
to be getting going. We'll miss the opening act
of the play.'

I woke with a start. Dickens' voice in my ear. An empty
table. That was good. I didn't want Inspector Field. Not now.
Not while I still had to work through my thoughts.

'Damn the play,' I said. 'I have more important things to
think of.'

Dickens sighed, smiled, shook his head at me, but put down
the coat that he held in his hands. He sat down again and took
out a cigar. Looked at it and then put it away.

'Oh, come on, Dick,' I said impatiently. 'If you want a cigar
why don't you damn well smoke one? Don't be such a fanatic.
Go mad. Allow yourself three cigars in the day. Just once! Won't
kill you, you know. Just relax. And get me some more of
that purl.'

Dickens laughed quietly to himself. 'No more purl for you,
my young friend. You've had enough. You'll be out in the
middle of the floor challenging all newcomers to a fight to
the death if I get any more of that ale for you. Have a cup of
coffee.' And without waiting for a word from me, he went
off into the bar in search of the landlord.

I sat very still, smiling to myself. My brain was miraculously
clear. I could see it all. The drawing room. The paintings. My
father's landscape. The admiring visitor. There had been something very stagey about that eye glass, I thought. It had been

waved around like a banner proclaiming that its owner was short-sighted and yet, on entering the dining room that night he had picked out his own name, Mr John French, from right across the room, had glanced down the room, and had taken his seat in between the art gallery owner, William Jordan and the beautiful gambler, Mrs Helen Jordan. Perhaps, after all, as soon as he had entered my mother's drawing room, he had seen every detail of the painting with its intriguing title, *Taken in Adultery*, and had, like everyone else in the room, guessed that his own elderly features were hidden behind the mask of white paint, that he was the one looking in through the door at his beautiful, very young wife and her handsome, red-headed, young lover. It must have been a terrible shock to see this picture. John French would have thought that he was safe after he had killed the artist and had destroyed the picture *Winter of Despair* which may have shown the body of his young wife, or perhaps the body of the young man and the girl looking down upon him. The picture had been badly mutilated and it had been extremely difficult to glue the scattered pieces together again. It was impossible to be sure of the identity of the drowned body. Nevertheless, guesses could be made when the other pictures were seen side by side with it. All that it now revealed was that there appeared to be a body floating in the Thames and that an audience stood above on the Hungerford Bridge, looking down upon the corpse. All details had been so slashed and mutilated by the sharp knife that it had proved impossible to identify anyone.

But, nevertheless, I thought that I was beginning to see the truth.

'You're looking very pleased with yourself,' observed Dickens as he came back accompanied by the landlord and the coffee.

I waited, quietly smiling to myself, until the coffee had been poured and we were left to ourselves again.

'I'm doing a bit of thinking around the problem, rather than confronting it full face,' I said grandly.

Dickens raised a sceptical eyebrow and buried the lower end of his face into the mug of coffee. Above the rim, two dark eyes flashed at me, but he said nothing.

'Just thinking the whole matter out logically,' I said and then kept him waiting while I swallowed some coffee. And some more, then some more. It was very strong indeed and I felt that the soft, fuzzy sensation of infallibility began to ebb from my brain. Nevertheless, when I put down the cup I tried to reassemble my thoughts.

'I've been thinking about that threat that ruffian shouted, telling me to stop asking questions. Well, it must be questions about the murder of Milton-Hayes, mustn't it? So who sent him to threaten me? If you or I, Dick, wanted the services of Silken Sam, would we know how to go about summoning him to our presence? What would we do? Put an advertisement in *The Times*? Inquire at our local post office?' I went on devising other ridiculous scenarios but then when I saw that he was getting impatient, I finished up with, 'No, we wouldn't know where to find him, but I wonder would Mr French be able to find him?'

I left a short pause and saw him turn this over in his mind. I waited for a question, but he said nothing and so I went on.

'I do know something, though. Ruskin, or was it Millais, one of Charley's friends, anyway told me once about the origins of the very rich Mr French.' Whichever it was, Ruskin or Millais, I remembered thinking at the time that he was telling me in the hopes that I would warn my brother against this affair with pretty little Molly French. 'French wasn't born rich. He was just a clerk as a young man,' I went on. 'Just a clerk working down at the docks. Noting down deliveries, all that sort of thing.'

I waited again for the question but as he still said nothing, I supplied it myself.

'So how did he become such a rich man? Well, it appears that no one exactly knew. There he was for years, a young clerk, living in lodgings, scurrying to and fro to the docks. And then, ten or fifteen years later, he is living in a big house in Hampstead, servants, butler, housekeeper, groom, everything that money could buy. Everyone could see how rich he was. Perhaps he made money importing goods, but if so, how did he get a start? Where did he get the capital to do that? But,'

I said gravely, 'now listen to this, Dickens, since no one knew how he became so rich, no one knew how he made his first fortune.' I thought back to that conversation months ago. 'I think it was Millais that told me this,' I said slowly. 'I was drunk at the time. I know that we were in that holster near to Lincoln's Inn at the time and Millais tried to persuade me to talk Charley out of the liaison with the pretty little wife. Said that old John French was a dangerous man. I laughed at him at the time. I remember doing that and I remember saying, how could an old codger like that do any harm to a young fellow like Charley who must be a foot taller than him and no more than half his age.'

'And Millais said . . .?' Dickens' voice was dry, but I could tell that he was interested.

'Millais said to me, "Come on, Wilkie! You don't think that a man as rich as John French does his own dirty work".'

'I see,' said Dickens. Once more he took the cigar from his pocket and once again he put it away.

I did not comment this time; just waited for his answer, waited for him to sip his coffee and swallow it.

'Silken Sam,' he said, eventually, and there was a grim note in his voice.

'Exactly,' I said. I put my hand to my neck and felt the bruises on my throat. 'Who knows? They may have known each other for a long time. They were both in business down at the docks, weren't they? I don't know much about that sort of thing, but I'd say that there is money to be made down the docks in two fashions. One would be legally and the other would be illegally.'

'And did you pass on Millais's message?'

I nodded. And then grimaced. It had not been a satisfactory meeting between brothers. Charley was furious with me. Denied everything. I had made a mistake in approaching the whole matter in a cynical, rather jocose manner. I had not realized that he was so deeply in love, so tenderly in love with the girl. I should have been more thoughtful, more diplomatic and then he might have confided in me, instead of trampling all over his young love and driving him to leave the house and slam the door behind him.

'But Charley wasn't attacked. You would have known about that, wouldn't you?'

'No, he wasn't, as far as I know. I've never seen any signs of it. I can only suppose,' I said slowly, 'that Millais and Ruskin and all of that gang of painters knew far more about what was going on than did John French. He may have been quite complacent, may have expected that his wife would be quite content with the splendid carriage, the beautiful house, the silken clothes, the jewels, the servants. It may not have occurred to him that she wanted anything else.'

'And so the first time that his eyes were opened was when our charming friend, Edwin Milton-Hayes, invited him to look upon that picture, *Winter of Despair*, that's what you think, isn't it, Wilkie?'

'That's what I think. And I do believe that he picked up the knife and slashed the man's throat and then he destroyed the picture. May have meant to have removed it, but the servant girl returning interrupted him. But, in any case, he would have rendered it unrecognisable. Of course, he wasn't to know that there was another stash of paintings hidden away. He wouldn't have been a man that took much interest in art. The hinges on the side of the frame would not have meant anything to him, whereas . . .' I stopped and looked at him very carefully as I said this, 'Whereas, Dick, any artist would have immediately known that *Winter of Despair* was part of a diptych or a triptych.'

He nodded at that. 'I have never once suspected your brother, Wilkie. Put that out of your head. I'm a man who knows about people and I know that Charley has not got it in him to slash a man's throat.'

With an air of self-satisfaction he took out the cigar, lit it with a flourish and while staring steadily at me as though waiting for a comment, he sucked upon it wearing an expression of quiet enjoyment.

'I'm sure that you're right,' I said humbly. 'In any case,' I said, 'my brother would not have the money to employ a man like Silken Sam. He is completely dependent on my mother. And if he had asked for a large sum of money, whether to pay off a blackmailer or hire an assassin, my mother would have immediately asked my advice. And would probably have had to involve Coutts Bank, also. I don't suppose people like Silken Sam come too cheap, do they?'

'I don't know why you refer to me as an authority on the hiring of an assassin,' he said in an irritated fashion, but he went on smoking and soon, I could see from his brow, that the smoke was having a calming, soothing effect upon him.

'And that means that we rule out young Walter Hamilton, also,' he said pensively. 'He wouldn't have had the money. And I suppose that we can rule out the schoolgirl, too, as it was unlikely – however ill-cared-for and badly-behaved as she seems to have been – that she actually had access to Silken Sam.'

I felt that I should stand up for the girl who had seemed to me very charming, very mature, and very in love, but I did not reply to this. No point in leading Dickens away from the probable murderer and into the realm of the improbable. 'John French had the motive, Dick,' I said. 'He had the motive – that of protecting his wife and saving himself from ridicule in the eyes of the world – and he had the means of employing Silken Sam and probably, if he deals in imported goods, the means of being in contact with Silken Sam. I don't suppose that someone like my brother or like Walter Hamilton had even a notion of Silken Sam's existence.'

Dickens puffed at his cigar. There was a half-smile on his face. It was typical of the man that, once he had taken the decision to allow himself a third cigar, he wasted no time in regretting his decision.

'I think that your friend, Silken Sam, has given this matter a new turn,' he said after a few moments. 'I wonder whether Inspector Field has thought about that. It does seem to rule out all of the women in this intriguing case, does it not? We had decided, had we not, that, given the sharpness of the knife, a woman could have murdered Milton-Hayes. But I can't see little Molly French down in the docks looking for Silken Sam. Nor Florence Gummidge, nor, indeed, though it grieves me to say it, am I able to picture her unpleasant mother in the role.' Dickens contemplated his cigar, holding it aloft and went on thoughtfully. 'You know my friend Thackeray has the idea that all women are jealous of cigars and regard them as a strong rival. That's the trouble with Thackeray. All women are the same to him. Now I'm not like that. Women are individuals to me. And so it has occurred to me that there is one woman who might know of the existence of Silken Sam and might think of getting him to do her dirty work for her, and that is Helen Jordan. Gamblers know all sorts from the underworld.'

I looked dubious. 'I doubt that she would have the money; I've heard that she has been having very bad luck at the cards.'

Dickens shrugged. 'Stole it from her husband. I'm sure that she has done so in the past. He wouldn't have threatened divorce if she was only using the housekeeping money for gambling. Easy enough to put a stop to that – could pay the bills himself. No, she's either been stealing actual money, or, more likely, filling out cheques in his name or getting people to lend her money in the name of her husband.'

Dickens' face grew dark as he said this and I said nothing. I knew that he had problems like that with his own father and mother, both of whom were inclined to use their famous son's name in order to borrow money from all and sundry. I gave him time and, as I guessed, he came back to the problem quite quickly, his face alive and full of interest.

'What about the young man, though? The adventurous Lord Douglas? I'd say that he has some dubious acquaintances. He wouldn't be able to sell the fruits of his nocturnal wanderings if he didn't, would he?'

'Possible,' I said judicially. Within me a sudden idea had sprung and I trembled with excitement. 'But I've suddenly thought of someone else. We're forgetting, aren't we, though, what Silken Sam said to me. "You've been going around, asking questions? And who have I been asking questions of?'

'Me,' said Dickens.

'Well, I was thinking about our visit to the canon,' I said diffidently. 'We asked questions of him. Asked him whether he thought of the subject matter. All that sort of thing. And he was very ill-at-ease with us, wasn't he?'

And then when he still looked sceptical, I explained my meaning a little more.

'It just occurred to me that we have more or less identified all of the figures in the painting, all except one. We've
guessed that *The Night Prowler* depicts Lord Douglas and
his assistant is Florence. We've guessed that *Forbidden
Fruit* is Walter Hamilton and we're all sure about the three
figures in *Taken in Adultery* and we know that the gambler
in *Root of All Evil* is undoubtedly Helen, but we haven't
said anything much about *Den of Iniquity*, have we?' I thought
of saying that Sesina had directed my attention towards the
painting, but then refrained. Dickens would not take Sesina
too seriously.

But he was knitting his brows over my statement. 'A white-
haired man, dressed in shabby, old clothes,' he said slowly.

'Forget the clothes, easily purchased in Monmouth Street,'
I said confidently. Sesina, I remembered, had said that and I
was sure that she would have known all about Monmouth
Street.

'But the hair.' Dickens' mind had instantly leaped to something that had taken me a long time to work out.

'Yes,' I said. I guessed that he was doing as I had done,
going in spirit around that tableful of guests.

'Only two men with white hair,' he said then. 'John French
and William Jordan.'

'Wrong,' I said. 'Three. He wore a cap, a filthy-looking old
cap. Made him look different.'

'The canon, you mean,' he said slowly. 'But . . .'

'He was wearing a biretta at the dinner and that's why you
didn't notice his hair, but substitute a canon's biretta for a
filthy cap and you will see that it could have been the canon.
A man that would be ruined if it were known that he frequented
opium dens,' I said decisively. 'A man who would undoubtedly
have changed his clothing before going there, changed into
those old rags. But, there is another thing. You know, Dick,
we may not have uncovered the full story about Milton-Hayes.
I heard a rumour that Milton-Hayes was not his full name and
so did you. Augustus Egg told you, did he not? He told you
that Milton-Hayes made a mistake once when he was about
to sign his name and that he wrote the letter R and then
possibly an A or a U. I suppose I might have had that at the

back of my mind when I watched my mother write a letter earlier today. You were there, too. You saw her write.'

'"Dear Canon Rutter," that's what she wrote wasn't it?' Dickens was thinking hard.

I beamed at him.

'I still don't see a respectable canon of the church going to an opium den,' said Dickens decisively. He had certain very positive theories about religion and those who practised it and I decided not to argue with him. In any case, there was that other idea which had swept across my mind and I'd been dazzled by its brilliance before I got engulfed in fog and violence.

'*Rutter* is an Essex name,' I said. 'Not a very dignified name. Makes one think of rutting deer and it would be too easily corrupted into something like *Ratter* if a man has the sort of friends who would enjoy a little leg-pulling. And,' I added, 'if you were shopping for an expensive piece of art to hang upon your walls, would you really want it signed by someone with such a ridiculous name?'

Dickens removed his cigar, held it in his hand and gazed at me for a moment.

'So you think that Edwin Milton-Hayes was really Edwin Rutter?'

'Or even Tom Rutter,' I said.

'And so, when he came to London, he changed his name to that impressive-sounding, double-barrelled Milton-Hayes. And you are thinking that the canon is a relative?'

'Possibly a brother,' I said. 'Not very unlike him, either. The hair could be prematurely grey, but the face is relatively young. The weight doesn't help either. Could be three or four, or even five or six years older, but they certainly could have been brothers. And, as for a motive, it could be something to do with money. Inspector Field did seem astonished at the amount of money in Milton-Hayes' bank account. Isn't that right?'

'That's right,' said Dickens, watching my face and puffing at his cigar.

'And Milton-Hayes was not married. Had neither wife nor child. Right?'

'Right,' agreed Dickens.

I thought that he had probably guessed where my thoughts were leading me, but he said no more. Just allowed me to spell it out, step by step.

'And so,' I said, triumphantly, 'given that his father is probably dead – after all Milton-Hayes was not a young man, why then who would inherit his wealth – and it was probably considerable – who would inherit it, but his brother?'

'And his brother being . . .'

'The canon,' I said eagerly. 'Why not the canon? He comes from Essex. Milton-Hayes came from Essex. Milton-Hayes had changed his name, probably from a name beginning with R U or R A, and Rutter is an Essex surname, so it's likely, well, possible, anyway, that they were related. Were brothers, in fact . . .' I allowed my voice to tail out when faced by his sceptical expression but my inner certainty did not waver. The men were alike, I thought. My father, who was not hopeful of a career as an artist for me, had nevertheless admitted that I had a good eye for detail. *'He sees!'* My godfather, the artist David Wilkie, had exclaimed those words at my christening – much to the amusement of my mother who was of the opinion that her husband's friend had mistaken me for a puppy or a kitten – but that seeing-eye had stayed with me. I was confident now that the something familiar that I had noticed about the canon had been, in fact, the resemblance to his brother, the man we had known as Edwin Milton-Hayes.

'So he kills his brother – partly to avoid blackmail or that picture being sold, but also so that he could inherit the fortune. Once the canon knew that not only was his brother making money from the paintings that he sold, but that he was making each piece doubly valuable by extracting blackmail before the picture was finished, well, then he would have been tempted to kill his brother, ensure his own safety from ruin and disgrace, but also inherit the money that his brother had accumulated.'

Dickens took the stub of his cigar from his mouth, examined it and then ground out the remaining sparks upon the floral ridges of the weighty brass ashtray on the table in front of us. He was frowning heavily.

'You may be right,' he said eventually. 'And yes, I did think that there was something familiar about the canon when your mother introduced us. And I did, also, think that the choice of pictures supposedly for a church hall was a very strange one. I wouldn't like any daughter of mine to frequent a church hall that showed a picture like that abominable *Forbidden Fruit* or even the gambling one or the opium den, or any of them, come to think of it.' He got to his feet and nodded across the floor to the landlord, delving into his pocket for his purse.

'Well, Wilkie,' he said. 'We're too late for the play, but not too late to pay a call.'

I waited while he paid the bill and we were both wrapped in overcoats and girded with our umbrellas by the solicitous landlord, and then as soon as we were outside the door, I said eagerly, 'Scotland Yard.'

He did not answer, but raised an imperious umbrella and then when a cab stopped beside us and the cabbie peered down from his roof-top seat, he stepped forward and said something into the man's ear.

EIGHTEEN

Sesina spotted him instantly. There had been some attempt at a disguise. He wore a coat that wasn't his. An old frock coat, too small for him, stained with green mould and strange white patches – salt water perhaps – and on his head he wore a broken bowler hat, again stained and discoloured by sea water and age.

But at the back of his neck, beneath the rim of the bowler hat, a fringe of red hair appeared.

It had been Sesina's monthly afternoon off. She had gone to Covent Garden, wandered around the stalls, bought a wizened apple to chew and recognized eventually that she was not enjoying herself, but that she was lonely and wanted some company. Since her friend Isabella had been murdered she had not had a single friend. Who could make a friend of Dolly or of Mrs Barnett? Both of them were nearly three times her own age. Feeling depressed she had wandered into Drury Lane and there, just outside the door to the theatre was a notice: *'Experienced Housemaid Required. Good Wage Paid'*.

Sesina stopped and looked at the notice. She was experienced, well-trained, also, thanks, she had to admit, more to Mrs Morson in Urania Cottage than to Mrs Barnett or even Mrs Collins. It hadn't been a bad idea of Mr Dickens to train girls straight out of prison to be top-class servants. Gave them a way of earning money that didn't involve selling themselves on the streets. A mug's game that. End up in prison and then infected and before you knew where you was, you'd be in a grave with quicklime being shoved over you. Housework was boring, but better than that. She missed Isabella, though, missed someone to giggle with and to tease and to play jokes on.

Time she moved on, she thought, staring at the notice. A big theatre like Drury Lane would have to employ plenty of housemaids. Would be fun, she thought. And no emptying of chamber pots every morning. And might get a chance to become an actress. Sesina rather fancied the idea of being an actress. She thought that she'd be good. And she was so small that they could use her as a child if they wanted to.

'How d'you fancy it?' A hand went across her eyes, but Sesina wasn't fooled. She knew that voice.

'Oh, God, Hanny, take your filthy hand off my eyes.' She spoke automatically, but her heart warmed a little. Long time since she saw Hannah. Had left her behind when she crashed out of Urania Cottage.

'Going to apply?' Hannah had taken her hand away. In the old days in Urania Cottage, she'd have shouted her head off at Sesina, used her fists, too, but now she looked a bit mellowed. Always fighting in those days.

'You going to apply, Sesina – go on, do. I'm working there. Could put in a good word.'

'What, a job in a filthy play house!' Sesina enjoyed saying that, but her eyes lingered on the place. It would be empty during the morning, just the girls all together cleaning out the place, sweeping, dusting, washing floors, larking around and then a chance to see a play in the evening, helping the actresses, cleaning their rooms. Perhaps getting a chance to snaff a bit of rouge or face paint. Would be fun . . .

And then she thought about poor Mr Charles. She'd never see him again if she left the house in Hanover Terrace. Other side of London, wasn't it?

'Nah,' she said decisively. 'Got a good place next to Regent's Park. Treat me like one of the family. Might even get meself a rich husband. This would be a rubbish job. Have to find me own digs, too! Nah, I'll stay put.' She tried to keep a note of longing out of her voice and averted her eyes from the placard.

And that was the moment when she saw him. Dressed in clothes that were not his own, a hat too big for him, his face almost covered by it. But he had been spotted.

Behind him, not too far away was a policeman, not looking left nor right, but keeping his eyes fixed on that tall figure ahead of him.

Sesina acted quickly. 'That's my lover boy. Quick, Hannah, talk to that peeler, keep him busy while I have a word with Mr Handsome.'

She didn't wait to see what Hannah would do. She knew that they'd act as a pair. In a moment she was beside Mr Charles. From behind she heard Hannah's laugh. Had a laugh like a peahen, Isabella used to say. She'd do her part, though, would Hannah; Sesina knew that. Wouldn't let her down. Would enjoy it anyway. Depends on the policeman, though. Might be one of the serious types. The 'follow orders' type. Lots of them about. Sesina reached out, grabbed the sleeve of the old dirty frock coat and pulled hard. 'Down here, Mr Charles, this way, quick! There's a peeler after you. Quick!'

It was taking a chance, going down that alleyway. All right if she was just by herself, she'd be down it in two shakes of a lamb's tail, but he was like a sack of potatoes as she tried to haul him along. Would the peeler shake off Hannah and be after them? Had he spotted them turning away? Still, he'd be looking for a man on his own. Not a man and his girlfriend. Sesina looked up at Mr Charles anxiously. Very pale, but he didn't seem sick. What was the matter with him? She had to drag him along. At this rate she'd never get him away from the peeler. On her own, she'd be fine. It would take just about a quarter of an hour, she reckoned. But Mr Charles was going so slowly. A dazed look on his face. Like he didn't know what he was doing. She had to drag him along. Nearly to the end of the lane, now. She looked back over her shoulder and swore to herself. There was the peeler. Moving very fast, too. Hannah hadn't been able to hold him for long. She swore again, and this time aloud.

That was a mistake. He never liked swearing. Very pious, he was. Not at all like his brother, Mr Wilkie. It made him move, though. Went a bit quicker. Out of the lane now and into the busy New Oxford Street. Had his hand up now. A cab.

Quick, she thought, looking anxiously over her shoulder. The policeman was gaining on them. No cab stopping, all got passengers inside. Only what you could expect on a lousy wet foggy day like this. There was one. Slow old horse, but better than nothing. She made to follow him in, but he slammed the door in her face.

Didn't know what he was doing, poor fellow.

Sesina stood back into the protective shadow of a shop door and looked anxiously back at the peeler. No flies on him! He had seen everything and was going to follow. She watched anxiously as he climbed into the cab, hitching up his blue coat and taking off that very tall reinforced top hat that all the peelers wore to protect their heads. She looked after him anxiously and wished that she was around when Mr Charles arrived at Hanover Terrace. She'd keep an eye out in case the policeman arrived at the same time. He probably would. A better horse than the one poor Mr Charles had taken, she thought, but then was cheered by noticing the sheer number of carts, cabs, and omnibuses that cluttered the road. She was a fast walker and she could take short cuts through lanes and alleyways while the cab struggled through the traffic.

When she arrived at number 17 Hanover Terrace, all seemed very peaceful. The fog had lifted – never so bad here as it was right down near the river. The door knocker that she had polished this morning glinted in the last ray of sunlight. And then the cab with its slow, plodding horse turned into the terrace, and drew up in front of the door. Mr Charles got out. Took a long time delving into the pockets of that old frock coat. Looking for his purse. Her heart ached as she saw his white face. She tried to send a message to him and perhaps she succeeded because he abandoned his search of the borrowed frock coat and put his hand into the pocket of his waistcoat. Took out some coins. Not much of a tip, probably. The man went off without a word, whipped up his horse, splashed through a puddle, drenching his passenger.

Poor fellow. Hardly noticed. Almost stumbled on the edge of the pavement. Her heart ached for him. Needed someone to look after him. She hesitated for a moment at the steps down into the area. There was a cosy light coming from the basement window. The stove would be glowing hot, ready for cooking the evening meal. Dolly wouldn't be there. She'd be up with Mrs Collins at this time in the evening. And Mrs Barnett always had a bit of a rest before she started on the dinner. 'Need my *lay-down*,' she'd say before she stumped off. If only she could get him into the kitchen, sit him down by the fire; let him warm up; run upstairs for a clean coat; bring down a towel and a hair brush; get him tidied up.

And then her breath shortened. Another cab had drawn up. A man in a blue coat, wearing a very tall top hat. A peeler. The very one. The one that had been following Mr Charles away back in Drury Lane.

'The peeler is after you, Mr Charles. Come down here. Come quick while he's not looking.'

He seemed a bit dazed, but she dragged at his sleeve and he responded, stumbling down the area steps after her.

Once they were in the kitchen she relaxed. Yes, she had been right. No one there. Gently she pushed him into Mrs Barnett's cushioned chair and saw steam rise from his sodden clothes. And then, half expected, but a sickening blow. The front door bell. Someone had pressed it and then kept their finger upon it. Someone in authority.

Sesina took one worried look at him. He seemed almost as if he were drifting off to sleep, sitting there and staring at the hot, red glow from the range. She'd have to leave him and answer the door.

'Stay there!' she said imperatively, but as soon as she reached the bottom of the basement stairs, she knew that she was going to be too late. Dolly's heavy footsteps came clumping down the hall. Still never mind. If it was that nosy policeman, Dolly would just tell him that Mr Charles was not at home. Was staying with his doctor.

Nevertheless, Sesina crept up the stairs and stood with the door to the hall just barely ajar.

No need to strain her ears. He was loud and clear.

'I've a warrant for the arrest of Mr Charles Collins. I've just seen him go down the steps to the basement.'

Sesina did not wait to hear any more. She flew down the stairs, into the kitchen, grabbed his arm, and hauled him to his feet.

'Come on, Mr Charles, come on, the police are after you. They want to put you in prison.'

He heard that. He gave a half sob but she did not hesitate, just kept dragging him from the kitchen. As usual, he gave in.

A sound of a door opening above their heads. The door from the basement steps into the hall.

'I'll hide you.' She whispered it into his ear, but he made no sign of hearing her. She didn't wait for a response. Just exerted every muscle in her body to drag him along, across the landing and into her own room. Rapidly she stripped back the bedclothes, shed her shawl and her dress. And while he stared at her with horror in his eyes, she pushed him hard right in the centre of his back so that he stumbled and fell across the bed. The iron frame jumped but stood firm under his weight. In a second, she had gathered up his legs, thrust them onto the sheet and heaped the blankets on top of him.

'Nobody here.' Dolly sounded quite placid. But then Dolly always did take little notice of anyone who spoke to her, unless it was Mrs Collins or perhaps Mrs Barnett.

'I saw her and I saw him.' Rough-sounding man, that peeler. Most of them were. Stubborn, though.

'Perhaps she's gone to her room. Sesina, Sesina!' Dolly raised her voice in a shrill cry. There was a sound of her heavy footsteps crossing over the landing.

Sesina didn't hesitate. She unbuckled her shoes and in a second was beside Mr Charles in the bed. A work of a second to pull the blankets over the two of them, pull them right over his head. She began to sit up, to arrange an expression of annoyed surprise on her face, when suddenly he hit her. Hit her across the face.

'Get away from me, you slut.'

Her head jerked back and there was a blinding pain beneath her left eye. She heard herself give a low moan, but he was on his feet, striding towards the door, flinging it open and shouting, 'Do you want me, my man? Here I am.'

NINETEEN

Neither Dickens nor I said a word on our way to Scotland Yard. The expression on the face of my companion made me worried. I knew how much I would have to rely upon him, upon his forceful manner, his air of always being in the right and above all his influence over Inspector Field. But now Dickens bore the look of someone who was deeply troubled. I sensed that he felt unsure and that was not a usual state of mind for one of the most important men in London. From time to time, he sighed, crossed his legs and then rapidly uncrossed them again. He tapped on the window, a staccato, disjointed arrhythmic sound that set my nerves on edge. I said nothing, however. Let him work through his doubts while we were here in the privacy of our cab. Dickens was a born actor. Once we had arrived at Inspector Field's office I was sure that he would rise to the occasion and play his part.

As we left Whitehall and turned into Scotland Yard I got a shock. There emerging from the door was a familiar figure. A well-dressed clergyman, settling his glossy hat upon his head and looking about him for a cab. I shrank back into the seat and looked across at my companion. Dickens made no move and did not open his mouth. And so I said nothing.

Inspector Field greeted us with great warmth and immediately sent for a pot of tea and apologized for not being more hospitable, giving us a complicated explanation about rules against alcohol. I hardly listened to him. Dickens bore a remote detached expression which filled me with foreboding and my fears were realized when he interrupted Inspector Field with an air of false bonhomie.

'Don't worry about me, inspector, I just chanced to accompany my friend, but it is Mr Collins who wants to talk to you.'

I anticipated an expression of surprise on the inspector's face, but he immediately turned a commiserating and kindly face towards me.

'I'm very sorry, Mr Collins,' he said with an apologetic note in his voice. 'I'm afraid that your brother left me with no alternative.'

Brother! My heart seemed to stop for a second and then to go on beating very slowly. I felt a cold sweat on my forehead and the large face of the inspector seemed to shimmer before my eyes. I took out my handkerchief, wiped my glasses and then, as unobtrusively as I could, dabbed the moisture from my brow.

'My brother,' I said hesitantly. What had happened? Surely by now Piggott had my brother safely somewhere in the middle of the English Channel and was well on the way towards the Isle of Wight.

'He gave himself up, you see, Mr Collins. One of my men was following him, of course. A pair of them noticed him on the Strand. They work in pairs, Mr Dickens, you see.' Inspector Field was imbued with the idea that the famous Mr Dickens was fascinated by every detail of the workings of the police force. Dickens, however, said nothing. Just looked gravely and sympathetically at me and it crossed my mind that he showed no surprise.

'My brother . . . but . . . I thought that he was . . . in the hands of his doctor.' The words came out in a series of disjointed gasps.

Inspector Field smiled with a false sympathy that made me feel slightly ill. This time, I openly mopped my brow and looked across at him.

'Yes, yes,' he said. 'And a little trip on a boat. My men saw him disembark at the Temple Stairs. No doubt,' Inspector Field cleared his throat noisily, 'no doubt his doctor thought a little air would do him good. Should have let us know, of course. We thought that he was at death's door.' The inspector looked at me reproachfully and I looked angrily back.

'Where is my brother now?' I asked.

Inspector Field cleared his throat. A false sound if ever I had heard one. The man was enjoying this. And when the words came, I was not surprised.

'I'm afraid that we have him in custody, Mr Collins,' he said. 'He confessed, you see. Confessed to murdering Mr

Milton-Hayes. Said that the man was a scoundrel and the earth a better place without him.'

'But he didn't; he couldn't have. We know who did murder Milton-Hayes, don't we, Dickens? And we know why he did it. You must listen to us, inspector.' I cast a look of appeal towards Dickens.

He roused himself, but when he spoke his words were about Charley.

'Did you believe him, inspector?' And then when the inspector did not reply, he elaborated. 'Did you believe Mr Charles Collins when he confessed to the murder, the savage murder of a friend and fellow artist? Did you really think that he was the sort of person who would take up a knife and slit a man's throat?' He sounded interested. Just as though he were working out a plot for a novel.

The inspector smiled weakly and looked embarrassed. 'Well, you know, Mr Dickens, we don't go in for that sort of thing here in Scotland Yard. Hard evidence is what we go for. And there is a lot of hard evidence that points to Mr Charles Collins.' He cleared his throat and avoided my eye. 'You see, Mr Dickens,' he said confidentially, 'the young man was having an affair with a married lady, a lady with a rich husband and this artist fellow, this Mr Milton-Hayes, had painted a picture of it, *Taken in Adultery*. One of the other artists, a man called Ruskin, explained it all to us.'

'And you thought that Mr Charles Collins was the sort of man to commit murder, did you?'

I sat back. I felt sick and bewildered and hoped that Dickens would handle the matter. I looked hopefully at the inspector. Was he beginning to look a little uncertain? I couldn't be sure. There was a mask of professionalism on his face that seemed to show the official point of view and exclude all indecision.

'Well, you see, Mr Dickens,' he said, 'that's not really a matter for us. Remember the young man has confessed to the murder. His guilt or his innocence is now a matter for the judge and the jury. And, of course, the judge and jury can be persuaded by a good lawyer.' He looked then across at me.

'If I were you, Mr Collins, I would engage a good lawyer. Don't spare money on him. Would you like to see your brother now?' He half rose, but I did not move and I shook my head. My mother, I knew, would spend her last penny on a lawyer for her youngest son, but that might be too late.

'We, myself and Mr Dickens, know who did do the murder and also why he did it.' I said the words as firmly as I could and he sank back into his chair again. There was a look of resignation on his face that spoke more highly of scepticism than any argument could have done. I looked despairingly across at Dickens and this time he did not fail me.

'Collins and I were studying the pictures, inspector, and he has been very knowledgeable about the figures,' he said. 'We agree, I think, that they were painted in order to blackmail the subjects; that Milton-Hayes used his knowledge of the follies of some young men and young women. Mr Collins, of course, knows this world of those so-called Pre-Raphaelite artists and was able to identify most of the subjects. But –' Dickens held up an admonitory finger as the inspector was about to speak – 'but,' he continued, 'one man, one painted figure, did not appear to belong in that world of young people. And that was the grey-haired main figure in the picture entitled *Den of Iniquity*. I'm sure that you remember that particular picture, inspector, do you not? The grey-haired man, dressed in old clothes, right in the centre of that scene of iniquity, that opium den, surrounded by other unfortunate addicts.' Dickens paused, eyed the inspector closely and then continued, giving every word an impressive weight.

'We have identified that man, inspector. It is Canon Rutter, the would-be purchaser of those five pictures. No, let me finish. I know what you are about to say. The resemblance is slight, the clothes all wrong, the suggestion quite far-fetched. Why should a man murder another on such scanty evidence which could be laughed away? Well, I'll tell you something interesting. We believe, my friend and I believe, that Milton-Hayes was an assumed name and that the artist's real name was Rutter. If you were to delve into the matter, you would find that Canon Rutter was closely related, even perhaps as nearly related as a brother, to Milton-Hayes. And, you know yourself, inspector, you remarked upon it, I remember. Milton-Hayes, through nefarious practices like this latest attempt at blackmail, had become a very rich man. A man,' finished Dickens, one finger raised and his voice solemn, 'a man,' he repeated, 'that would have been worth murdering if one was sure of inheriting his fortune. It makes, and I'm sure that you'll agree, inspector, it makes for a far more powerful motive for murder than a mere boyish indiscretion such as my friend's young brother might have committed.'

And Dickens, as always convinced by the sound of his own voice and the logic of his reasoning, sat back looking satisfied.

Inspector Field, however, showed no signs of surprise. 'You're quite right, Mr Dickens,' he said. His voice held a note of admiration. 'Don't know how you worked it out, to be sure, but you are quite right. Mr Edwin Milton-Hayes' real name was Jem Rutter and yes, his brother was Canon Rutter.'

'You worked it out.' I was conscious of a feeling of disappointment. I had been proud of how I had worked out that relationship and was disappointed that the inspector, a man of small brain, as I had always thought, had also done so.

'No, no, we don't have too much time for that sort of thing, Mr Collins. No, I heard it from the man himself. Came to see me.'

'What, the canon!' And then I remembered. Yes, we had seen him outside. I remembered the well-dressed clerical figure. He had stolen our thunder. I sat back in despair. The man had forestalled us.

'I had another look at the pictures after he went,' said the inspector.

Not stupid then, I told myself, with hope slightly rising, but then that hope subsided when he added, 'But, confidentially, Mr Dickens, I don't think we'd get anywhere, to be very honest with you both. A judge wouldn't like a clergyman in court, the jury wouldn't like it, my superiors in Scotland Yard, well, they wouldn't like it at all. The man has been open and honest, explained that it was his younger brother who didn't want the relationship to be known, thought the name would be bad for business, make people laugh at him. That's what this Mr Edwin

Milton-Hayes thought, apparently, and it all makes sense.' The inspector stopped and looked at both of us with his eyebrows raised.

'On the other hand,' said Dickens. 'If my friend's younger brother is accused of this murder which he did not commit, then his mother, a very well-off lady, will secure the services of the top lawyer in London, even perhaps Sir Cresswell Cresswell himself.' Dickens rolled the name on his tongue and eyed the inspector. 'And, of course, the young man's family and friends would take care to brief Sir Cresswell Cresswell on all the factors that make it most unlikely that Mr Charles Collins was the person who killed Mr Milton-Hayes. Witnesses would be called; private affairs would be revealed; questions in the House of Commons; newspapers making insinuations, very distressing for a hard-working, ambitious man like yourself.' Dickens looked sympathetically at the man behind the desk and then waited.

The inspector was a man of decision.

'As you say, Mr Dickens, the affair is shrouded in mystery. The problem is,' and now he spoke with an apologetic note in his voice, 'the problem is that Mr Charles Collins has at least twice confessed to the murder of Mr Milton-Hayes.'

Dickens did not hesitate. He waved his hand. 'Temporary derangement of the mind, inspector. Dr Beard is highly respected among the professional men of the city. His evidence will more than reassure.' He stopped there and did not add anything to the end of his sentence. He, like me, knew that if poor Charley was taken to court, the result might be catastrophic. I could see him wagering all on this last throw and it worked.

Inspector Field nodded. 'I think you are right, Mr Dickens. No point in putting the unfortunate young man through a nerve-wracking experience. I think, gentlemen, if you will secure a cab then I will bring Mr Charles Collins out to you. No point in too much fuss or formalities.'

Dickens had a satisfied look as we drove away. I kept an arm around Charley's shoulders. We would drive him straight to Frank Beard's place. No yachts this time. Piggott was not up to detaining Charley against his will, but Frank Beard would look after him until his nerves had improved. My mother could visit him there and try to coax him from the depression and delusions that now held sway over him. There was only one thing wrong and, as I felt Charley's head drop on my shoulder and heard his breathing lengthen into the long, slow breaths of slumber, I spoke my thought aloud.

'Does this mean that no one is to be accused of the murder?' I heard a very bitter note in my voice and was surprised at myself. After all, I hadn't even liked the dead man, and I certainly did not relish the thought of anyone being hanged for his murder.

I was, however, rather taken aback when Dickens said in a low, firm voice, 'Believe me, my dear Wilkie, that it would be much the best thing if the subject was now dropped and was never to be mentioned again between us.'

TWENTY

S esina chose her time carefully. Mr Wilkie was having a small party that evening for some friends. Mr Dickens, of course, had been invited, and had arrived an hour earlier than the other guests and both were having a low-voiced conversation in the downstairs parlour. Mrs Collins had finished getting ready for the party, had sent Dolly back to the kitchen and now was alone in her sitting room.

Sesina had written the letter in Mr Wilkie's study on the evening before when he was out. Though it was very short, she had taken care with it, placing the lines at an exact distance from each other, just in the way that Mrs Morson had taught them when she and her friend Isabella were living in Urania Cottage. She speculated on taking one of these new-fangled envelopes to enclose it, but decided that the use of candle and sealing wax added another complication.

And so it was a single folded sheet of paper that she handed to Mrs Collins.

The woman was taken aback, but unsuspecting. She read the letter through, took slightly longer over it than she need have done; it was, after all, a very short letter. And then she read it aloud.

'I'm sorry to have to hand in my notice, ma'am.' Sesina felt that there was a nice note of sincerity in her voice. Might as well keep the old lady happy for the moment. See how things went.

'And we're very sorry to lose you, Sesina.' Mrs Collins eyed her with a certain degree of puzzlement. 'I can't persuade you to change your mind, can I? You haven't found the work here to be too difficult, I'm sure, have you?'

Very cautious. Not sure. Eyeing Sesina, sensing the excitement, perhaps. A bit stiff, ready for anything. Still, you had to admire her. That woman would do anything for that son of hers, anything to look after him, to keep him safe.

Not worth it, thought Sesina dispassionately. Going to have trouble with him all of her days. She and Mr Wilkie were going to have to look after him for his entire life. Never did grow up, that fellow, she thought and was surprised to find how she could feel so detached-like about Charley Collins. One blow and it had knocked all of the nonsense out of her head. Surreptitiously she touched the bruise beneath her eye. She had tried rubbing a bit of cornflour over it to hide the blackness, but it had not been a success and so she had washed it off.

'You see, ma'am,' she said and heard a note of sincerity in her voice, 'this is a job in a playhouse. I've always wanted to be on the stage and this might give me my opportunity.'

Now the woman relaxed. A slightly contemptuous look came over her face which Sesina resented.

'You'd want to put that nonsense out of your head, Sesina,' she said patronisingly. 'Goodness knows how you'd end up if you work in a playhouse. You'd be on the streets in a couple of years. I really don't feel that I can give you a good reference if that's what you have in mind.'

Sesina smiled sweetly. 'Oh, but I think that you will, ma'am, and a nice little present, too. Just to show your appreciation. And, of course, to ensure that I keep my mouth shut.'

'Don't be impertinent.' Once again the woman eyed the bruise, but Sesina observed a slight shrug of the shoulders. She could read the woman's thoughts. What was a blow? A blow from a young gentleman. Happened in lots of households. Maidservants were two a penny. Lots of them were knocked about on a regular basis. No, Mrs Collins, thought Sesina, I have a better trick up my sleeve than that. It was time to come out with her prize card.

'I recognized you that morning, you see, ma'am,' she said with a slight smile. 'And, of course, that was Mr Charley's cricket cap that you was wearing. I recognized that, too. I've seen it in his wardrobe when I've been dusting. Keeps all his old school stuff, does Mr Charley.' She gave the woman a moment to swallow this and then went on. 'I was following Mr Charley, you see, ma'am. Trying to make sure that he came to no harm. There he was, running like a lunatic away from Mr Milton-Hayes' house, down Park Road and you dodged into a back alley. Not that he would have noticed you. Too much on his mind that morning. Always does just think of himself, doesn't he?'

Mrs Collins' eyes had widened and she had drawn in a deep breath. But then, courageous as ever, she pulled herself together.

'I really don't know what you are talking about, Sesina,' she said sharply.

'Oh, but I think you do, ma'am. You see I'm not stupid. I've put it all together. I remember what you were like that morning of the murder. Dolly said that you were in a state. Have to hand it to you. You was wearing lots of stuff on your face, of course. Rouge and all. Of course, you'd have been a bit pale – Dolly said that you were ever so pale, that morning. Was worried about you. Hard to blame you. Must be a bit of a shock to a lady like yourself to cut a man's throat. Don't suppose that you hesitated much, though, did you? Not when it came to Mr Charley. Would do anything for him, wouldn't you? Be afraid that he might commit suicide if he was disgraced. Just the type, isn't he?'

Mrs Collins drew in a long breath and Sesina eyed her with amusement. Quite the actress, wasn't she? That's how she managed to pull it off. Pretending to be surprised that the man hadn't turned up for dinner and knowing all of the time that she had slit his throat that morning. You'd have to admire her, thought Sesina. But then she hardened her heart as she thought of how she had been sacrificed.

'And, of course, you thought that you'd turn the police away from Mr Charley and on to me. Had that constable following me everywhere, didn't you? Asking me questions. Suggesting all sorts of things. That's right, isn't it, ma'am? You tried to drop me into it. It would have suited you, wouldn't it, if the police had taken me in for questioning, had accused me? Anything, just so long as your darling little boy was safe.'

'No, no. You're wrong, Sesina. Mr Dickens and Mr Wilkie were coming up with other names . . .' Her voice tailed out and Sesina smiled contemptuously at the thought of that pair beating their brains. Got nowhere. Barking up the wrong tree, they were.

'I'll have twenty pounds and the best reference that you can think of,' she said. She had thought about asking for more, but best to take what she could easily and get out quickly. 'And no going behind my back and saying something different if anyone comes to call on you about the reference. I know all of those tricks and I won't hesitate to go to Inspector Field with the whole story.' Sesina sat back and studied the face opposite to her.

You had to admire her, sometimes. A woman who made up her mind quickly. Got up. Went to her writing desk, wrote out the reference, took up the pounce sprinkler and scattered the cuttlefish powder onto the wet ink, shook the paper, handed it over to Sesina and then waited while she read it through.

'And the money,' said Sesina. The reference had been very good but she wasn't going to praise it. It was the least that woman could do. Getting away with murder; that she was. She hardened her heart when she remembered how Mrs Collins had gone to such trouble to make the inspector think that Sesina was guilty. All that talk about getting a letter from someone. All made up. 'Twenty pounds in small notes,' she added.

Mrs Collins unlocked another drawer and took out four brand-new, crisp, five-pound notes and handed them over. Bigger than she would have liked, but it would have to do. Sesina took it from her without a word of thanks. She thought of giving the woman some advice about her son, Charley, ship him off to Australia or something, but then she shrugged her shoulders. None of her business.

'I'll take my uniform and my Sunday clothes,' she stated. And then she left the room rapidly, shutting the door quietly behind her. A quick visit to her room. Everything that might be useful packed into two bags. Moving quietly. Checked the stairs before she went and then out through the area door.

But there he was. Standing at the foot of the steps to the hall door. Smoking a cigar and gazing across at Regent's Park. Turned when she came up, though. Eyed her, just as though he had expected her. Looked at her Sunday clothes, and at the couple of bags that she was carrying and then he nodded his head.

'You're off, then, Sesina.'

'Yes, Mr Dickens.' No harm in saying that.

'Got any money?' He put his hand in his pocket. Would take out one of his sixpences. Or perhaps it might even be half a crown.

She couldn't resist it. Showed him the four five-pound notes. And looked for astonishment on his face.

But just a smile and a nod.

'You worked it out, then.' That was all that he said. But she felt disappointed. Not going to let on, though.

'Worked it out, Mr Dickens,' she repeated in her most innocent manner.

He took one last suck from his cigar, extinguished the flame on the pointed edge of the railing and flung it down onto the paved surface of the area. Someone would have to sweep it up, afterwards. Not her, though, she told herself with a feeling of pleasure. Not her. Dolly would have to do it. He saw the half-smile on her face and he gave another nod.

And then he lifted his umbrella, and when the cab stopped he opened the door and stood there holding it.

'Get in, Sesina, I'll drop you off wherever you are going.'

She thought of saying 'Australia', but he would take that seriously and so she got in and said loudly and clearly, 'Drury Lane'. And then she sat down, like a lady, and looked across at him.

He said nothing, but he wore the expression of one who is thinking hard. Paid the cab, once they arrived, added a tip, but got out with her and seemed ready to walk by her side. She shrugged her shoulders and walked on. He'd find out sooner rather than later. That was him.

He stopped her, though, before they reached the theatre, touched her on the shoulder and turned to face her.

'Of course! Now I understand! Somehow I always felt that she had her finger in the pie, but I couldn't quite work out how. Young Mr Charley didn't have the guts to do it himself, but he's just the type to go crying home to his Momma. And, of course, now that I come to think of it, Mr Wilkie remarked on the strange affair of only one picture being present at the murder scene. *Winter of Despair* should have had its partner, whether it would have been *Taken in Adultery* or *Den of Iniquity* or *The Night Prowler*. The fact that only *Winter of Despair* was mutilated seemed to show that the partner picture had been shown to the murderer on a previous occasion. But why had the murder not taken place then? He drew one conclusion; obviously you drew another, and in view of those four five-pound notes, and your interview with my hostess, I would reckon that yours was the correct one. Tell me, Sesina, how did you guess?'

Sesina thought for a moment. She should, she thought, tell him to mind his own business and then walk off, but the desire to impress him was too strong within her. She smiled a little.

'I don't suppose that you have seen Mrs Collins in her dressing gown, sir,' she said innocently. 'Ever so slim, she is.'

He picked up on her meaning instantly.

'Of course,' he said. 'So that's how it happened. Mr Milton-Hayes blackmails young Charley, asks him for a large sum of money, too large for his mother to find – she is subject to the trustees and Coutts Bank; her husband was a careful man – she'd have to tell them why she needed so much. They would not have paid it out, not for blackmail. And so she dressed up; that's what you are hinting, aren't you, Sesina. Dressed up as a young man. Always the actress, that's her. Played the part of a lifetime. And you saw her, did you?'

Sesina smiled. She had got him intrigued. 'I followed Mr Charley to Mr Milton-Hayes' house,' she said. 'He was in a terrible state. The hall door in Dorset Square was open and he left it open. I was behind him when he saw the body. The man was only just dead. The blood was still trickling. Mr Charley, well, he just lost 'is head. Turned and ran. And I went after him, kept up with him. And then, on Park Road, I spotted, just ahead of us, a lad wearing Mr Charley's cricket cap. Later on, I guessed who it was. You see, he keeps all his things since school, keeps them on a shelf in his wardrobe. She was just ahead of us, dressed like a young lad, running fast, ducked into an alleyway.' Sesina faced him defiantly, noting the excitement in his eyes and how he gnawed the side of his forefinger. 'Nothing could ever be proved against her, sir,' she said. 'I've got what I want and I won't give evidence against her. If you try to make me give evidence, I'll tell the judge I made up a story just to give you an idea for a book – I can convince any judge, sir.'

He chuckled and then broke into a laugh. 'I can guess that. I remember how well you can lie. Even if I went straight to Inspector Field himself, you'd deny every word of this conversation and so would she deny ever having left the house. And, do you know, Sesina, I wouldn't do it. I didn't have much of a mother myself and most of the mothers that I know are fairly useless, but, by Jupiter, that worthless young Charley has a mother who would lay down her life for him and who am I to interfere? Keep in touch with me, Sesina!' And, with a flourish of his umbrella, he was off, striding down Drury Lane.

Sesina took out her glowing reference and went into the theatre and towards the manager's office. Mr Dickens hadn't acknowledged her cleverness, but he would seek her out again if he needed help. She knew him. He liked people with brains. People like her.

There was a girl there, ahead of her, a very young girl, quite nervous, talking to the manager.

'My name is Ellen Ternan,' she was saying. 'I wonder if there is a part for me in *The Little Pickle*. My sister Maria is in it and she thought . . .'

AUTHOR'S NOTE TO THE
GASLIGHT SERIES

Whenever I read a novel that includes real people from the past, I usually wonder how much is true, and how much is the author's imagination.

So, this is what is true. Charles Dickens and Wilkie Collins are true figures from the mid Victorian age and everything that is mentioned about them, their age, their families, their habits of work and entertainment, their favourite restaurant, even, I dare to say, their speech patterns, all of these things are as true as I can ensure after years of reading their fiction – I've read every single one of Dickens' novels, time after time, over a period of more than seventy years, and most of Collins' books, also – but also reading letters, biographies and books of criticism. I am not a scholar so never was moved to add to this enormous pile, but I suppose that being such a Dickens fan, I have always had it in my mind to weave his larger-than-life personality into one of my stories. However, that idea stayed at the back of my mind until I read his letters – hundreds and hundreds of them. And one set of letters sparked off a story in my mind. They were mainly addressed to the rich and philanthropic Baroness Coutts who had financed his scheme to set up Urania Cottage, a home for girls who had strayed into prostitution. Some of the girls started a new life with the help of the training they received in Urania Cottage, but others could not stand the quiet life and the discipline and they left or were dismissed. Isabella Gordon (from *Season of Darkness*) was one of these.

I think it was the phrase that he used describing how she was sent to her bedroom to await the committee's decision: '*She danced up the stairs before Mrs Morson, holding her skirts like a lady at a ball*' which first made Isabella come to life in my mind. What had been her future after she was expelled from Urania Cottage, I wondered? And what had been the future of her best friend, Sesina, whose real name, intriguingly, was Anna Maria Sisini? Of Italian origin, perhaps. She also left Urania Cottage, *'would corrupt nunnery'* remarked Dickens, though he laughed at the idea of his housekeeper worrying about such a *'pint-sized'* and *'little dumpy atom of a girl'*. Dickens wrote dozens and dozens of letters about the girls to Baroness Coutts and they have provided me with all the details which I have quoted in the book when Sesina remembers their time in Urania Cottage. The subsequent history of Sesina and of poor Isabella Gordon are, of course, just figments of my imagination.

The plot of book two, *Winter of Despair*, was inspired by Augustus Egg's triptych, the first picture of which depicted the fall from grace of a woman, her expulsion from the family home and from her two daughters, the second showing the loneliness of the abandoned young girls with the moon shining in through their bedroom window and the third the mother's subsequent ruin where she is portrayed, under the light of the same moon, as a prostitute living beneath the arches of Adelphi. Having seen this picture in the Tate Gallery when I was in London I became so interested in the set of artists known as the Pre-Raphaelites that during a holiday in Wales I bought from the marvellous second-hand bookshops in Hay-on-Wye no less than ten books about the Brotherhood and settled down to a summer's reading about these talented young men whose every picture told a story. The leap from a picture that told a story to a picture that might tell a secret, might be used as blackmail, came to me early on in my reading, but, of course, I've never read anything that would suggest that any picture was used for that purpose.

My portrayal of Charlie Collins, Wilkie's younger brother, is partly based on a few comments in Catherine Peters' biography of Wilkie, but also from the fact that Dickens was deeply upset when his younger daughter, Katie, accepted a proposal of marriage from Charley. For some reason Dickens was deeply unhappy and very much against the marriage. There were rumours about Charley, some suggesting that he may have been homosexual, though that seems unlikely. Others that he was involved with a married woman – there is a letter from the artist Millais alluding to this – but mainly, I think, because he was a hysterical individual who did little with his talents, but lived on his mother's money. Not a man to appeal to someone who was as driven and as hard-working as Dickens.

The details about Mrs Collins' ambitions to become an actress and about her fond relationship with her sons came also from Catherine Peters' biography though the ending to my book is purely a figment of my imagination. Again letters from her, and to her from her son Wilkie, give a flavour of her personality and of her devotion to her sons and her enjoyment of their artistic friends. I could hear her voice in my head as I began to write about her. Letters are such a wonderful resource for any author – the authentic voice of those who are long dead ring through them.

I wonder whether emails and text messages will survive for the biographers and story writers of the future!

Books that I have found useful while researching for this series:

Dickens:
Dickens: Peter Ackroyd
Charles Dickens: Michael Slater
The Life of Charles Dickens: John Forster
The World of Charles Dickens: Angus Wilson
Dickens: Simon Callow
Charles Dickens: A Life: Claire Tomalin

Wilkie Collins:
The King of Inventors: Catherine Peters
Wilkie Collins: Peter Ackroyd
Wilkie Collins: A Life of Sensation: Andrew Lycett

Pre-Raphaelite Brotherhood:
Pre-Raphaelites: Heather Birchall
A New and Noble School: Quentin Bell
The Pre-Raphaelite Tragedy: William Gaunt
Victorian Narrative Painting: Julia Thomas
John Ruskin, The Later Years: Tim Hilton

General books about the 1850s:
The Victorian Servant: Pamela Hern
London Labour and London Poor: Henry Mayhew
The Victorian Home: Jenni Calder